She thinks once h

A
TRICK OF
THE
LIGHT

ROSIE ORR

A Trick of the Light
© 2025 Rosie Orr

Published under the **Blue Murder**
imprint of Oxford eBooks.
www.oxford-ebooks.com

ISBN 978-1-910779-46-0 (Paperback)

Oxford eBooks
Blue Murder

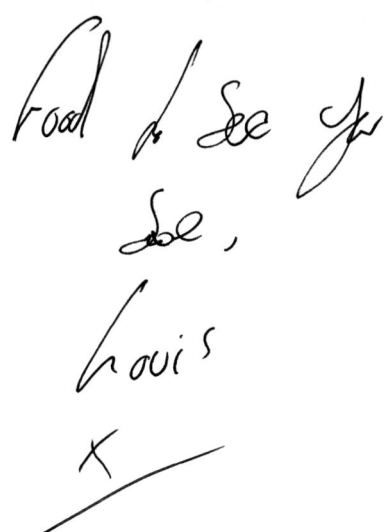

Food to see you
See,

Louis

x

Dedication

for Polly and Joe
with love and gratitude
★ always ★

PROLOGUE

How had it come to this? Life would have been so different if only Tom...

Both twenty-two when they met, he was a medical student at the Royal Free, Cassie was studying jewellery design at Central St Martin's. She moved in with Tom three months later. Soon they were sharing a tiny flat in Wood Green, Cassie making (and selling) exquisite jewellery on the kitchen table, Tom working increasingly long hours in A&E at Barnet General.

Too proud to accept Cassie's father's offer of another car when Cassie's little Fiat finally puttered to a halt, Tom rode a bike to work.

On Christmas Eve, three years later, she was concentrating on icing the wonky fruit cake she planned to surprise Tom with when the landline rang. Giving the spatula a messy lick, and dropping Royal icing down her jumper, she answered, hoping it would be Tom telling her he'd just come off shift and could she unearth that pepperoni pizza from the bottom of the freezer and stick it in the oven – he was starving.

It wasn't Tom. It would never be Tom again.

The policewoman told her that Dr Thomas Dearborn had been knocked off his bike on his way home by a drunk driver who had gone on to plough into a shop front. When at last the taxi Cassie somehow managed to call finally arrived, she'd set off at a run through the maze of dimly-lit and indecipherably signposted corridors, calling Tom's name over and over again, pushing away anyone who tried to stop her, to be greeted at last by the distraught nurses who'd been working with Tom just a few hours earlier, and the fellow doctors she'd so recently been laughing with at the Christmas party, to learn that it was too late.

They'd planned to marry when Tom qualified as a paediatric surgeon. Now, instead of wondering whether a wild silk column gown would be preferable to a chic little A-line number, she was trying to decide whether Tom would have wanted a single white rose bud or a simple bunch of wildflowers laid on his heartbreakingly simple bamboo coffin.

That had been five years ago. The following year her beloved grandmother died, leaving Cassie her little terrace house in Oxford. She'd had no relationships since Tom, and no wish for one.

Three weeks after her twenty-ninth birthday, she met Ivo at a party. She'd gone reluctantly to accompany a girlfriend, Ivo was there because he was in Oxford to audition for an upcoming drama at the Playhouse. Cassie was about to leave – her girlfriend was sparkling in a group near the drinks table – when she found him standing beside her. Smiling. She learned that he was ten years younger than her, funny – he made her laugh with scurrilous tales about well-known actors – and was sofa-surfing in London while he went to the auditions advertised in The Stage. Unlike Cassie, he had no father, and his mother survived on various cleaning jobs, showing no interest in her son's career.

He was turning away to leave – he had to get in character for tomorrow's audition – when he turned back and asked if Cassie could possibly meet him for a drink the following evening, so he could look forward to having somebody fascinating to talk to – jewellery, she said? Wow, amazing – before he headed back to London.

He arrived at the pub in tears. He'd been forced to turn down the part; the director was an idiot who couldn't direct a reading of a MacDonald's menu – it would have damaged Ivo's career beyond repair to work with him. He's desolate that he can't stay for a drink after all - he has to get back asap, as the guy whose sofa he's currently kipping on works shifts, and gets violent if Ivo disturbs him. It's frightening...

That night he slept wrapped in a duvet on Cassie's kitchen floor.

Two weeks later he was sharing her bed.

For a while, at least, she thought she was in love with him.

CHAPTER ONE

THE EVENING STRETCHED ahead, full of uncertainty.

Please God let it be third time lucky. All he needed was a break...

At half past eleven Cassie was still waiting. She'd given in to hunger just before ten and eaten her share of the chicken casserole she'd prepared, but the wine was untouched and the champagne remained stowed in the fridge. Her feelings had ricocheted from hope (he'd got the part and was celebrating with Larry, his agent) to despair (he hadn't got the part and was drinking spirits in some bar with money borrowed from a stranger – he was good at that, conning strangers).

She switched on the radio, grateful for the comforting familiarity of the announcer's voice, and wandered around the kitchen, touching the old pine dresser with its rows of mismatched floral plates, the bookcase overflowing with the reference books on flora and fauna she used for her work, the painted wooden chairs ranged round the scrubbed table.

She glanced at the clock.

Twenty to twelve.

Somehow that sounded a lot worse than half past

eleven.

The thing to do was keep busy. Look casual when he walked in, as if she wasn't worried sick. Maybe she'd get on with the commission she'd begun work on at the weekend. The design was complicated; a tiara with a silver wire headband that tapered at the sides, with clusters of diamond and seed pearl flowers supporting a crystal pendant. It was based on an elaborate brooch the client had seen in an old Italian painting, and she'd need all her concentration to get it right. Returning to the kitchen she settled down at the cluttered workbench under the window, loaded Spotify and found Adele. Opening her notebook at the complicated design she laid out her tools, chose a length of silver memory wire and selected a pair of tiny long-nose pliers. She was about to set the first pearl in place when she heard a key in the front door. Getting up, she hurried to the oven and checked on the state of the remains of the casserole. Not too bad…She unwrapped the baked potato from its foil and put it on a plate. Turned to get the butter from the fridge, and jumped.

Ivo stood leaning against the wall, scowling at her. Somebody had told him recently that he looked like James Dean, and ever since he'd worn a black leather jacket and cultivated a heavily oiled quiff, jeans hanging low on his narrow hips. The sulky smoulder he currently affected had come so naturally, he told Cassie, that he sometimes wondered whether there wasn't something in this reincarnation stuff. He spent a lot of time slouching about with his hands in his pockets, gazing with a tortured air into the middle distance.

'Ivo?' Cassie took a step towards him. Hesitated. She risked a smile; he ignored it. Her smile faded. Once, she'd have rushed to meet him, full of joy at the mere thought of seeing him. Now she'd learned to be wary – to gauge his mood before hurrying to embrace him, or telling him news of her own day. Turning away, she took his plate of chicken casserole from the oven and put it on the table beside the baked potato, careful to set it down gently and arrange the cutlery more neatly beside the checked napkin.

'Christ. Could smell that crap from the end of the road. Made me want to spew.'

'But you asked for it this morning –'

He rolled his eyes. 'Like I could think about *food* when I was concentrating on my *lines*?'

'Sorry.' She went to the work bench and took a sip of cold coffee. 'So, how did it go?'

'Go?' He shouldered himself away from the wall, slouched over to the table and sat down. Pushed his plate away from him with an expression of disgust, got up and found the wine. Poured a glass, drank it down fast, and reached for the bottle again. 'If you mean *did I get the fucking part*, the answer is no.'

Her heart sank. 'Oh, Ivo, I'm so –'

'Reason's obvious, knew as soon as I got to the hall. Bastard who got it knows the director.'

'God, that's –'

'Show's transferring to New York in November. *New York*!!' The glass was drained. 'It should've been me.'

'Of course it should –'

'Knocked myself out preparing for that role! Stayed

in character all day, like Day Lewis and Heath Ledger do. Rehearsed in graveyards, practising different speech impediments –'

'Speech impediments? I didn't know Shakespeare said he had a –'

Ivo threw himself down at the table again. Ran a hand through his hair, hard. 'Fuck's sake! Stands to reason he's got some sort of affliction or he'd have a better job – I mean grave digger, for chrissakes!'

'I –'

'Attended actual funerals wearing the gear! Filthy ripped moleskins, jacket with one sleeve hanging off, dead rabbit dangling out the pocket. Even carried a rusty spade till some pretentious bloody *vicar* told me to get lost –'

'A *spade*…?' Cassie tightened her grip on her coffee mug, trying hard not to laugh.

Ivo looked up sharply. 'Research. Authentic, right?'

Right. Better not to think about the time he was offered *back row third from left in crowd of Senators watching when Caesar gets stabbed*, and spent the weeks preceding the opening night traipsing about Oxford wrapped in a sheet, stopping occasionally to practice throwing up his arms in horror and falling to the ground with a loud (very loud) shriek. Personally Cassie thought (but didn't dare say) that the audience would probably think he'd simply tripped over his toga and roar with laughter, and was relieved when the director decreed that the Senators would simply (and silently) freeze with shock.

'Gotta feel grave-digging *here* – in your gut.' His mouth twisted. 'Huh, like *you'd* understand.'

'No, I do, honestly –'

He laughed. 'Get real! All *you* have to do is knock a couple of bits of tin together, stick on a few gobs of coloured glass and charge some rich bitch 2K a pop…'

She flinched as Ivo held the wine bottle to his lips, drank, and banged it down hard on the table again. Getting to his feet, he staggered over to the workbench, picked up the dish of pearls and sat down again at the table. 'Wouldn't even matter if sales of crap jewellery dropped off a bit – darling Cassie'd still have a dear little house thanks to good old Granny, *jammy bitch…*'

Cassie jumped to her feet, stung. 'That's not fair –'

'Too bloody right it's not fair.' He grabbed the bottle. 'Saw some poor homeless bugger sleeping in a doorway near the coach station on my way home.'

'I know – God, it's awful.' She headed for the kettle. 'I'll make us some coffee.' She turned away as water rattled into the kettle, didn't see him pick up the crumpled copy of the Oxford Times left on the corner of the table, flick through it then stop abruptly, staring at a grainy black and white photo of a new hostel for the homeless. Didn't see the tears of self-pity that filled Ivo's eyes, or see him wipe his nose painfully with his leather cuff.

He cradled the bottle as if it was a baby. 'Could be me one day….' He gave a sob.

'Come on, sweetheart – you'll ace the next audition.' She hunted for the bag of demerara in the cupboard and re-filled the sugar bowl while he watched her, expressionless.

After a moment he sat forward slightly in his chair.

'You've never been scared, have you?'

She hesitated. Shivered, remembering.

running through the dimly lit
maze of hospital corridors

She'd never told Ivo about Tom. She knew he'd hate it – not only because Tom had been a brilliant doctor, and they'd been happy – but, she'd finally come to realise, because it wasn't about *him*. 'Not really…' He was watching her closely. She hesitated, then gave a rueful shrug. 'Though that film you made me watch last Christmas was scary as hell, what with the spooky haunted house and the weird kid – Martin? No, Miles – channelling the phantom gardener.'

He relaxed. 'Ah yes, The Innocents…' He gave the smallest of smiles. 'With the apparition in black – pale and ominous – standing motionless beside the lake. The dead governess, Miss Jessel. Watching. Waiting…'

Cassie shuddered. 'God, I *hate* ghosts.' It was true, she did. *A long white curtain wafting in the moonlight on the warm evening breeze…* She managed a smile and looked away quickly, glad she'd never told him. 'But apart from that film, suppose I can't say I've ever been really scared.' She concentrated on clattering the mugs down from their hooks. Didn't hear him murmur '*Well maybe it's time you were*', as he smiled back, more broadly this time.

'Ivo, don't be cross, but please eat something –'

'– and everything'll be all right. Sure. Good idea.' He sat down and pulled the cooling plate of chicken casserole towards him. Raised a forkful to his lips.

Cassie relaxed. 'Honestly, I'm sure you'll get the next job you go for –'

'Yeah?'

'Yes –'

'*Sure…*?' He gave her a tremulous, hopeful smile.

She smiled back at him, willing him to feel better. 'Sure. Today just wasn't the right showcase for your talent, that's all.'

He stopped smiling. Narrowing his eyes, he thrust the forkful of food into his mouth and chewed angrily, mouth half open. Gravy ran down his chin. 'Yeah? And what makes you so sure of that, you patronising bitch?' He dropped the fork, scooped up some pearls and began to flick them at her one by one. 'Precisely what qualifications do *you* have, eh?'

'Ivo, don't, *please* – I –'

'Why not? I like doing it.' He lifted the glass and swallowed the last of the wine, eyeing her over the top of the glass. 'Problem, is it?'

'I need them for my work –'

'For your work! Well, of *course* I'll stop!' Picking up the dish, he got to his feet, held it out to her. Pretended to slip. Pearls spilled all over the floor, rolling behind the furniture, lodging in the cracks in the flagstones. Ivo clapped his hand over his mouth in mock dismay.

'Oh *no*! Oh, whatever have I done? The poor little pearls –' He started to laugh.

Cassie looked at him. His features, softened and blurred by alcohol, were distorted with fury; smears of chicken gravy had congealed on the front of his leather jacket. She remembered for a brief moment the first time she'd met him. The impossibly handsome features, the rueful self-deprecating smile. The wild ambition he assured her was matched by his stupendous talent. His jokes. The anecdotes he told, acting all the parts, doing all the accents. His delight when she presented him with the little brushed silver hoop earring set with a tiny diamond she'd made for him.

His tenderness the first time they made love – *if she could only get him to bed, maybe he'd fall asleep.* She started to speak. Met his eyes and thought better of it. Getting to her knees she began to crawl about the floor, collecting what few pearls she could. As she stood up, Ivo drew a bottle of whisky from his jacket pocket and set it on the table. He'd stopped laughing.

She went cold. 'Ivo, no. Please – you know it's only going to make you sick –'

He unscrewed the cap. 'Just the one time, you said?'

'Sorry?'

'*Ghosts.*' He took a long swallow of whiskey. Sniggered. 'For chrissakes – that's *pathetic.*'

Picking up his loaded plate, he looked at it reflectively then swung back his arm.

'Scared now?'

The plate hit the wall behind her head. Shattered and fell to the floor, leaving a trail of gravy and vegetables trickling slowly down the dark red paint.

For a moment Cassie stood stunned, watching a disc of carrot slide past a sliver of – onion, was it? – then fall with a faint *plop* on the floor. She whirled round. 'For Christ's sake, Ivo, you bastard – what the hell do you think you're doing?' She burst into tears. 'My grandmother left me those plates!' She fell to her knees, trying to gather up the broken pieces. 'You know how much I love them –'

A jagged fragment cut into her palm. 'Shit –' She hurried over to the sink, laid the pieces of broken china gently on the draining board and turned on the cold tap, hard. Turning away she held her palm under the freezing water. 'I can't take much more of this –'

She gasped as he seized her from behind, spun her round, grabbed her by the front of her blouse and pulled her to him. He thrust his face close to hers, hissing. *That makes two of us, you pathetic bitch –*'

His breath stank of whisky, there was a cut on his chin where he must have cut himself shaving. His eyes were half shut, unfocused. She had to stop him, calm him down. 'Ivo – I'm sorry, I didn't mean –' His grip tightened on the front of her blouse. A button popped, and fell to the floor. She swallowed. 'Look, try and put this morning behind you. I know it's painful, but it's just one audition – there'll be others –'

'*One audition*?' He propelled her backwards towards the old pine store cupboard, and shoved her hard against the doors. The handles slammed into Cassie's back, agony exploding in her kidneys, shooting up her spine, a dazzling display of scarlet fireworks fading to black as she collapsed. 'You call my chance to become a household name in New York *just one audition*?' Reaching out an arm, he dragged her upright and slapped her face, hard. 'So how about now? You scared *now*…?' He drew back his fist and punched her in the stomach.

She crumpled to the floor and lay doubled up, gasping for air. After a moment she managed to haul herself into a kneeling position, shaking her head slowly from side to side, trying to clear the red haze floating in front of her eyes.

'Bitch.' He turned away and picked up the bottle again.

Stumbling to her feet, she staggered down the hall to the bathroom. Closed the door and locked it. *Mustn't cry.* Her stomach ached dully – it was hard to stand upright. Something warm was trickling down her chin; bent double over the washbasin, she managed to turn on the cold tap, soak a flannel in cold water. Painfully, she dabbed at her lower lip, and touched tentative fingers to her throbbing cheek. Explored the inside of her mouth with her tongue – her gums hurt, please God none of her teeth were loose…No, they seemed to be okay. She risked a glance in the cabinet mirror above the washbasin. Her reflection stared back at her, eyes blank with shock. Blood welled from the cut on her lip – it must have been caused by the heavy gold signet ring he wore. Her right cheek, a startling scarlet in her paper-white face, was already swelling.

Opening the cabinet she found a dusty pot of arnica behind the welter of male skin care products and teeth-whitening kits and fake tan creams. She applied some to the bruise that was already forming, then dabbed again, wincing, at the cut on her lip. Rinsed out the sink.

She looked in the mirror again, thought of Ivo's overweening narcissism, his constant sniping at her work. His rudeness to her neighbour Zadie.

Now she came to think about it, she almost wanted to laugh aloud. Because there was really only one question; why the hell had she put up with him for so long?

She'd go back to the living room now, before he had a chance to drink any more whisky, and tell him quietly it was best if he left.

Attempting an encouraging smile at her reflection – stopping when she realised it made her lip start bleeding again – she returned to the kitchen.

Ivo was sprawled on a chair, holding the whisky bottle up to the light. 'Nearly empty, 'fraid.' He got unsteadily to his feet. 'Lend us a twenty, Cass. Need 'nother one for medic' – medic'nal purposes.'

'Ivo.' It came out in a whisper. She tried again. 'Ivo, I think you should leave.'

'Leave?' He frowned. '*Leave*?'

She swallowed. 'Yes. The thing is, I don't think we make each other very happy these days, and –'

'You're telling me you think I should leave?' He stared at her incredulously.

'Yes –'

He burst out laughing. 'Hell, I'm not going anywhere.' He tilted the bottle to his mouth and drank. Set the bottle down carefully on the table. 'But hey, tell you what –' He shook his head as if to clear it. Swung round to face her. 'If *you're* so anxious to split, Cass m'darling – queen of my heart, light of my life – *you* can fucking leave.'

He moved towards her. Cassie backed away – *he's going to hit you again, and this time* – but he ignored her as he passed, stumbled against the cooker, and left the room.

She could leave? But it was *her* house, her grandmother had left it to her, he couldn't...

She hurried into the hall. 'Ivo…?'

She could hear muffled sounds coming from the bedroom. Thank God; he'd thought better of it and was packing his things. She felt a brief pang of pity for him – apart from his clothes the only thing he owned was his collection of Spotlights and the silver cigarette box an uncle had given him on his eighteenth birthday. He'd kept it stuffed with spliffs and uppers ever since. She'd give him his taxi fare – maybe he could go to his brother in Bermondsey until he organised something more permanent. She returned to the kitchen, found her bag and rummaged for her purse.

'There you go.' She jumped as a large suitcase was hurled at her feet. It burst open as it hit the floor, spilling a tangled jumble of her own underwear and sweaters over the floor. 'Make yourself a cup of coffee if I were you.' He ran a finger under her chin, smirking. 'This could take a while.' He turned and lurched towards the door.

Cassie lifted a shaking hand to her mouth. Her lip had started to bleed again; her cheek was numb. She could hear Ivo in the bedroom, opening drawers, slamming cupboard doors. She made her way carefully across the kitchen, holding on to the backs of chairs for support. Black dots danced in front of her eyes, her back hurt when she breathed in. At last she reached the dresser, and fumbling among the debris of old bills and pizza flyers, found her mobile. *Hurry*. She'd hit nine twice when she heard him behind her. Grabbing the phone, he hurled it across the room, swore when it landed on a cushion. 'Who the fuck you calling?' He seized her wrist. 'Christ, not that stupid bitch Zadie!'

She tried to pull away; he tightened his grip so that the linked bracelet on her watch cut into her wrist. '*The police.*'

His jaw dropped.

'They're on their way.'

'On their...?' He drew back his arm.

She was at the table and grabbing a knife from the row of jeweller's tools before she knew she'd even thought about it. She spun round and faced him, holding the knife in front of her in both hands, the tiny, lethally sharp blade pointing upwards. 'They'll be here any minute.'

'You cow! You bloody –'

She gripped the handle tighter. 'Go now and I'll say it was all a mistake, a joke, I never meant to call them–'

'You're going to be sorry.' He took a step towards her. 'Very, very sorry.'

She risked a glance at her watch. Her wrist was red and throbbing. 'Any minute.'

He backed away towards the door. '*You'll pay for this, you bitch*!' He seized the pepper mill as he passed the table, threw it in her face and lurched out.

She waited until she heard the front door slam.

Holding her breath she made her way painfully upstairs to the bedroom, lifted the edge of the blind and peered out. Ivo was weaving his way down the road, heading for the high street. As she watched, he tripped over a drunk who'd bedded down for the night outside the pub on the corner. He kicked him a couple of times, hard, and staggered on. As he disappeared from view Cassie was pretty sure he was laughing.

Returning to the table, she replaced the knife neatly

in the row of tools and sat down. Aligned the blue sugar bowl with the jug of red and yellow striped tulips, and brushed a speck of lint from her sleeve.

Then she laid her head on her folded arms and burst into tears.

CHAPTER TWO

SHE'D FINALLY STOPPED crying and was staring into space when the silence was broken by a distant sound from the street – a car backfiring? A drunk kicking an empty bottle? *Or worse, something nearer…*Suddenly she was on her feet, searching for her phone, Googling Oxford Emergency Locksmiths, finding:

KEYKWIK, EMERGENCY RESPONSE TIME 35 MINUTES

Hands shaking she dialled, and managed to hit the right numbers at the third attempt. Haltingly explained the situation when the call was answered, and learned there was a *Premium Call Out Charge* for unsociable hours, plus it would cost £150 to change a mortice, usually took about an hour – double that, course, if she was wanting two doors fixed – plus *Cost of Parts*. Her eyes widened as she made a rough calculation. Damn Ivo – it would make a massive hole in her savings. Still, it would be worth anything to feel safe. *Cash or Card*? She assured the speaker that card would be fine (she'd learned long ago not to keep a lot of cash in the house) and was told that Merv, tonight's *On Call*, would be with her in two shakes of a duck's tail and he'd call when he was outside her house so she could be sure it was him.

In less than half an hour her phone rang, the caller's thick Oxfordshire accent so strong that for a brief moment she was sure it was Ivo, but within minutes Merv – a very old man in sagging overalls and a stained flat cap – had proved his credentials, shuffled inside, thumped down a battered carpet bag containing his tools, and violently sucking his teeth, inspected first the back, then the front door. Back in the kitchen again he accepted a mug of strong tea with three sugars and a pile of chocolate digestives, gave her a crash course on locks – *you'll want chains, course, ladies always like a nice chain* – and advised her to have a sit-down – *don't mind my sayin but you're lookin fair done in, my duck* – while he got on with the job. Gratefully she sank back in her chair while he rummaged in the carpet bag, chuntering on about how the weather did his arthritis a power of good, then set to work. She'd almost fallen asleep by the time he'd finished, demonstrated the new mortices and chains, cleared up what little mess he'd made, and presented the spares with a flourish. She gave him another mug of tea while he calculated the bill and proffered the card machine, waiting patiently till at last – hands still shaking – she found the right card, managed to insert it the right way up, then fumbled in her bag and found a crumpled ten-pound note in her wallet. Leaning against the back of a chair for support – she was feeling seriously weak, now – she handed it to the old locksmith, thanking him for everything with tears in her eyes. As he shoved the bill in an oil-stained pocket he beamed, held out a hand with a palm so rough it resembled sandpaper, and headed for the door. Watched critically while she closed it behind him, locked it with one of the gleaming new keys, and slid the shiny new chain smoothly into place.

Thumbs up, a cheery wave and he was gone.

CHAPTER THREE

SHE'D LAIN AWAKE most of the night, her cheek throbbing, trying to staunch the blood from her lip with a crumpled tissue, and despite clutching the new spare keys, struggling upright every time she heard a noise outside, or a creak on the stairs. Now sunlight was filtering through the gap at the bottom of the blind, she could hear birdsong, the sound of traffic. A new day at last, thank God. Carefully she climbed out of bed, threw the blood-stained pillow on the floor, tried to stretch, abandoned it when the bruises on her back hurt too much. Still, nothing was broken, which meant that at least she'd be able to get on with her work; she had several orders for birthday presents to complete by the end of September, plus another wedding tiara she hadn't even made sketches for yet. Averting her eyes from the open cupboard doors, the smashed porcelain jug and the cross-stitch cushion she'd laboured over at school when she was eight, leaking stuffing where he'd kicked it against the wall, she pulled on her shabby kimono and shuffled into the bathroom. Used the toilet, gently brushed her teeth and ran a comb through her hair, avoiding her reflection in the mirror.

Downstairs in the kitchen Cassie checked that the blinds were still securely closed and stood motionless for a moment, grateful for the comforting familiarity of the old pine dresser with its rows of mismatched floral plates, the overflowing bookcase, the painted wooden chairs ranged round the scrubbed table. But there were bitter reminders of last night's supper beside the jug of tulips; Ivo's untouched baked potato beside the butter dish, the congealed trail of gravy and vegetables trickling down the dark red wall. She turned away – stopped as she caught sight of the suitcase he'd flung at her feet, remembering how it had sounded as it burst open to disgorge a tangled mass of clothes. Her favourite sweater, she saw now, was among them, and an expensive cream silk shirt with one sleeve almost severed.

She didn't cry until she caught sight of the camellia plant under the table, the stem broken, its petals crushed, earth spilled all over the flagstones. *Bastard.* When she'd done her best to salvage it, and stood it on the kitchen windowsill beside the wilting lemon tree, she switched the kettle on – she'd clear up the rest of the mess after she'd made a restorative mug of tea. Taking a bright blue mug decorated with smiling yellow suns from the shelf, she risked raising the blind a little way and glancing out of the old sash window above the sink at the little area where she kept her ancient bike (must get the chain mended) and Granny Jackson's equally ancient Wheelbarrow with the Wonky Wheel. There was a hole in the peeling wooden fence abutting the area, shared with next door; through it she could see the kids, Brooklyn and Bronx, kicking a football around, yelling at the tops of their voices. The yells were punctuated by their mother Zadie's even louder screeches coming from their open kitchen window, competing with Magic Radio at top volume – the same place the powerful cooking smells were emanating from. Some sort of fry-up. Jerk chicken? Beef patties, maybe. Cassie smiled. Thank God for normality... The kettle boiled and she stood gazing out of the window, thinking about her design for the pendant while she drank her tea. An engraved silver and red polychrome enamel teardrop, the silver twining round the enamel like a vine? She frowned. Maybe midnight blue instead of red?

Pulling the blind down again, she hurried over to her workbench, switched on a powerful magnifying Anglepoise, opened the small safe and began to sort through the exquisite array of precious and semi-precious stones. Jumped as a shadow fell across the bench, followed by a sharp knock on the back door. She clapped a hand to her mouth. Winced. *No. Please God, please God, no...*Holding her breath, she raised her eyes to the window. The shadow was still there, unmoving. Waiting...As she watched, the handle turned. Slowly twisted the other way. Suddenly the new lock and chain didn't look anything like strong enough. If only she hadn't switched the lamp on, it was obvious she was there...Her phone, must find her phone...Pushing herself away from the bench she backed away, knocking over the stool with a clatter. *No...*

'Cass...? You in there, girlfriend...?'

Cassie felt a rush of relief so great she thought she'd

be sick. *Zadie*! Almost falling over in her haste, she ran to open the door. Her neighbour stood there, skinny candy-pink camisole atop tight black leather trousers, punishingly tight little bunches of bleached hair secured with yellow plastic beads, nails a gleaming magenta. 'Hiya Cass! A'right?' She adjusted a bra strap, shiny silver bangles clattering on her wrists.

'Yes, course –'

'*Come to warn you.*'

She must have heard the row last night, come to complain it had frightened the kids. She sighed. The people on the other side must have heard it too.

Zadie moved closer, frowning. 'Christ, what happened to *you*, girl?'

Cassie put a hand to her cheek, touched her lip. 'Oh nothing, I just – I –'

'That bugger Ivo, wasn't it?'

'No, honestly –'

'Heard the sod creatin again – thought at first it was the telly. Would've sent Lloyd round, but he's doin the Southampton run all week.'

'Sorry –'

'Not you who should be sorry, mate.' She looked round the kitchen, swore as she took in the chaos. 'Time you showed that toe rag the door.'

'I did. I've had enough, this time.'

'Glad to bleedin hear it. Locks been changed yet?'

'Yes, last night –'

'Sorted.' Heeling the door shut behind her with a crash, she held out a hand for the new key, locked the door and slid the chain into place. 'Thinks he's God's gift, that one – saw him one mornin creepin about in the gutter, goin apeshit about some bloke called Derek's skull –' She demonstrated. Cassie laughed. It hurt. 'Asked him if he was okay. Creep said fuck's sake sod off, he was '*in character*'.

'Right. Didn't get the part, I'm afraid.' She sighed. 'Again…'

'Took it out on you, right?' She fiddled with the yellow beads. 'Thing is, is name should've given you a hint, I mean *Ivo*…not English, is he? Bound to be temperamental with a moniker like that.'

'Ivo's not his real name, Zades – he changed it for the stage.'

'You're kiddin me. So, what…?'

Cassie lowered herself gingerly onto a chair, careful not to lean back. 'Have to kill you if I tell you.'

Zadie's eyes widened. 'Give, girlfriend.'

'Ready?'

'Ready.'

'Keith.'

'*Keith*…?'

'Figured it's no name for a Star. I mean think about it – *Keith de Niro* doesn't really do it, no?'

'Got that right.' She headed for the kettle, then turned, grinning. 'Cass.'

'What?'

'*Keith Cruise*.'

They looked at each other, Zadie screeching with laughter, Cassie snorting painfully, touching a finger to her sore lip. Zadie stopped laughing as she saw her wince. 'That bastard – I'd nip back for the arnica but I slapped the last of it on Bronx's knee when he come off his bike last week.'

'I'm okay, honestly – looks worse than it is.'

'Ask me, you need a refill.' She picked up Cassie's mug as shouts of hysterical laughter from the garden were followed by a worrying silence. 'Shit, think you had it tough with *The Celebrity Known as Ivo* – aka *The Wanker Previously Known as Keith*? Try a night with my kids.' She sighed. 'Better get back, soon as I've told you why I come round.'

When Zadie had made the tea and rummaged around for the biscuit tin, and Cassie had thrust the clothes back in the suitcase and cleared away the reminders of last night's meal, they settled at the table. Zadie leaned forward, narrowing her eyes. 'So...'

Cassie dipped a gingernut in her tea and waited.

'*She's back.*'

'Who's back?'

'That cow Erica.'

'Hello? Thought she'd gone?' Cassie slipped a piece of soggy biscuit in her mouth.

'Me too. Only bumped into her yesterday, didn't I – bossy bitch was bawlin Bronx out for skateboardin outside her house. *Her* house!'

'But hasn't she got her own place now the divorce has gone through?'

'Yeah, she had – some fancy doss up The Smoke. Contract fell though at the last minute, though, so she's back drivin Dave nuts while she finds somewhere else.'

'Hmm. Wasn't exactly my favourite neighbour.' She managed a smile. 'Remember when she tried to make everyone in the street paint their front doors toning pastels?'

'Always bitchin about Lloyd's Ford Fiesta bein up on bricks –'

'Still, David seems nice. Bumped into him a while ago, said hello.'

'Handsome or what. Wish Lloyd'd wear linen jackets.' Zadie stirred more sugar into her tea and took an appreciative slurp. 'Still, they're all buggers, aren't they. Lloyd gets up to all sorts when he's home – you know, gamblin online and that –' She began to list Lloyd's shortcomings in some detail.

Cassie began to sketch the jug of tulips on the back of an envelope stamped council tax reminder, as she half-listened to Zadie's catalogue of complaints.

'– always sayin he's goin to give up long distance and start deliverin for supermarkets – pay's more that £50K a year now there's a shortage of truckers –'

'Wow –' Cassie added cross-hatching to the leaves.

'– trouble is there's loads of drop-offs all day, plus he'd have to work weekends –'

'Hey, maybe Ivo should give it a try...'

Zadie gave a snort of laughter. 'Still, look on the bright side, he's good with the kids at weekends when he's home, watches Love Island with 'em and that...'

Even louder shouts issued from the back garden, soon accompanied by thunderous kicking as the fence was scaled. Zadie rolled her eyes. 'Bleedin ball's come over.' Downing the rest of her tea, she shoved back her chair and got wearily to her feet. 'Gotta love you 'n' leave you, they'll be hollerin for their dinner any minute.'

As she grabbed another biscuit, there was a thud as a lemon fell off the potted lemon tree standing on the windowsill above the sink. Cassie sighed. 'Won't be any left soon. Shame, it was stunning when it arrived.'

'Present from some punter wasn't it? Weird.'

'Roland. Sweet, really – he proposed to his girlfriend at a restaurant called The Lemon Grove –'

'That little caff up Cowley Road?'

'Somewhere posh in Gloucestershire I think – anyway, she said Yes and he commissioned a gold link bracelet with loads of tiny lemon charms. Nightmare, took weeks to get the mould for the lemons right and as for the glaze…Anyway, she was thrilled apparently, and he sent the tree as a thank you.' Getting up, she headed for the sink and prodded the wilting tree's soil. 'D'you think I'm watering it enough?'

Zadie grinned. 'Don't look at me, girl. Only plant I got's a plastic rose come free with my fancy underwear catalogue.' There was the sound of fighting from the garden. 'Better get some nosh down the buggers.' She headed for the door. 'And watch out for that Erica. Be round any minute tellin you your windows need a clean.'

Cassie looked after her, waving, as she crossed the grass and stopped at the rockery beside the shed. Grabbing a handful of oregano from the profusion of lavender and herbs that spilled from every crevice, Zadie turned. 'Better give this lot a drink, girl, before they cark it too…' Blowing a kiss to Cassie, and chivvying the squabbling kids ahead of her, she disappeared through the wooden gate and down the little lane that ran the length of the terrace's back gardens. Cassie pushed open the creaking shed door and stood still for a moment, breathing in the pungent aroma that always reminded her of road works, affectionately regarding Grandpa Jackson's shaky push mower and basket full of old-fashioned trowels, the shelf with its jam jars of paint brushes and neat row of tools, including the gleaming putty knife, price tag still dangling, that he'd never had a chance to use before his heart attack. On the shelf below sat the almost full outsize container of Roundup Total Weedkiller with its heavy duty pump applicator that Granny Jackson refused to use once she discovered it killed daisies as well as plantains, beside the bright pink vat of Bloom 'n Gro Advanced Fertiliser she used on the rockery plants. There was a giant pack of Best Quality Enriched Plant Soil she'd been planning to use on a projected window box, plus several obsolete tins of paints, their lids jammed permanently shut. The ancient watering can stood in a corner; beside the bucket and mop. Cassie scooped it up, brushed the cobwebs off the spout, and after inhaling a last comforting creosote-infused breath, closed the door behind her. Leant against it for a moment, relaxing; eyes closed, enjoying the sun's warmth on her upturned face, the fragrance from the climbing roses on the kitchen wall that pervaded the whole garden. No need to check the bright red desk diary she kept on the workbench; she remembered that a client was ringing to discuss the diadem she was planning for her wedding (*wild roses were to be the motif – pink guilloche enamel and amethyst for the blossoms, rose gold for the entwined stems if the budget ran to that*), and someone was coming to do a Gas Safety inspection. The postcard was stamped '**Urgent** –

Overdue owing to Change of Customers Name'. She sighed, hoping it wouldn't take too long. Meantime, better go and finish sorting out those stones. The blue topaz was particularly promising…

Opening her eyes, she stretched carefully, bent and picked up the watering can. Heading to the kitchen sink she filled it with water, lugged it back to the rockery and splashed the contents about liberally. Cassie stood for a moment, considering. The tips of the chives were looking decidedly brown – clearly a chef's extra would be no bad thing. Mission accomplished, she returned the watering can to the shed, hesitated as she passed the climbing rose on her way back to the kitchen. Surely the creamy flowers and delicate leaves must need a drink too, given the weather? She returned, limping, to the shed, and despite her throbbing back repeated the operation, chef's extra included.

As she trudged back to the house she glanced over the fence at Zadie's back yard, referred to with pride by Lloyd as The War Zone. Most of the space was taken up by an outsize trampoline with a trailing safety net that had seen better days, and a rusting barbecue strewn with similarly rusting, lethal-looking cooking implements. The surrounding patch of yellowing grass was littered with broken bikes and battered toys, mainly outsize plastic weapons and decapitated characters from Toy Story.

As she neared the back door, she risked a glance over the fence on the other side, admiring the elegant conservatory. An enormous palm tree stood opposite the door, flanked by a pair of orange trees, all glossy dark green leaves and glowing fruit, while a veritable jungle of exotic plants thrived behind the gleaming glass panes. Cassie grinned, enjoying as always the contrast with Bronx's battle-scarred Starship Enterprise, half submerged in a dried-up sand pit liberally embellished with cat poo, and Brooklyn's latest acquisition, one *Wedding Barbie Doll*. It had recently left been behind by a visiting cousin, and was now limbless, sequinned gown reduced to tatters, sparkly diadem replaced by a rubber hatchet protruding from the back of her skull.

As she gazed, a figure appeared at an upper window. Tall. Thin. Wearing her trademark black. *Erica*. Quickly Cassie turned away, involuntarily casting a critical glance at the kitchen windows, grateful the back door was wide open so she could stroll unhurriedly, *casually* inside. As she approached she noticed the sunlight glinting on the chain, and – she stopped dead. The *chain*…? Why on earth was there a…? And then she was running, *remembering*, breath catching in her throat, heart pounding, until she was inside, door safely locked, chain rammed into place. She collapsed into a chair, breathless, as somewhere deep inside the house, her phone began to ring.

CHAPTER FOUR

No sign of her phone in the kitchen. Wait – she remembered now. After she'd double checked the front door when she went to bed she'd slipped it under her pillow, in case… in case… She ran upstairs, sank down on the bed, breathless, and pulled out the phone. *Little clusters of wild roses or a variegated row? Paste instead of enamel?* She took a deep breath. 'Hi Jessica, sorry to keep you waiting –'

A sob. 'Cassie?' *Ivo.*

Without even thinking about it, she pulled the thin summer duvet towards her, held it against her like a shield. 'No! *No* – I can't –'

'Come on, Cass, you know I didn't mean it! I was upset, disappointed – you don't know what a bitch of a day I'd had, didn't even –'

'Ivo, *please* – it's over –'

'One more chance, that's all I ask.' Another sob. 'Sweetheart, I've got nowhere else to go –'

She pulled the duvet higher, clutched it tighter. 'No, Ivo. It's final. I told Zadie, she said Lloyd'll be back soon, and if you –'

A furious hiss. 'Break *that* sack of shit's neck one hand tied behind my back.'

'Look, I've got to go, I'm expecting a client to call –'
Oh God. Would she never learn?

'Fuck's sake, your bloody customers are all you ever think of. S'pose it's another loser too dumb to see your crap junk makes Accessorize look like fucking Fabergé.'

She heard a series of gulps as he drank. 'Christ, sometimes I wonder what I ever saw in you. Mouth like a cat's arse…thighs like a fucking sumo wrestler…' There was a crash as a bottle was set down and he began squealing in a piercing falsetto, '*Ivo, sweetie, I want you to leave, I mean we simply aren't…aren't…*' He laughed mirthlessly. 'Jesus, I'm good. Got that prissy little voice of yours down to a tee.' He took another swallow of whatever it was. 'Too fucking right we aren't. Should've done a runner months ago – let you cramp my style way too fucking long.'

'Ivo, please –'

'Anyway, never could stand your bloody awful little shack. Cushions everywhere. Stupid fucking plates painted with stupid bloody flowers, chrissakes.' He sniggered. 'Not so many of those left now, though…' He hiccupped. Farted loudly. 'Gotta go, Cassoulet. Oops! Sorry, Cassandra. Whatever. And know this, you fucking bitch.' Suddenly his tone was conversational. Friendly. '*You're gonna be sorry.*' A click, and he was gone.

Carefully she smoothed out the creases in the duvet cover. It wasn't till she stood up that she realised she was shaking. Stupid to let him panic her – surely she knew better than anyone that Ivo was all talk? Time to put last night behind her, get on with the day – she had a life, for God's sake, work to do, plans to make. Maybe Zadie could be persuaded to go to the multiplex to see that new thriller with her when Lloyd was home again. And if work went well on the hair ornament she'd head for the Zumba class on Thursday, go for a coffee with Helen and Mia afterwards.

She'd collected the last of the pearls from between the flagstones when her phone rang again. This time it *was* her client, and once the details of the diadem had been agreed on and she'd promised to text the following afternoon with sketches and a price estimate, she sat down at her work bench to make notes

know this, you fucking bitch

Halfway through she jumped up to check that the back door was locked, the chain safely in place. Mistakenly wrote 'gold' instead of 'silver', twice. Corrected it.

you're gonna be sorry

Springing up again she hurried to make sure the front door was still locked, the chain safely in place. Come on, of course it was – she was being ridiculous. Returning to the kitchen, she tried to whistle to cheer herself up. Impossible, with a damaged lip. Wincing, she began to draw.

She'd just completed the design for the diadem's delicate wild roses when she froze. Had that light tap, or click come from upstairs? The hall…? *Ivo*? No, he'd have raised hell when he found his key didn't work. Slowly she got to her feet and crept up the stairs – relaxed when she saw brown envelopes and a couple of flyers scattered across the mat. Still, the Gas bloke could arrive at any time, better get changed. Hurrying into the bedroom she pulled on a pair of jeans, added a white shirt – *damn, no time to iron it* – then padded to the bathroom, patted concealer over the bruise on her cheek and dragged a brush through her hair, ignoring a second light tap – *the postman must have forgotten a catalogue or something* – thought of applying a touch of lipstick and decided against it – time to look business-like, *in charge*. Back in the kitchen she tuned the radio to a classical music station, opened the Italian art book containing the portrait of the rather dull-looking medieval noblewoman wearing the hair ornament she was planning to incorporate into the tiara design, and placed it ostentatiously in the middle of the work bench. She found the pair of horn-rimmed spectacles she used to wear for work before she graduated to contact lenses, and began to slip them on. Dropped them as she heard the click of the back gate. *No, please God, no…* Holding her breath she edged the blind aside a fraction and peering out, saw a tall thin youth approaching, wearing dark blue overalls and a grey long-sleeved fleece beneath an over-sized hi-vis jacket. He carried a dark blue toolbox bearing a yellow logo that Cassie was too far away to read, while an official-looking lanyard hung round his neck. *The Gas bloke, thank God.* Quickly she retrieved the spectacles and jammed them on her nose, wincing as her bruises flared, and raised the blind. Conscious of his impassive gaze through the glass she inserted the new key, freed the chain and threw open the door.

'Hi there! You must be the – er – Gas Man.' She

attempted a welcoming smile. 'Great.'

He cleared his throat. 'Gas Safety, Miss. Tried the front door just now, thought you were out.'

'I'm so sorry, I forgot what time you were coming –'

He stepped inside. 'S'posed to have got an appointment card –'

'Oh, I did, it's in there somewhere –' She gestured towards the pile of bills on the end of the kitchen table, making an ineffectual attempt to tidy the flyers scattered beside them. 'You're definitely in the diary, it's just it's been a bit of a morning –'

He coughed. When she looked back, she saw he was sweating. She held out a hand. 'Let me take your jacket, you must boiling in this heat –'

'No, I'm fine, thanks.' Fumbling in a pocket, he produced an official-looking card and held it out.

'– um, Eddie.' She headed for the ancient cream gas cooker with its four worn gas rings and wonky oven door, wedged between a crammed storage cupboard redolent with the scent of dried fruits and spices, and a set of shelves laden with porcelain cups and saucers and green glass cake stands. 'Afraid it's pretty old – thing is, it was my Grandmother's.' When she first moved in she'd planned to change it, but she was fond of the memories of Granny Jackson's smoky Guinness stews and fruit cakes heavily laced with brandy it evoked, and until recently she'd hadn't had much trouble with it.

Until recently. The evening of Ivo's birthday at the end of July, to be precise, when he'd requested a twice-baked cheese souffle for supper. Nervous – she could just about manage an edible tomato quiche and a passable roast chicken – but determined to make the evening a success, she bought the finest quality ingredients and studied the recipe until she could recite it by heart. Luckily Ivo was out all afternoon, buying the state-of-the-art music system he'd persuaded Cassie to give him for his present, and by early evening a green salad was chilling in the fridge beside a chocolate cheesecake, and the table was laid with the best cutlery and wine glasses. She'd added a jug full of sprays of the diminutive white roses that climbed up the wall outside the kitchen, and set beeswax candles beside each place setting.

At half past seven he returned, full of good humour, his pockets stuffed with leaflets about music systems and an eye-watering bill, which he thrust at her with a pantomime wet kiss on her cheek. She could smell alcohol on his breath, but saw with relief that his eyes were only slightly bloodshot; if she could get some food into him, all might be well. Quickly she stirred the cloud of egg whites into the mixture, tipped the result into the well-buttered souffle dish she'd bought specially for the occasion and opened the oven door. A wall of heat met her – excellent, it had been heating at Regulo Six for the last half hour. Sliding in the souffle dish she tried to close the door gently. Held her breath as the catch stuck. Tried again; no luck. No choice but to give the door a light shove – still no joy. Again, harder this time. A pause followed by a loud click, thank God. She turned. Ivo had taken the Prosecco she'd stowed in the fridge earlier and was already downing a glass. 'Hope you're hungry – won't be long.' She helped herself to wine, raised her glass –

'Happy birthday, sweetheart' – and sat down to look at the sheaf of leaflets he pushed towards her.

Twenty minutes later she took the salad from the fridge and set it on the table, refusing more wine and trying not to notice when Ivo tipped the last of the bottle into his glass. Please God he'd show an interest in the souffle – the main thing was to stop it collapsing. 'Just going to close the back door, can't have a draught ruining my masterpiece.' She saw his frown, managed a laugh to show she was joking.

'Thank Christ for that.' He took a long pull at his wine. 'Smell of that bloody rose bush makes me want to puke.' He plucked the little white roses from their jug with an exaggerated shudder, and tossed them in the direction of the rubbish bin. 'Get rid of this lot too, if you don't mind.'

Cassie opened her mouth, thought better of it and shut it again. Cleared up the mess of broken stems and bruised petals and dumped it in the bin, stiffening as Ivo gave a tortured sigh. 'Gonna suffocate, this rate. Open the window, can't you?'

'Ivo, you know I can't.' The sash cords had broken years ago, and the weights had dropped, making it difficult to close the window safely. Repairs would be costly; despite Granny Jackson's protests, Grandpa Jackson had solved the problem by coating the already weak catch and entire wooden frame with several layers of white gloss paint. It had been impossible to open ever since. 'I'm really sorry – we can open the door again soon as we've eaten.'

'Ought to be condemned, this place. Bloody death trap.'

Slipping on the oven glove she forced an artificial show-biz smile – '*Ta da!!*' and opened the oven door with a flourish. Froze. No wall of heat this time, no tempting aroma, no perfectly risen souffle. The oven was a dark, chilly cave, the souffle dish held a slop of cheese sauce topped by a puddle of deflated raw egg whites. She turned helplessly to Ivo, apologising, explaining that the pilot light must have gone out when she forced the door shut. He stared at her expressionlessly as she apologised again, promising she'd do better next time, and tried to put her arm round his shoulders. How about she phoned for a Thai takeaway, it'd be here in no time and he loved Pad Thai, didn't he?

He stood up and pushed her away. 'Nothing but a Bunsen burner in a bloody tin, your stupid bitch of a Gran's cooker – the crap she produced must've been barely fucking edible.' He grabbed the second bottle of prosecco from the fridge and shoved it in his pocket. Slouched towards the back door. 'Okay to leave it open? Permission granted, is it?'

'Please don't go! I've tried so hard – there's chocolate cheesecake, and indoor fireworks –'

He stopped as he passed her. 'Just no souffle, right?' He smiled. 'Shame.'

It was the first time he hit her.

Next day she phoned the Gas Board.

Still, there was no way the Gas Engineer – *no, Gas Safety* – needed to know any of this. She pushed her glasses higher up her nose and straightened her shoulders. 'Well, here's Exhibit A.' She attempted a laugh. 'Don't suppose you see many cookers as old as this.'

Silence. She turned. He was still standing just inside the back door, gazing transfixed at the array of works-in-progress on the work bench. Sunlight glittered on the coils of copper wire, shone on the rows of tiny metal tools, gleamed on the scattering of seed pearls and semi-precious stones. '*Wow…*.' His voice was light. Quiet. His skin was paper-white, with a smattering of faded acne scars, his fair hair cut short in a punishing crew cut. Cheek bones any model would kill for, very pale blue eyes. She'd just decided they were actually grey when her visitor looked up. Reddened. 'Sorry, we're not s'posed to make personal –'

'No, honestly, it's fine.'

There was a brief silence while he gazed at the far end of the bench, reinforced to support the heavy-duty bench grinder, the soldering kit and ring-sizing machine, the lethal-looking saws and blades.

'So…' She gestured towards the cooker, wishing she'd remembered he was coming so she could have cleaned up the hob. 'Look, it's really embarrassing, afraid I let some milk boil over recently, and I haven't had time to –'

'S okay, you'd be surprised the mess some people –' He stopped, and padded over to the cooker. Peered at the worn badge below the overhead grill. 'New World Forty-Two, eh.? Can't be many of these still around – must be what, more than sixty years old.'

'It was my Gran's. I expect you think –'

He looked at the mess of burnt milk on the hob. 'Gotta a damp cloth and some washing up liquid?'

'Sure –' As she hurried to the sink, he flipped open

the lid of his toolbox and began to lay out an array of complicated-looking gadgets on the counter beside the cooker. When she returned he held out a hand, palm upwards. 'I'll do it.'

'Please let me – it's my mess, it won't take a sec –'

'Got to think of the pilot light. 'S risky.'

'Oh.' She handed him the cloth and embarrassingly sticky Fairy Liquid container, watched helplessly as he bent over the hob, frowning. *Oh God.* 'Could I get you a cup of tea? Coffee?' *Stupid, he must be boiling in those overalls.* 'Or I've got some great cold –'

He jumped, banging his head on the shaky overhead grill. 'No – I mean no thank you.' He rubbed a hand down the front of his fleece. 'Best if I get on with it, if you don't mind.' He began to scrub delicately round the back burner.

'No of course not – I'll just –'

Just what? She turned away. He clearly felt uncomfortable with her being there, but there was no way she was leaving him alone with all that stuff on her work bench. Might as well use the time to sort out her accounts, pay a few bills. Pulling out a chair as quietly as possible she sat down at the table, hauled a bulging folder of paperwork towards her and settled down to work. The first time he passed her to rinse out his cloth in the sink she attempted a friendly smile, but he blushed so painfully that on his next trip she pretended to be concentrating on organising her receipts.

Half an hour later, tools clanked as he rummaged in the toolbox, followed by a loud tapping as he investigated the inside of the oven. She'd given up on the accounts and was happily sketching the camellia on the windowsill when the tapping stopped, followed by an exclamation. She looked round. He was holding a complicated-looking object covered with blackened grease up to the light, shaking his head. 'Oven burner. Not looking too good.'

'Oh dear, I can see it is a bit –'

'Needs replacing. Door handle too, obviously.' He pushed the door to, gently.

'Lord, didn't realise things were that bad. Is it okay to use it?'

'Only if you want to blow up the whole street.' He repacked his tools neatly and looked up with a surprisingly sweet smile. 'Only kidding.'

He pressed the automatic starter, shook his head when it clicked fruitlessly. 'Spark generator's gone.'

'Been kaput since I moved in. Still, matches work fine.'

Reaching down, he tried to open the oven door. It stuck. Cassie went to stand beside him, pretending not to notice when he moved away slightly. 'There's a trick to it, let me show you –'

'No need.' He applied pressure to the handle, twisted it gently and stood back as the door swung open. Knelt and peered inside. 'Door seal's gone. Thought so.' Frowning, he ran his fingers along the rubber gasket surrounding the oven's hatch. He drew in his breath sharply. 'Worn all the way round, looks like.' He probed and prodded, looking concerned. 'Couple of torn sections, too.'

'God, sounds awful.'

''Fraid it is. Total new seal required. Thing is you're

probably getting at least 25% heat loss the way things are.'

Cassie remembered Ivo's birthday dinner. She tried to laugh. 'Actually, sometimes they don't cook at all...' She flinched, and closed her eyes briefly – opened them again to find him staring at her, looking concerned.

'Better check the rest, Okay?' He began to check the rest of the oven, looking increasingly worried as most of the components malfunctioned. Shooting an apologetic glance at Cassie, he drew a small device from his breast pocket and began to dictate. 'Gas burner caps worn. Grill control knob ditto. Gas injectors...nozzles...ditto.' Cassie put a hand to her mouth. He continued his inspection. 'Gaskets, O rings...' He shook his head.

'Don't tell me.' She managed a laugh. 'You're going to tell me it's only fit for landfill, right?'

'Unsafe gas appliances...' He shook his head. 'Serious health risk. Can lead to CO poisoning.'

'C. O....?'

'Carbon monoxide poisoning.'

'God.'

'Causes headaches nausea breathlessness dizziness leading to loss of consciousness leading to ...' He finally took a breath. 'Collapse. Not pretty.'

'No, no of course not.'

Thank God her father wasn't there. He'd been appalled when she'd refused his offer of a new Shaker kitchen including cooker and fridge (*and how about a central island and a wine chiller while we're about it, Cass darling?*) when she moved in, not to mention the complete rewiring Granny Jackson had always refused point blank to let him organise, since she didn't Hold With Change. But Cassie loved the little house with all its idiosyncrasies as it was; exchanging the curtains –

it was shimmering in the moonlight, rippling and billowing in the breeze for all the world as if it was alive

– for blinds at all the windows was the only alteration she wanted. Though she was pretty sure her father would have gone ahead and simply ordered the stuff – and insisted on being there to see it safely installed, too – if he'd heard the list of ailments the young man had just mentioned.

There was a brief silence.

Cassie thought of Granny Jackson's expression as she lifted a tray of mince pies from the oven, the star-emblazoned pastry cases golden, the aroma of dried fruit and brandy filling the kitchen. 'I suppose there's absolutely no way –'

A regretful shrug. 'See thing is, a model this old, be nearly impossible to get the parts.'

'Course. It's just … I miss her.' She shrugged. 'Silly really, but having her cooker here makes me feel as if she's still – you know –'

'Sure.' He smiled. 'Tell you what. I'll take a look at the rating plate, check the serial number, and ask around – maybe I'll strike lucky.' As he added the information to the lengthy list of faults, the landline, listed with her phone number on her website, rang. She jumped, and hurried over to the workbench.

'Sorry – won't be a sec, probably a client.'

He nodded politely, turned away and began to collect various items from his toolbox, while Cassie discussed possible designs for the choker the client was requesting – *absolutely nothing sparkling, so common, I'm thinking opals – and I must have five rows, five's my lucky number d'you see?* – and arranged a visit at the end of the week. With a sigh of relief Cassie entered the details in the desk diary, and began to retrace her steps. Stopped, smiling as Eddie concentrated on tying an *UNSAFE APPLIANCE* label to the cooker's door handle. Cassie felt a wave of gratitude as he carefully wound several lengths of bright yellow *DANGER DO NOT USE* tape round the body of the oven, and stood back to admire his handiwork.

Cassie stood up, and moving closer, smoothed down a jagged tape end. 'Ought to enter it for the Turner Prize.'

He retreated to the table, took a pad from a pocket and started to fill in a form. 'Need half a dead cow in the oven and a sparkly skull on the grill if you want to win that.'

She tried not to look surprised.

'Right. Be back Saturday with some replacement parts, hopefully.' He glanced at his watch. 'Lunch time suit you?'

'Great, thanks.' She fetched the diary again and made a note. Looked up, smiling. 'And I'm really grateful for –'

A double take at her sketch of the camellia, a pause beside the workbench as he passed. Then head down, he hurried through the open back door and was gone.

'– everything.'

She stared after him for a moment, then shrugged. 'Oh well. Guess it's lucky it's salad weather.' Opening the fridge carefully (of the same vintage as the cooker, it had been one of Granny Jackson's proudest possessions), Cassie steadied the door as it swung open violently, then jammed. She scanned the shelves; a heel of cheddar, a rhubarb yoghurt and half a jar of red pesto. The contents of the freezer were hardly more cheering, apart from a container of vividly coloured, rocket-shaped lollies she occasionally passed over the fence to Brooklyn and Bronx. Though last winter she'd found a recipe in one of the supplements for French onion soup – easy and delicious – and had made a vast quantity, and frozen it. The following week it was chicken soup – not so easy, this time, and she forgot the seasoning – but she made a double batch and froze that, too. Ivo spat out his serving later that week and hissed that he'd wait till he was old and toothless and propped up in some bloody care home before he ate slop like that, and what the fuck was wrong with fillet steak, twice-cooked goose fat chips and a couple of bottles of a decent claret?

She slammed the fridge door. *Bastard.* Definitely time for a trip to the shops – her cheek was throbbing and a change of scene would do her good. Some interesting cheese, free range eggs, fruit and salad, a couple of lemon sorbets and maybe some chocolate. No, *definitely* chocolate. Plus she needed a couple of drawing pens and pastels for her sketches – better call in at Broad Canvas before they closed. Upstairs to the bathroom first; glancing in the mirror as she washed her hands she saw that the concealer had almost worn off her cheek, her lipstick-free mouth and heavy spectacles doing little to improve things. God, no wonder the Gas bloke – Eric? *No, Eddie* – was so nervous, you could see he thought she was a weirdo. She wouldn't be surprised if he got them to send a replacement next time...After repairing the damage to her appearance she collected the post from the doormat, ran downstairs, tossed the scatter of letters and flyers on the table beside the rest of the mail, closed all the blinds, grabbed her favourite purple string bag and locking the back door behind her, emerged into the late afternoon sunshine.

CHAPTER FIVE

A FEW OF the little late nineteenth century terrace houses in Poplar Street were still occupied by tenants of her grandmother's generation. Dusty net curtains shrouded the windows, window boxes were crammed with pots of wilting purple heather. Here and there an empty plastic crate stood beside the doorstep, waiting for a milkman who no longer called. A couple of houses at the end of the street were in urgent need of landlord's repairs – leaky gutters, broken slates, peeling paint – and occupied by students, most of whom seemed to stay on in Oxford during the vacations, bikes dumped haphazardly in tiny front gardens, tattered protest posters taped to windows, music drifting from open front doors. A cheerful Asian family occupied the house on the corner; today the younger women stood chatting on the front path, plump in their gold-embroidered saris, enjoying the sunshine. As usual, tantalising cooking smells drifted from the kitchen.

The rest of the houses had cars parked outside, neatly clipped bay trees in pots beside the front doors, pine slatted blinds at the windows. Mostly occupied by people from the university, or creatives or business executives, like her neighbours, David and Erica. *Toffs*, as Zadie on her other side would say. Grinning, Cassie waved as Brooklyn and Bronx raced past, pushing a squeaking supermarket trolley crammed with a selection of unidentifiable stuffed animals, narrowly avoiding Erica as she screeched to a halt at the kerb and alighted from her gleaming black Mini.

Pretending not to notice, Cassie rounded the corner into Cowley Road, cheered even more as an ice cream van trundled into view, bells chiming discordantly, and with a final ear-splitting peal, turned into Poplar Street. She knew from experience that the driver (Rasta braids elaborately beaded, gold fillings gleaming) would brake sharply to a halt and leap into place at the window, beaming, as kids appeared from nowhere and raced towards the van, screaming with joy, hotly pursued by their mothers. She knew, too, that Erica would be close behind them, threatening to report the driver to the council, of whom she knew some *extremely* important members, for the *disgraceful* breach of the peace...

She headed for Sainsbury's first, grateful for the comforting familiarity of its cluttered shelves and cut-price offers, and bought her groceries. Then she strolled the length of Cowley Road, enjoying the sun's warmth as it eased the pain of her injuries, stopping occasionally at the little Asian shops to buy fruit (brightly coloured mangoes and hairy little lychees) and salad (red onions and misshapen yellow tomatoes), smiling her thanks for a ruddy-skinned pomegranate a stall holder slipped into her bag with a wink. Secure in the knowledge that nobody would be waiting irritably for her return in order to demand something complicated and expensive for supper, and criticise whatever commission she was currently working on, Cassie began to relax. Allowed herself to linger outside the window of the expensive artisan gift shop, admiring the silver cufflinks and luxurious silk scarves. In the Indian emporium, the friendly manager was busy arranging his newly arrived delivery of incense sticks, and in a burst of optimism Cassie purchased a vividly coloured package of Special Exotic Lotus, charmed by the beaming dancing girls, their costumes consisting of a mere silver chain or two, decorating the label.

There was just time to hurry past St Clements roundabout, past Magdalen and on up the High Street, then right down Turl Street to Broad Street and a quick dash into Broad Canvas for her art materials. After a wander among the racks of paints and brushes and displays of complicated craft materials, she added a large sketchbook and a box of pastels to her purchases. It wasn't until she got outside, and tried to juggle the bags bulging with her earlier purchases with her booty from Broad Canvas, that she realised the walk home would be challenging. Retracing her steps she headed back to the High Street again, resisting the urge as she passed Toast to stop and admire the pale blue linen sundress displayed in the window, concentrating instead on forcing her way through the crowds of tourists thronging the pavements.

Crossing the High Street, she made her way to the bus stop and with a sigh of relief joined the queue.

She found herself behind the elderly white-robed Muslim with aquiline features she often saw chatting to his friends outside the Cowley Road mosque, and a scrawny youth in a tattered hoodie clearly on his way to join his mates for a spliff or two in the bus shelter outside the health centre. Prising her travel card out of the junk in her wallet as the bus arrived, she returned the driver's greeting and lugged her bags down the aisle to a vacant seat by the window.

As the rest of the queue shoved and jostled its way on board, she stared out through the grimy glass, pondering her design for the diadem. It was rush hour, now, and the traffic in the High Street was heavier than ever, buses lurching past the speeding taxis and delivery vans, bicycles weaving through the trickle of jay-walking tourists. She'd just decided to experiment with crystal spacers for the diadem as soon as she got home when the bus juddered to a halt at the traffic lights by the corner of Longwall Street, opposite the Grand Café with its elegant Georgian proportions and pale blue paintwork.

The lights changed to amber, and the bus began to edge forward slowly. Cassie pulled a crumpled tissue from her pocket and rubbed at the stains on the glass, trying to get a better look at the impressive display of giant meringues in the café window. Leaned closer to the window for a final glimpse – and stiffened. A figure had emerged from the café and joined the group of pedestrians waiting to cross, a figure clad in a black leather jacket, despite the heat. A figure sporting a heavily oiled quaff and a sulky smoulder as he jabbed savagely at the traffic light buttons, scowling at the traffic as it began to pass. Where was he going? *Where*? Oh God, surely he couldn't be on his way to Poplar Street…?

A few more seconds and he'd see her. Forcing herself to look away from the window, she rearranged the shopping on her lap, fast, contriving to give the bag of salad a nudge, and pretending to jump as the pomegranate tumbled out. Exclaiming at her clumsiness she dived to the floor, and spent as long as possible searching for it, resurfacing as the traffic lights receded into the distance. A quick glance over her shoulder – no sign of him. With a sigh of relief she flourished the battered fruit at the young girl who'd taken the seat next to her, a sleeping baby with a large pink bow bobby-pinned to the sparse kiss curl adorning its forehead clasped in her thin arms. Cassie managed a friendly smile. 'Great colour, isn't it? Seeds'll be great in salads!' Looking nervous, her neighbour edged as far away from Cassie as she could, a nail-bitten hand shielding the baby's hand protectively. Oh for God's sake, it was a pomegranate, not a bloody hand grenade! She turned her head slowly back towards the window in a dignified sort of way, ostentatiously admiring the view as the bus gathered speed across Magdalen Bridge, over the Plain and on into the blessedly noisy Cowley Road. As they stopped every now and again to pick up yet more blessedly noisy shoppers, Cassie peered inside her bulging string bag from time to time, taking comfort from the reassuringly domestic contents. At last the bus bucketed to a halt at her stop. Getting to her feet, she clambered unsteadily past her neighbour, bestowing what she intended to be an admiring smile on the infant as she squeezed passed. Unfortunately it chose this moment to break into piercing screams, causing its mother to cast Cassie a baleful look, and making it as embarrassing as possible for her to fight her way down the aisle, crowded now with female passengers eyeing her suspiciously.

Despite herself she was running as she approached her turning, the carriers and string bag banging painfully against her ankles, her hair, damp with perspiration, falling in her eyes. The uneven pavement with its dusty little plane trees, the mismatched houses with their tatty student protest posters and inappropriate pastel front doors, had never been more welcome. *Nearly there.* Zadie was standing outside, clasping a filthy limbless, one-eared stuffed rabbit and laughing with Cassie's neighbour on the other side. Damn. She couldn't just ignore them, though she was desperate to get inside and lock the door behind her. Though maybe if he saw her talking to people, saw that she wasn't alone, he'd think twice before –

'Hey, girlfriend!' Zadie eyed the fruit and vegetables poking through the string bag and elbowed her in the ribs. 'Ha! Health kick is it now?'

Cassie tried not to wince. 'Sure thing. Long as I'm still allowed the vino –' She managed to return her other neighbour's smile. She'd done little more than exchange a friendly wave in the past – he was in London a lot, apparently – but now she took in an untidy shock of hair – dark brown, with a hint of grey – and a slightly hawk-like nose. Blue eyes, no, more sort of dark green – good teeth – with a tiny chip in the front one.

'Second that.' He held out a hand. 'David. Good to meet you properly.' Cassie dropped a bag and took it. It was warm and dry, his clasp firm.

'Cassie.' She wished her hand wasn't damp with sweat after all the running, and faintly sticky with pomegranate juice.

He was looking at her intently. 'Nasty bruise you've got there. How –'

She ran a hand casually through her hair. 'Oh, it looks much worse than it really is. Walked straight into a cupboard door. Stupid...So how's things, Zadie? Kids okay?'

Zadie brandished the remains of the rabbit at her. 'Come out to find Terminator. Fell out the trolley when they was muckin about this afternoon, Dave here found him arse over tit in the gutter.' She bestowed a kiss on what might once have been the creature's nose. 'Never get Brooklyn off to sleep without him. Speakin of which, gotta go, they'll've found the X Channel before you know it –' She began to hurry away, then turned back suddenly. 'Tell Dave about that lemon plant, Cass. Cryin shame the way it's moultin, and Dave's an expert what with his oranges and that.'

'Lemon...? He glanced behind her, frowning. She swung round nervously. Nothing, just an old man shuffling in their direction on the other side of the road. Her companion raised a hand. 'Hi, Bill, how's it going? Be over tomorrow to fix the catch on that gate for you.' He turned back to Cassie. 'Right, about your –' He stopped as the tasteful Skittles Green front door of his own house whipped open, to reveal

Erica standing with her hands on her hips, scowling. 'David! I need you to come and make the gazpacho, please.' Ignoring Cassie, she folded her arms. '*Now!*'

He sighed. 'In a minute, Erica.' As Erica slammed the door, hard, Cassie grabbed her bags and began to edge away. 'So nice to see you, time I was –'

'Hang on – what's all this about a lemon plant – or tree, I take it?'

'Honestly, it's nothing, it's just these little lemons keep falling off even though I put it on the windowsill to catch the light –'

'Happy to call round and take a look, if you'd like me too?'

'No really, I'm sure you're far too busy to –'

'Be a pleasure. Tomorrow morning any good? About eleven?'

'Well, if you're sure?'

'Look forward to it. Back door okay?'

'Fine.'

He strolled towards his front garden. Cassie admired the pale paving stones and the ivy-covered trellis concealing the row of bins as he rummaged for his keys and let himself in, noting that despite the ire that undoubtedly awaited him, he made absolutely no attempt to hurry. Feeling unaccountably happy, she reached in her pocket for her own keys – and realised suddenly, with a lurch of terror, that she was standing in the middle of the pavement by herself, now Zadie and David had gone. What was she thinking? Ivo could slope into view at any moment – worse, he'd seen her talking to people and had retreated to the corner of the street, waiting to pounce as she opened the front door.

Moving fast she retraced her steps, turning left at the end of the street, and along the short distance to the path leading behind the back gardens. For the first time she was aware of autumn approaching; the heat of the day was fading, and there was a chill in the early evening air as dusk began to fall. The path was shadowy, the gates and fences demarcating the gardens' boundaries blurred, the shapes of the overhanging shrubs and bushes indistinct in the deepening gloom. She moved towards her own gate, alert for a half-concealed figure, a drift of stale cigarette smoke. Jumped as a ragged white shape slid from a nearby ditch and fled; relaxed as she recognized Blanco, number 8's tomcat. Heart hammering, she stood for a moment, then silently opened the gate and entered the garden, closing it carefully behind her. Focused on the grey shape of the back of the house, accepted after a while that she could see nothing untoward and tiptoed – *tiptoed* in her own garden, for God's sake! – towards the back door, grateful for the bright light that sprang into life in Zadie's bathroom and the accompanying burst of Bob Marley, and the lamplight glowing in her neighbour's – *David's* – kitchen on the other side.

Her keys were in her hand, now, and then the door was open and she was inside, *home*, slamming the door behind her, locking it, dropping the shopping bags, pulling down all the blinds, switching on the lamps, taking the stairs at a run and checking the front door. Downstairs again, she streamed Nina Simone – kettle on too, she'd never needed a mug of tea more. A quick check of her phone; two messages from clients, two unanswered calls from Ivo. Sinking into a chair she looked around the kitchen, cheered by the positively cheerful-looking tape festooning the ancient cooker, then over at the work bench, grateful for the familiar array of materials, the evidence of works-in-progress.

As the kettle boiled, she hauled herself to her feet and switched off her phone. Time to get on. There was work to be done.

Three hours later she set down her tools with a sigh. Enough; work was coming along nicely and she was tired and hungry. Taking the new ingredients from the salad drawer she chopped and sliced, arranging the bright colours on a plate shaped like a lettuce leaf she'd found in a charity shop, sprinkling them with pomegranate seeds that glowed like garnets. A quick sprinkling of dressing, a grab for the Ryvita packet when she realised she couldn't warm the stale bread rolls lurking at the bottom of the bread bin in the oven, plus a large glass of Merlot.

Nina Simone had given way now to Billie Holiday; she sat slowly eating her supper, wondering how David's gazpacho had gone and thinking about the shops in the Cowley Road, wishing Granny Jackson was still here so she could give her one of the expensive silk scarves she'd seen for her birthday. Suddenly she heard a commotion outside, and jumping to her feet clutching her knife, headed for the stairs – *surely she checked the chain just now, didn't she?* – stopping when she heard Zadie screech at one of the kids to *get inside right now, buster*, followed by the slam of her back door. Relief swept through her. Draining the Merlot, she got to her feet and put her plate in the sink, and was rinsing her wine glass when she caught sight of the lemon tree. Oh God, it was looking sadder than ever, plus three more wizened fruits had given up the ghost and fallen onto the draining board. What on earth would David say when he saw it? Probably report her to the plant equivalent of the RSPCA. Water, that was the thing. Filling the wine glass she emptied it carefully into the dusty soil, replaced the little tree on the windowsill and stood back consideringly. Better, definitely better. By way of demonstrating good will she added another glassful, in imitation of the *chef's extra* her grandmother used to chuckle over as she added another measure of brandy to the Christmas cake mixture.

Time for bed, before she fell asleep leaning on the sink. She stood irresolute; finally decided to leave all the lights on, plus the radio. Loudly. After double checking the locks and chains, she showered, cleaned her teeth, pulled on a tee shirt, set the alarm for nine, slipped keys and phone under her pillow and crawled into bed.

She fell asleep almost at once, but woke at twenty past three mired in a nightmare where she was running for her life under a darkening sky, pursued by a swarm of angry wasps. Opening her eyes with a start, perspiring, she sat bolt upright, frantically brushing at her arms and legs, gradually becoming calmer as she took in the shadowy shape of the wardrobe, the chair with her clothes draped over the back. Weak with relief, she straightened the damp sheets – then stopped, listening. *That muffled buzzing was no dream*…Holding her breath she forced herself to lift up the pillows, almost laughed aloud as she saw her phone and heard its cheerful ring tone, loud and clear now – *stupid*, must have forgotten to switch it off – stopped laughing as she checked caller ID, and saw Ivo's name. *Of course, who else would it be in the middle of the night?*

Too late now; she'd have to let it ring out. Replacing the pillow, she reached out, switched on the bedside light, picked up a favourite book of Redouté Rose watercolours and turned to an exquisite image that reminded her of her beloved white climbing rose blooming beside the back door. She sighed. Impossible to escape the buzzing; leaning over the side of the bed she retrieved the pillow she'd discarded a couple of nights ago, thrust it on top of the first one and went back to her book, grateful when after a couple of minutes the noise stopped. Groping beneath the pillows she pulled out the phone, and was about to switch it off when it began to ring again in her hand – shrilly, insistently this time – as if the caller – *Ivo* – knew she was there. Instinctively she started to shove it back under the pillows – then hesitated. Maybe it would be better to answer it, say coldly that if he didn't leave her alone she'd call the police right now and report him for harassing – *no, stalking* – her. Pressing 'answer' she took a deep breath. 'Ivo…?'

The only response was agonised sobbing – choking gasps for breath – more sobbing, interspersed with heart-broken attempts to speak. She pressed her hand to her mouth, horrified.

'Cassie, *darling* Cassie – I love you, dearest, *sweetest* angel, I'm just a poor fool who doesn't know how to show it –' a strangled groan '– tell me what you're doing right now, my beloved, so I can picture you …'

'Nothing – I – just looking at my book of roses, the Redouté one –'

A strangled sigh. 'The one on the bedside table?'

'Well yes –'

'Oh, it hurts so bad to think how adorable you must look! I miss you, Cass – I can't live without you – remember how good we used to be?' Stumbling reminders followed, of lazy summer picnics in punts, visits to intense arthouse films, coach trips to London in the early days to network with his theatrical friends, passionate love-making in sunlit fields.

Now he was reliving the visit to Ann Hathaway's cottage garden in Stratford, where he'd managed to declaim most of Henry Vth's famously bracing speech to a crowd of bemused Japanese tourists before the guide moved him on, when he was interrupted by a terrible bout of coughing 'Oh God – I'm ill, Cass – I swear I'll *die* if you won't let me come home.' He started to sob again. 'Please *please, my angel…my darling…*'

She sat with tears running down her face, longing to hold him, comfort him. It was true, they *had* been good in the beginning, and it wasn't Ivo's fault if he had an actor's over-sensitive temperament – everyone knew creative people were touchy. She should have been more understanding, more supportive. Dropping the phone, she fumbled under the pillow for a crumpled tissue and blew her nose, remembering

Ivo's delight on his birthday near the beginning of their relationship when she presented him with the little gold hoop earring containing a single tiny diamond she'd created for him. The time she'd had flu and he'd offered to make her a mug of hot lemon. Okay, so he'd forgotten to actually *do* it, and headed out to the pub, but it was the *thought* that counted. She dabbed at her wet cheeks, careful to avoid the bruises, and thought of his childlike sense of fun, the jokes he loved to play. Like the Christmas when they were first together and he presented her with an exquisite little red leather box and sat watching her avidly, smiling, while she opened it, expecting – *no, hoping, with all her heart* – that it would contain a ring. Ivo roared with laughter when he saw her discover that the adorable little box merely contained a foil-covered chocolate cherry, and quickly hiding her crushing disappointment, made herself laugh too…

Her trouble was she was too conventional, too – well, *dull*. Maybe she could try to be more – She winced. Cramp. She could hear him faintly, sobbing even more pathetically, calling her name. Her heart ached with pity. *Hurry* – she'd change her position, get some support for her aching back, then talk to him. Reassure him. Promise him…Pushing the sweat-sodden pillow aside she edged to the side of the bed, leaned over, and gasping with pain as her muscles protested, grabbed a pillow she remembered falling to the floor the other night, and fell back against the headboard. Easing herself into position she glanced down, preparing to slide the pillow behind her to act as a support.. Stopped as she saw the rust-brown stains spattered all over the faded cream linen pillowcase, clotting the delicate lace edging. Sat staring. Remembering. Picking up the phone she took a deep breath. 'No, Ivo.'

An agonised groan. 'Cass –'

She touched the smallest stain lightly with a forefinger. Shuddered. '*No.*'

Clicking the 'off' button, she shoved the now blessedly silent phone under the mattress, and switched off the lamp. Lay rigid for a moment, trying to control her breathing. Check. *Check now*…Switching the lamp on again, she eased herself off the bed, dragged on her kimono, and wrapping it tightly round herself, crept out onto the landing, glad she'd left all the lights on. It didn't take long to check the front and back doors were securely locked, the chains neatly in place.

Back in bed, she clasped the book of Redouté paintings to her chest for comfort, pulled the damp duvet over her head and curled herself into the smallest ball she could manage.

Tried to sleep.

CHAPTER SIX

SHE WOKE MUCH later than planned next morning. Sunlight filtered round the edges of the blind, a lorry driver shouted at kids playing in the road, engine revving menacingly, somewhere a dog was barking. Her cheek throbbed where she'd slept on the wrong side by mistake, worse, jumbled fragments of some bizarre dream refused to fade, making it hard to think clearly. Better get up – wasn't she supposed to phone a client? No, that wasn't it. Think…'*Happy to call round, if you'd like?*' Oh God, David! '*About eleven?*'

She grabbed the clock. *10.40.* Throwing off the duvet she yanked up the blind, threw on jeans and an oversized striped shirt, realised the shirt was Ivo's – tore it off with an exclamation of disgust, resolving to pack it up with the rest of his stuff later – tossed it in the corner, replaced it with a sleeveless tee shirt and ran into the bathroom. Tugged a brush through her hair, wishing she had time to wash it as she'd planned, settled for securing her straggling curls in a scrunchie on top of her head and cleaned her teeth, trying unsuccessfully to avoid her painful lip. Quick glance in the mirror. *Mistake.* Oh well, he was coming to check out the lemon tree, it wasn't a social visit.

With a sigh she patted the now customary concealer on her cheek, picked up her mascara then put it down again.

Downstairs, fast. Raise blinds, unlock back door, undo chain. *Freeze.* Re-lock door, re-set chain. Put kettle on for coffee, switch on radio, tidy the – No time, there was a gentle tattoo at the back door. Forcing herself to relax – Ivo would never knock like that – she went to open it.

David stood outside, holding a carton full of jars and cans, their torn labels portraying improbably colourful plants. 'Hi there. How's the patient?'

Cassie shook her head. 'Don't think I'll be offering anyone homemade lemonade any time soon.'

Smiling, he stepped inside, and stood looking around. 'Wow, great kitchen. Love the dresser and those fabulous antique dishes.'

the plate hit the wall behind her head. Shattered and fell to the floor, leaving a trail of gravy and vegetables trickling slowly down the wall

'Royal Worcester, aren't they?'

She tried and failed to imagine him hurling one at the wall. Blinking back tears, she nodded. 'They were my Gran's.'

Pretending not to notice her distress, he frowned mock seriously. 'Right. Where's that lemon tree?'

Cassie gestured at the sink. He began to follow her, stopped as he noticed the workbench. 'Didn't know your partner was a jeweller?'

'*He's not.*' She attempted a casual shrug. 'My partner, I mean.'

He adjusted the lid on a particularly rusty can.

'Sorry, didn't mean to –'

Oh God, she'd embarrassed him. 'No, really – it's just we…split up recently, and –'

'Nightmare having to explain, I know.' He looked away. 'Still, all good things come to an end.' He looked back again, grinning. 'Thank God.' He cast a brief look at her cheek, and stopped grinning. 'Even the not so good ones, too.'

She looked away. 'So, let me show you the –'

But he was looking at the work bench again. 'So… this is *your* work?'

She nodded, waited for him to make a supercilious remark, wishing Zadie had never mentioned the bloody lemon tree.

'It's stunning. Do you sell in stores, or…?'

'Got a website – do it all on-line these days.'

He moved nearer, peering at the saws and blades, the stone-setting tools, the array of semi-precious stones. 'May I…?'

She hesitated. 'If you really…Coffee?'

He bent over the drawings for the tiara. 'Love some.'

By the time he'd finished admiring the works-in-progress and asking technical questions about her tools, the kettle had boiled and she was hunting for a new pack of filter papers when there was a thud from the direction of the windowsill. Turning, he caught sight of the denuded tree and the wizened little fruit rolling across the draining board. 'Oh dear. Better take a look. Can I ask where you bought it?'

'It was a present.' Better not tell him it was thriving when it arrived, bursting with bright green leaves and flowers like little white stars, and, incredibly, loaded with miniature lemons. Looking concerned, he picked up his basket and approached the sink. 'Dwarf Meyer, I'd say. Should do fine indoors, long as it's got plenty of light –' better not tell him that these days she kept the blind closed '– and it's not standing in a draught. Plus it's important not to let the soil dry out, obviously.'

Cassie discreetly brushed a dead fly and a tiny flake of white paint off the windowsill as he prodded the soil gently. 'Ah, no danger of that, I see.' He raised an eyebrow. 'Not natural swimmers, Dwarf Meyers, far as I know – too much water, especially cold water, makes the roots rot.'

'Oh, I thought –'

Looking purposeful, he stripped off his black pullover, dropped it on a chair, and rolled up his cream flannel shirt sleeves. 'Got any old teacloths? Kitchen towel?'

Cassie tried not to stare at his tanned forearms. 'Yes, but –'

'Let's have 'em. Maybe a bucket, too, if you've got one –'

'God, sorry, I don't think I –'

'No worries, a washing up bowl will do fine.'

Suddenly the landline rang. She jumped. *Leave it*! She stood, irresolute. Ivo always called on her mobile – it was probably a new customer, or maybe the potential client who left a message recently asking if Cassie could make a pair of drop earrings for her daughter's upcoming eighteenth birthday. Either way, she couldn't afford to lose commissions.

She turned to David, who was watching her, looking

concerned. 'Sorry, better get that – won't be a sec.' She reached for the phone, hands shaking, and found it was the client, Mrs Langley Smith, after all. After discussing possible options they agreed she'd pop in that afternoon at four to decide on the final design, and after giving her directions Cassie returned to the sink. David was examining the lemon tree, the washing up bowl, now overflowing with a disgusting-looking sludge, at his feet. 'Sorry to take so long – new commission. I'll finish making that coffee now.'

'I've replaced most of the wet soil with compost, plus perlite to encourage drainage.' He shook his head. 'Thing is with lemon trees, they're relatively easy to care for, but if you overdo the TLC...'

Cassie bit her lip. 'It's my fault – I thought a Chef's Extra would be a good idea –'

She was pretty sure he hid a smile. 'Still, look on the bright side.' He patted a branch and pretended not to notice when another lemon fell off. 'Probably be fine once it settles down. I'll just give it a quick pick-me-up ...'

She put the coffee pot on the table while he ministered to the little tree with a range of impressive-looking cartons and sprays and stood, hands on hips, surveying his handiwork. 'Ought to do the trick.'

'Do you really think it'll –'

'No worries, it'll be fine.' His lips twitched. 'Better go easy on the watering for a few days, though.'

'Oh, I will.'

'Keep that window shut too, when the temperature drops in the evenings, 'kay? Kiss of death, that could be.'

'You bet.'

She passed him a mug as they sat the table. 'Thanks.' He lifted it to his lips, hesitated and set it down again. 'Look, tell me if this is out of order, but you said just now that call was about a commission, and I wondered if I might be allowed to make a request, too?'

Cassie took a sip of coffee, not noticing as it burnt her lip, and tried not to look too pleased. 'Sure. What sort of thing were you thinking of?' Suddenly it was easy not to look at *all* pleased. Of course – he wanted a present for ghastly Erica. A hideous black jet scorpion brooch ought to fit the bill…

'…I thought maybe a pendant? With a single iris – or maybe several, if you think that would be better? They're her favourite flowers –'

Cassie banged down her mug. 'Really sorry, afraid I'm up to here with orders at the moment –'

'Oh.' He pushed back his chair. 'No problem, hope you didn't mind my asking –' He gestured at the workbench. 'Just wanted to give her something really special. It's her seventy-fifth birthday in a couple of months, you see –'

'Pardon?'

'My mother.'

Cassie tried to rearrange her expression. 'What a lovely idea. Irises, you said?'

'Well yes, if you think it might be possible?' He sat down again. 'Thing is the old girl only just survived bloody Covid. She's doing fine now, but for a while there…' He cleared his throat. 'Her hair's silver, and she often wears lilac and mauve, so I thought…'

'A pendant sounds perfect. But I'm pretty sure iris

are out of season at the moment, so I won't be able to find any to draw...' She thought for a moment, then clicked her fingers, jumped up, prised a volume from the crowded bookcase, opened it at one of van Gogh's joyful paintings of iris and passed it to him. 'Something like this?' She watched while David gazed at it, noting the fine lines radiating from the corners of his eyes, wondering how he got the tiny scar on his cheekbone. 'Let's see...Art Nouveau-style paste, velvety purple and pale blue petals delicately outlined in black? Suspended on a fine silver curb-link chain?'

He looked up. 'You could do that?'

Laughing, she retrieved the book, laid it open on the table. 'We do our best to please.'

'Fantastic!' Glancing at his watch, he drained his mug and got to his feet. 'Got to go, deadline's calling.'

She followed him to the open back door. 'Cassie, thank you.' He gripped her hand, started to say something else, then released her hand and strode away across the grass

Pushing the mugs aside she sat down at the table and gazed at the painting again, thinking, planning. It wasn't until she went to the workbench to make a list of the extra materials she'd need and phoned the order in to her suppliers that she realised with a shock that the back door was wide open. In an instant it was closed and locked, the chain slid into place, the blinds drawn. She glanced at the clock. Her client was due at four; forget iris pendants, there was just time to dress a bit more professionally and set out some photos of previously commissioned drop earrings, with examples of settings from *delicate* to positively *grand*, beside an array of precious and semi-precious stones. She'd given Mrs Langley Smith directions to the front door; just before four she'd raise the blinds and open the back door to the late August heat. Even Ivo wouldn't dare to make trouble in front of a witness.

By half past five, after several cups of Earl Grey tea (kept especially for clients – Cassie personally thought it tasted like warm cologne) and agonised indecision (after endless procrastination, clients inevitably plumped for their original choice) it was decided that circular blister pearls above pear-shaped amethysts with tourmaline spacers would be perfect, and after noting down the details Cassie saw a delighted Mrs Langley Smith out. As soon as she'd locked and chained the front door she ran down to the kitchen, secured the back door again and yanked all the blinds down. The earrings were needed in two weeks; as she entered the details in the diary Cassie noticed with horror that a hinged bangle she hadn't even begun work on yet was due to be collected the following week. Damn Ivo; it wasn't like her to lose track of her orders. This was for a simple rose gold bangle, but with a lobster clasp; better make a start on it right away. Changing into baggy dungarees with a sigh of relief she dumped the teacups in the sink, noticing with a frisson of pleasure that the lemon tree was looking healthier already. Perhaps over supper, later, she'd take another look at van Gogh's irises…

Switching on the lamps, she turned off her phone and settled down to work.

It was well past midnight when she set callipers, steel

rule and calculator aside and stretched, yawning. And once again regretted it – her lip was still sore, her back muscles ached more than ever. She'd carry on tomorrow; the tourmalines would be tricky. She was too tired to bother about food, a mug of tea was all she wanted. She tidied the bench, and was pouring boiling water on a tea bag when she heard something. A sound, outside. Faint, very faint, but definitely there. *A footstep…*? No, more a muted scuffle. Where was her phone? *Think…*Yes, she'd left it on the counter. Eyes on the back door she backed towards the counter. Stretched out an arm to retrieve it – and screamed with pain as she knocked over the mug and scalding water cascaded over her sandalled foot. *Oh God he'd have heard her…*

Suddenly Cassie was incandescent with rage. How dare the bastard scare the hell out of her, and what was he doing in her garden? Right, there were laws against stalking. Shaking with exhaustion and pain, she limped to the back door and pulled on the blind's cord, hard. As it shot up she darted forward, slammed her hands flat on the glass either side of her face, and glared out. No good, dammit, all she could see was her own contorted reflection. Whirling round she switched off the Anglepoise lamps and stood motionless for a moment, blinking as she tried to adjust to the sudden darkness. Quick, grab the heaviest file from the end of the bench, that way she'd be ready when…*when*…She swallowed. Then she was stumbling to the back door again – fumbling with the lock and chain – wrenching it open and stepping outside, fists clenched, holding her breath. A nail-paring moon drifted above a bank of impenetrable dark cloud, the trees down the lane reduced to a blur of indistinct shadow, the little shed somehow little no longer, seeming to loom much closer in the gloom. Suddenly she heard the scuffling sound again, even more sinister for being closer this time –

And then a blurred white shape was streaking along the fence, ghostly in the darkness, leaping over the gate as Cassie jumped, her shriek outdoing its yowls as it vanished down the lane in hot pursuit of its hapless prey. *Blanco*. Bloody *Blanco*… Hardly able to stand, Cassie leaned against the wall, trembling, and closed her eyes. Felt her knees give way as, almost suffocated by the climbing rose's fragrance pervading the warm summer night, she found herself sliding towards the grass, longing to sleep – eyelids jerking open as somewhere far down the lane a dog began to howl mournfully. Grabbing hold of the trellis she hauled herself up, wincing as she scratched the back of her hand on a spray of thorns, and stumbled indoors.

She stopped as she caught sight of something lying under the table, something dark, crumpled. A scarf or something of Ivo's, probably, better fish it out and add it to the rest of his stuff. She'd ask Zadie if she could dump his bags with her when Lloyd was home, no way was she letting Ivo come back here to collect them. With a sigh she dealt with the lock and chain, switched on a lamp and closed the blind again. Hot chocolate, that was what she needed. Wishing it was possible to heat milk on the de-activated cooker, she switched the kettle on. While she waited for the water to heat up again she tidied the workbench, admiring the simple curves of the rose gold bangle, looking forward to burnishing it to a soft gleam in the morning. Leaving the lamp on, she collected mug and phone and trudged towards the stairs. Hesitated. Might as well retrieve the damn scarf now. Pulling out a chair she retrieved the object and stood gazing at it. *Not Ivo's scarf after all; David's pullover.* She ran a hand over the soft black wool, enjoying the faint aroma of woodsmoke and some sort of citrus aftershave. She hung it over the back of the chair, smoothing out non-existent creases. She'd return it tomorrow on her way to the Botanic Gardens; a morning spent sketching among the array of exotic flowers and plants would restore her equanimity before she got down to serious work on the earrings in the afternoon.

She was smiling as she climbed the stairs; still smiling while she got ready for bed, slipped beneath the duvet and reached to switch off the lamp. Hesitated, no longer smiling, as she remembered the white shape streaking along the fence, ghostly in the darkness. *So it had been Blanco, this time, but what if…?* She got out of bed again, whistling 'America' from West Side Story in a jaunty manner to give herself courage, checking the front door as she passed, then hurrying downstairs to make sure that the back door was secure. Back in bed once more, she murmured heartfelt thanks to KeyKwik Merv, with his sagging overalls, stained flat cap and unsurpassed technical skills, and smiling again, fell asleep at last to dream of velvety purple and pale blue paste iris petals, delicately outlined in black, suspended on a fine silver curb-link chain.

CHAPTER SEVEN

BY NINE O'CLOCK next morning the bangle was burnished to perfection, and by ten Cassie was ready to leave. It had taken a while to decide what to wear (jeans and her favourite pale green button-neck tee shirt, with the top three buttons casually undone), hair up or down (down, brushed till it shone) makeup or not (definitely, but subtly understated – her lip had almost healed, but the bruise on her cheek had begun to turn an alarming shade of mauve, needing considerably more concealer). It had taken even longer to iron the tee shirt; Granny Jackson had had no truck with labour-saving gadgets and a yellowing socket on the landing outside the bathroom was the only place appliances could be plugged in. An ancient wooden ironing board, its cover resplendent with faded cabbage roses, leant against the wall, its shaky joints a trap for unwary fingers more lethal than those of any deck chair. Cassie had learned to do her ironing on a towel spread on the floor, and while the resulting imperfections didn't bother her, she had soon learned it was wiser to take Ivo's shirts to the dry cleaners.

Switching off the iron she set it upright on its metal stand to cool, ran downstairs, stuffed keys and wallet in her shoulder bag, added pastels and pens, grabbed her new sketchbook, slung the black sweater over her arm, ran back upstairs to check the bolts on the front door, and leaving the blinds down, unlocked the back door. Stopped. Thought for a moment, then set down bag, sketchbook and sweater. *What on earth was she doing?* Ripping off the tee shirt she crumpled it up, pulled it on again and fastened all the buttons. Yanked her curls into a scrunchie on top of her head, found a tissue and wiped off the apricot lip gloss.

Good to go at last – she couldn't wait to get to the Gardens and stroll about peacefully admiring the shrubs and trees, stopping here and there to sketch. It was quite annoying to have to drop off the sweater, really, she'd just knock on the door, hand it in and hurry on her way. If there was no reply she'd fold it up and slip it through the letter box.

Locking the back door behind her, she set off. Took a deep breath, knocked on the tasteful Skittles Green door and stood waiting. No reply. Ignoring a ridiculous feeling of disappointment, she folded the sweater carefully, and was about to lay it on the step when the door suddenly opened.

David stood there, scowling, holding a wafer-thin smartphone to his ear. Cassie held out the sweater. 'Hi – just wanted to –'

Giving her a quick smile he beckoned her inside, then scowling again, turned away and strode off down the hall, talking into the phone and motioning Cassie to follow him. She hesitated for a moment, then followed, closing the front door behind her. He'd disappeared into the kitchen, still talking into his phone – from the sound of it he was having a row with someone. In no hurry to follow, Cassie lingered in the hall for a moment, looking about her at the stylish stripped pine floorboards and the orange and scarlet kilim hung on the chalky white walls. Better go in the kitchen, leave the sweater on a chair, and hurry away.

David stood with his back to her, looking out of the French windows that gave onto the garden with its immaculate conservatory. From what she could hear, he was having a row with his editor about some photos that were being planned to accompany a book he was working on; David apparently thought the photographer was rubbish. Embarrassed, Cassie looked around the kitchen, all clean white lines and gleaming glass-fronted cupboards stacked with brightly striped earthenware plates; a pile of oversize books, unopened post and a battered laptop littered an old wooden table. A framed poster advertising a jazz concert featuring Ella Fitzgerald hung above the Belfast sink, potted bay trees stood on either side of the French windows.

'Okay, Pete, I'll get back to you tomorrow when I've had a chance to think about it, right? *Ciao...*' David turned round and chucked the phone on the table with a sigh. 'Hi, Cassie, great to see you – sorry about that.' He ran a hand through his hair. 'Problems with my editor.'

'Sorry to interrupt, it's just you left this behind yesterday' She edged towards the table, balanced the sweater on the corner, and backed towards the door.

'Hey, I was looking for that this morning, it's really kind of you to bring it round.' His skin was very tanned; when he smiled, little white lines crinkled at the corners of his eyes. 'Everything all right? No fatalities in the night, I hope?'

She stiffened. 'Pardon?'

'No kami-kazi lemons?'

She relaxed, smiled back. 'No, everything's fine, thanks –'

'Great.' On the counter a percolator started to bubble. 'Coffee's ready. Join me?'

'No, thanks, honestly – you're working –'

'Been at it since seven, I could do with a break.' He indicated a chair. 'So, how's the jewellery making going?'

'Great, just off to do some drawing at the Botanical Gardens, then I have to work on a pair of drop earrings this afternoon.'

He poured the coffee. 'Sounds complicated.'

She was describing her design when there was the sound of the front door opening, followed by footsteps clicking smartly down the hall.

'David? What on earth's going on?'

Cassie looked round. Erica stood in the doorway, tall, rake-thin, immaculately made-up, blonde hair cut in a perfect bob, glaring at her. David stopped laughing and got to his feet. 'Erica – you know Cassie –'

'Cassie?'

'Our neighbour.'

'Ah.' Narrowing her eyes, she looked Cassie up and down. 'And how is your lodger?'

'Excuse me?'

'The charming young actor renting your spare room because of Oxford's proximity to London?'

She ran a scarlet-nailed hand through her hair; it fell immaculately back into place again. 'Such energy! Such charisma! Quite the young Sean Penn, in my opinion.'

Cassie dumped several spoonfuls of brown sugar in her coffee and stirred it, hard. That would have been Ivo's *artfully ruffled hair, lazily drooping eyelids and permanently thrust forward jaw* phase.

Erica gave a thin smile. 'We had quite a chat last time I bumped into him, just after he was offered the lead in Julius Caesar at The National – such a pity his mother died and he was too distraught to accept it…'

'Mmm. He's moved away now.' Cassie stood up, fast. 'Thanks for all the help, yesterday, David, much appreciated.'

Erica's glance darted between them. 'Yesterday?'

David sighed. 'Zadie suggested I call round to sort out Cassie's lemon tree, it –'

'*Lemon* tree? Heavens, I thought they went out of style years ago.' She dropped her keys on the table with a clatter. 'Is that coffee freshly brewed?'

'Sure –'

Cassie got to her feet. 'I must be going.'

David smiled at her. 'No, please – do finish your coffee.' Reluctantly, Cassie sat down again as Erica took a mug from a cabinet and passed it to David. Ignoring Cassie, she began to leaf through the pile of post beside the laptop. David filled the mug and set it on the table as Erica looked up. 'Sweeteners, darling, please – really, is that too much to remember? And by the way, I need one of your books on Venetian architecture, I want some photographs of Verona for my sixth form lecture on Romeo and Juliet.'

Cassie drew in her breath. 'Oh, the actual balcony? How fabulous!'

'The actual...?' Erica stared at her incredulously. 'The balcony's a fake.' She gave a little laugh. '*I thought everyone knew that.*' She glanced at her watch, and picked up her keys. 'No time for coffee after all, I'm afraid.' She smiled sweetly at David. 'I'll help myself to that book.' She swept out of the kitchen. Footsteps clicked down the hall, then tripped lightly up the stairs.

'Thanks for the coffee.' Cassie rose and collected her things, almost tripping over a chair leg in her haste to be gone.

'Pleasure.' No longer smiling, David saw her out. 'And if those pesky lemons give you any more trouble, give me a call.'

She looked back as she reached the end of the road. He was still standing there, looking after her.

CHAPTER EIGHT

Cowley Road was busier than ever this morning – lorries overtook crawling buses, bikes sped past gridlocked cars, pedestrians crowded the rubbish-strewn pavements, traffic fumes stifling in the August heat. Cassie slowed as she neared St Clements roundabout, and stopped outside The Ballroom Emporium, gazing unseeing at the stunning window display of glittering ball gowns, all sequinned fishtails and diamanté-encrusted halter necks.

I thought everyone knew that

Bloody Shakespeare – she wouldn't mind betting most people thought the balcony was the genuine article. Stuffing her sketchbook into her bag, she turned back the way she'd come. Somehow she'd lost the urge to visit the Botanical Gardens. No, she'd go back home, get down to work on those earrings. At least she knew how to do that…

There was silence from Zadie's side as Cassie crossed the grass, relieved to be home – Zadie must have taken the kids to the park. She'd noticed Erica's car was gone as she entered Poplar Street and turned down the path leading to the back gate. No sign of David, either. She stifled a grin as she fished her keys from her wallet; he was probably sinking a beer or three at the Rusty Bicycle. As she straightened up she stood motionless, hand outstretched, about to insert the key in the lock, and sniffed the air. Sniffed again, harder this time…Then she was in the kitchen, slamming the back door behind her – gasping for air, breath catching in her throat, coughing as she raced up the stairs, tripping twice, bruising her ankle badly the first time and almost dislocating her thumb the second as she grasped fruitlessly at the banister before falling to her knees as she reached the landing. Horrified, she reached for the smouldering overturned iron, set it upright, ripped out the plug and getting to her feet backed away, hand clapped over her mouth, gagging at the smell of scorching, shocked at the ragged black hole that gaped like a wound, burnt into the worn green runner, and the exposed floorboards beneath.

It was a while before she stopped shaking. Surely she'd switched off the iron before she left? She'd never been careless about it before, *never*. Though… it was true she'd been hurrying to get ready, anxious to be on her way to the Botanical Gardens. And to get rid of the sweater, obviously…The ancient iron was clicking furiously as it began to cool down. Tears stung her reddened eyes as she imagined what would have happened if she hadn't changed her mind and returned home. Oh God, sorry, *sorry*, Granny Jackson. Still, no point in beating herself up about that now. Think positive. Tomorrow she'd have a look on Amazon, buy a new iron and a decent ironing board. A new runner for the landing, too.

Feeling better, she got to her feet. First a visit to the

bathroom to splash cold water on her face, then – *no*, Christ, in her haste she'd left the back door open. She glanced automatically at the front door as she rushed past, and veered to a halt. *What the..?* She was certain she'd checked the chain before she left, she remembered running back to make sure. *Didn't she…?* Oh just do it now, okay? Just DO IT. Downstairs again, limping, to retrieve her bag from the grass and the key from the back door – then lock herself in, fast, fix the chain and lean against the counter, panting, trying to get her breath back. Making a detour to switch on the kettle, she limped to the bottom of the stairs, desperate to get to the bathroom and bathe her eyes. Stopped dead as she heard a sound. Metal sliding on metal. Stealthy. Almost silent. From behind her? No, in front. *Upstairs.* Grasping the banister she hauled herself up the stairs, heard another sound when she was almost halfway up.

The click of the front door closing.

CHAPTER NINE

HEEDLESS OF THE pain Cassie raced up the stairs, and after a struggle, hauled the front door open and practically fell out onto the pavement. Nothing. Just a kid attempting wheelies on a decrepit mountain bike in the middle of the road, and two elderly Asian women chatting outside the house on the corner. Cassie retreated, defeated. Locked and chained the front door and stood leaning against it, trying to think. Stress caused people to become forgetful, right? And stressed she certainly was – who wouldn't be with a bastard like Ivo trying to psych them out. But how the hell had he got in? She'd check the minute she'd bathed her eyes, stinging unbearably now from the acrid fumes. She limped across the landing, practically fell into the bathroom – and stopped dead. She could still smell scorching, but there was something else underlying it behind the door. The faint odour of male sweat, plus some sort of cheap aftershave or cologne. He must have been taken by surprise when he heard her come in, hidden in the bathroom while she ran downstairs to lock the back door. Slipped out just in time.

Splashing water on her face she went downstairs to

the kitchen. She'd almost reached the back door when a shadow loomed against the blind. Oh God, he'd come round the back. A knock on the glass – he knew she was in there. Her phone was in her bag, on the floor near the door, where she'd dumped it. Crawl – quickly, *quickly* – forget ankle and thumb, grab bag and – he was knocking again. Hands shaking, heart thudding so fast she felt sick, she fumbled for her phone, dropped it –

'Ms Fitton? You in there, mate?'

Vic, with a delivery from Precious Gems supplies! Weak with relief at the familiar sound of his voice, she hauled herself to her feet and was about to open the door when fear that it might be Ivo after all – he'd often signed for deliveries when she was out, and did a brilliant imitation of Vic – made her hesitate.

'Come on, lady, need you to sign.'

Wait. Check it's really him.

'What's my account number?'

'Say what?'

'My number, should be stamped on the back of the package.'

'Bloody ell, old on…' Irritated fumbling. '07792554.' Sigh. 'You'll be wantin a bleedin password next.'

She pushed the blind aside a fraction. Vic stood there, unshaven as usual, grinning behind his gold-framed aviator sunglasses, sleeveless Iron Maiden tee shirt exposing his luxuriant grey chest hair and copiously tattooed forearms. 'Delivery, 'kay?' He held out a securely wrapped and stickered package and shook it.

Exhale slowly. Raise blind, open door. Try to smile.

He surged forward. 'Top o' the range diamonds this time, is it?'

'Thanks, Vic –' She took the package, reached for the door handle. 'Better get on with some work now I've got these! See you soon –' She began to close the door.

'Hang on – what the fuck's that smell?' Whipping off his sunglasses he took a step closer to the doorway and inhaled dramatically.

'No, it's fine – just the iron, I forgot to –'

'Let it overheat, am I right? Wanna be careful – bound to be dodgy wiring in an old shack like this. Death trap, ask me.' He poked an experimental finger in his ear. 'Jeeze, wimmen…' He extracted the finger, examined it and wiped it on his tee shirt. Frowned. 'So how come the boyfriend ain't fixed it? Too busy poncing about in his Calvin Kleins spouting poetry and that?'

'Ivo? He's in er London, now…' *If only.*

'Glad to hear it, you're better off without a tosser like that – thought he was God's bleeding gift, pardon my French.' Shaking his head, he started to push past her into the kitchen. 'Not to worry, your Uncle Vic'll sort it for you. Better let me take a look.'

'No, honestly, Vic, it's really kind of you but a new steam iron's on the way.' Well, it would be soon. 'And I'll be having the wiring checked, too.'

'If you say so.' He was staring at the cooker. 'Blimey O'Riley. Gift wrap it, did e?'

'It's for safety reasons, he says there's a lot to fix. Anyway thanks again for the delivery, Vic – better sign for it, I've got to finish some work –'

He held out the little screen reluctantly, shoved the stylus at her. 'Work too ard, that's your trouble. Reckon it's time I took you out for a couple of margaritas.'

She took the screen, trying to think what to say, when she heard a voice calling.

'Cass..? You there, girlfriend?'

She edged past him into the garden. Zadie was leaning over the fence. 'My mum sent a load of homemade coconut candy.' She held out a plastic container packed with violently pink squares. 'Try it, pure sugar. Yum.'

'Thanks, Zades – looks great.'

Suddenly Vic was standing beside her, wearing his sunglasses again. Impossible to read his expression, all she could see was her own reflection in the lens. She signed and handed the sticky screen back, pretending not to notice when his sweaty fingers brushed hers, resisting the urge to wipe her hands on her jeans. 'Thanks, Vic, great. Have a good er week.'

She fumbled for the key – no sign of it, it must have fallen on the grass, or maybe she'd put it back in her purse – turned back to Zadie as Brooklyn and Bronx hurtled into the garden, shrieking as they took turns to kick a half-deflated football against the fence. She hesitated, wondering if she should suggest Zadie offered some candy to Vic. 'Sure thing, girlfriend.' Zadie grinned. 'Ask me, he's hot.'

Too late. He was already slamming the gate behind him.

By the time Zadie had finished telling Cassie what the kids had got up to at the park (*jumping off the top of the slide, seeing who could go highest on the swings*) and Cassie had described David's unparalleled skill with lemon trees, her subsequent visit to return his sweater and sodding Erica's loathsomeness (*yeah, up herself or what*), it was time for Zadie to prepare the tacos (*veg? Don't make me laugh*) for lunch. Heartened by Zadie's cheerful normality, Cassie returned to the kitchen. After securing the door and closing the blinds she hurried upstairs clutching her phone, checked the front door and made sure no-one was lurking in the bathroom before she used the toilet. Checked under the bed, trying and failing to laugh at herself, she rifled through the clothes hanging in the wardrobe. Returning at last to the kitchen, she positioned the phone close to hand beside the polishing machine, and settled down to work.

It was impossible. Every shout in the street, every car backfiring made her start. After a while she gave up and wandered about the kitchen, refilling the blue sugar bowl, arranging the plates on the dresser in a different order, leafing through the flyers in the pile of bills and reminders. A colourful communication from Domino Pizzas caught her eye; pity she hadn't noticed it sooner, there'd been more than one occasion recently when a massive pizza with double pepperoni with mushrooms would have hit the spot...She was rinsing the mug she'd left that morning in the sink when her phone rang. Ignoring the mug as it fell and shattered, she gingerly approached the workbench, saw with relief that it was Ruth from her Zumba class – blessed normality again, thank God. After Cassie had promised she'd be there the following week and they'd catch up over coffee afterwards, she cut the call and returned to the sink. She'd wrapped the last of the bright blue and yellow china shards in newspaper and was about to dump them in the rubbish bin when glancing up, she noticed the blind was hanging fractionally awry. Quickly straightening it – it had always been a couple of centimetres off, and she should have sent it back to the manufacturers when it arrived, but she'd been so busy with a last minute commission she couldn't spare the time– she dropped the damp newspaper parcel in the bin, and stroked a leaf on the lemon tree. It looked so healthy now she could practically hear it growing. Feeling better – much better – she made the tea, found Ella Fitzgerald on Spotify, settled herself at the workbench and began to concentrate on the tourmaline spacers.

Work went so well she carried on till after midnight, and stumbled up to bed barely noticing the smell of the burnt runner as she passed.

CHAPTER TEN

EXHAUSTED, CASSIE SLEPT without dreaming – to be woken at ten past nine by yells of excitement from next door: '*Look Ma, I'm flyin'!*' – '*Asteroids headin' this way!*' – '*Re-calibrate, Commander!*' She turned over and burrowed under the pillows, grinning, hoping the kids were disturbing sodding Erica, too. She was contemplating getting up, and wishing there was some bacon in the fridge for a sandwich, when the yells of excitement were suddenly replaced by a shrill scream of pain. Cassie froze. That scream wasn't part of any game, it was *real*. Oh God, Brooklyn – or maybe Bronx, the youngest, impossible to tell – was screaming, over and over again. Falling out of bed she grabbed yesterday's tee shirt and jeans from the floor, yanked them on, tumbled downstairs and out into the garden.

Hurrying to the fence, she peered over. Bronx was lying doubled up on the ground, clutching his face and sobbing. As Cassie gazed, horror-struck, Zadie came flying out of her kitchen, fell to her knees with a clatter of beaded braids and a jangle of outsize hoop earrings, and gathered him to her pink polyester cropped top. After a moment she managed to gently prise the hands away from the child's tear-stained face, and gasped with horror as blood streamed, bright red and unstoppable, from his small nose. Her face white, she glared up at Cassie, her eyes fierce. 'Get ice, Cass – a shitload. *Now.*' She bent over her son again, murmuring endearments.

Cassie did as she was told, fast, elbowing the fridge door shut behind her, wincing as the bottles of dressing rattled on their plastic shelf, tearing a clean tea towel as she ripped it from its hook, returning on the run with a bowl piled with ice cubes. She thrust everything over the fence to Brooklyn, who was crying too, now, appalled at the sight of the blood. 'We was only playin Space Commanders, man – gettin ready for take-off, 'n' we banged heads –' He sobbed harder. 'He goin to *die?*'

Zadie was calling, her voice urgent. 'Give it here, Brookie –' He stumbled over to her. Zadie snatched the bowl of ice, wrapped several cubes in the teacloth and applied them to the bridge of Bronx's nose, which far from stemming the flow only made him struggle harder and scream louder.

'Hey – anything I can do?'

Cassie turned. David was leaning over the fence on the other side of her garden, looking concerned. Zadie raised her head, petrified. '*Can't make it stop –*'

Cassie called to him, quietly. 'They were playing on the trampoline and bumped heads –'

Zadie rolled her eyes. 'Sugar rush – little buggers got hold of the home-made coconut candy Mum sent, polished off the lot. Made 'em go wild.'

He frowned. 'Ah.' He vaulted over the fence, sprinted

over the grass, jumped over Zadie's fence too and knelt down beside her, talking quietly to Bronx and showing Zadie how to gently pinch the bridge of the little boy's nose to make the bleeding stop. It didn't work. 'No worries, just need to tilt his head forward a bit, okay?' Zadie did as instructed, applying the ice pack more firmly, murmuring encouragingly to Bronx while Brooklyn hovered beside them, clutching a headless Darth Vader to his narrow chest for comfort. Cassie watched helplessly, wishing there was something she could do. Maybe she should fetch another teacloth? A glass of water?

David patted Zadie's shoulder, smiling. 'Reckon that should've done the trick – let's take a look.'

With a sigh of relief Zadie took away the ice pack. She recoiled in horror as a cataract of fresh blood poured from Bronx's nose, soaking his grubby little *Man U* tee shirt, imprinting Zadie's pink crop top with bright scarlet blooms. David's eyes widened momentarily, then he ruffled Bronx's hair, grinning. 'Hey, that's what I call impressive. Makes those Storm Troopers look like real saddos!' He said something very quietly to Zadie; she nodded, speechless. He strode over to Cassie.

'Bleeding's pretty bad. Just told Zadie, if he's bumped his head he needs to be checked out.'

Cassie indicated Brooklyn, who was watching his brother wide-eyed, hiccupping violently. 'Shall I take...?'

David nodded. 'Good idea.' He shepherded Brooklyn over. Cassie reached over the fence and prodded Darth Vader. 'Hey, Darth. You look a lot better without your head, if you don't mind my saying.' She grinned at Brooklyn. 'And we don't have to hear him talking funny, either!' She imitated the Dark Lord's scary breathing, making a big deal of it. 'Reckon he always sounds like he's got a sore throat and needs a seriously strong cough sweet.' The little boy stared up at her, a shaky smile beginning. 'Tell you what, how about you and Darth come round to mine and we'll make some chocolate fudge – how'd that be?'

'Dave?' Zadie was frantically trying to staunch the flow of blood. 'Could you call a taxi? Need to hurry –'

'No way – I'll take you in my car. Hang in there, guys – it's only five minutes to the hospital –' At the mention of *hospital*, Bronx began to scream hysterically, while Brooklyn shot back to Zadie and flung himself at her, clinging to her like a limpet. Zadie's shoulders slumped. 'Seen too many documentaries, see.'

David vaulted back over the fence and stopped beside Cassie. 'Great idea, your fudge, but there's no way the little lad's going to let his brother out of his sight now. Probably thinks they'll amputate his head or something.'

Zadie was struggling to her feet, clutching Bronx, and trying in vain to disengage Brooklyn.

'Cassie?' He touched her arm lightly. 'Any chance you could come too, give a hand with the kids? Certain it'll all be fine, but I'm pretty sure they'll want to X-ray Bronx to be on the safe side, and –'

'Of course I will! Anything! I feel awful just standing about doing nothing –'

David gave Zadie the thumbs up. 'Just nipping indoors to get my keys, see you outside.' He raised his voice. 'Cassie's coming too, guys, she's very excited. Apparently there are special machines where you can get cans of Coke, and chocolate and stuff.' Brooklyn stopped crying, and even Bronx's sobs became more subdued. 'Going to be a really interesting outing – if you're really lucky, Bronx, they might take a little picture of your head with a special camera, like they do for footballers when they jump really high and bang each other's heads. Wow, will your mates be jealous!'

He vaulted over first one fence, then the next, and disappeared through his back door.

Cassie winked at Zadie. 'Just going to collect my bag – got to make sure I've got loads of coins for those machines. See you in a sec, okay?

She was making sure everything was switched off – double checking the iron, despite the fact that she hadn't used it since the other morning – when she remembered she was expecting a delivery from Precious Gems. She scrawled a note for Vic, *had to go to A&E to help with kids from next door, nothing serious but I'll be gone some time, please deliver today's package with my next order*, stuck it on the back door, flew upstairs and checked that the front door was locked and chained, then down again to grab her bag, scrabble at the back of a drawer for sticky tape, slam the back door, secure it, affix the note to the glass where Vic'd be bound to see it, started sprinting across the grass, stopped dead, dashed back again to check she really had locked the back door, then, breathless, headed for the gate.

Thirty seconds later she was on the pavement.

David was waiting beside his car, a bright red Audi, the passenger doors already open. Helping Zadie into the back, he settled Bronx, snivelling quietly now, on her lap, with Brooklyn beside her, where he sat beaming, holding up the headless Darth Vader so that by some unfathomable magic he could see out of the open window. Cassie slipped into the front seat, as a youth erupted into Poplar Street riding a rusty bike seemingly held together by string. He hurtled down the middle of the road, weaving from side to side as he passed, leaping up onto the pavement to perform complicated wheelies occasionally by way of diversion. She looked away quickly.

David glanced in the rear mirror, grinning; Cassie twisted in her seat. Erica was emerging from the ivy-covered trellis that concealed the row of bins in their front garden. wearing industrial-size rubber gloves and brandishing a can of floral air freshener. Screeching imprecations as the youth shot past uttering a terrifying war cry, she scuttled back into the house, slamming the front door so hard Cassie wouldn't have been surprised if it fell off its hinges.

Brooklyn craned his head out of the window. 'Wow! I'm gonna do that soon as I get a bike!'

Dr Thomas Dearborn knocked off his bike on his way home by a drunk driver

Cassie gasped.

'Yeah! I wanna do it too!' Bronx smeared his streaming nose down Zadie's front.

her colleague thought drugs were probably involved too

'It's dangerous, kids –' Her voice cracked.

David cast her a worried look, laid a hand on her arm for a moment.

Zadie's voice was urgent. 'Cass! Got any more tissues?'

'Okay, guys?' David put the car into gear. 'Show time!'

And they were off.

Cassie thought she probably wasn't the only one who wished the journey would last for ever. The interior of the car was pleasantly warm, the capacious leather seats comfortable, and Brooklyn had requested the radio be re-tuned from Classic FM to Kiss FM, which lent a certain holiday air to the trip. Calm had been restored by the time David swept into the John Radcliffe Hospital car park, miraculously identifying what seemed to be the only available empty space. 'Only a short walk, guys!' Cassie noticed he avoided mentioning the dreaded acronym A&E, sure to have figured big in most episodes of Casualty, and could have hugged him for it. As she climbed out of the car, David helped Zadie out, took Bronx and settled him comfortably in his arms, keeping his head well up and showing him how to press the compress to the bridge of his nose. They set off, Cassie bringing up the rear, her arm threaded through Zadie's, Brooklyn skipping ahead, chanting a rap song with very unsuitable lyrics that had been playing on the radio as they arrived. As they approached the gigantic white building looming above them against a cornflower blue sky, he stopped dead suddenly, squinting upwards. 'Hey, man –

looks like it's made of Cookies 'n' Cream! *Wowza – bazookas!'*

Cassie tried not to laugh. 'Bazookas, eh?'

Zadie rolled her eyes. 'Lloyd taught it 'em. Be something different next week.'

Cassie affected cut glass tones. 'Splendid, what?' and was rewarded by Zadie's laugh.

An old man was standing outside A&E's heavy glass doors, smoking a misshapen roll-up and racked with hacking coughs. He wheezed a greeting as they hurried past; with a wicked grin David hissed *'Guy's probably the chief surgeon...'* in Cassie's ear.

A short walk to the lift, then another walk to the waiting room. Cassie stood waiting near the entrance as David, carrying Bronx, with Zadie beside him, joined the queue at the reception desk, where two efficient-looking women were seated behind what looked suspiciously like bullet-proof glass. Cassie looked around, conscious of the effort that had been made to make the area welcoming, or at least bearable. The walls were painted white, and there was a huge brightly-lit aquarium in the far corner, while a giant flat-screen telly on one wall showed a muted weather forecast. There was a kids' area, littered with plastic toys, and opposite that was a row of glass and metal vending machines selling hot drinks and packets of crisps and sweets. Even the bright red sign saying EMERGENCY DEPARTMENT RECEPTION was cheerful, as if it would rather have been a Christmas decoration. In fact basically the place would have been fine if it wasn't for the patients.

The waiting room was crowded with row after row of

grey moulded plastic chairs barely supporting blokes with roughly bandaged hands, blokes with swollen black eyes and blokes with feet swathed in dirty tea towels. Women with arms in slings slumped in them, and toddlers with badly grazed knees and great blue and mauve bumps on their foreheads screamed their heads off in them. There was an empty wheelchair near the glassed-in counter that made her wonder what had happened to the occupant, and a bright yellow plastic sign saying WARNING WET FLOOR beside a smeary patch on the pale blue rubber floor. The smell of disinfectant was overpowering, and Cassie realised with a shudder that what had been mopped up was probably blood.

She was swallowing hard when a small hand was slipped tremulously into hers. Brooklyn leant against her legs, gazing wide-eyed at an enormous fat man in a torn kung fu suit in the middle of the front row, with weird tattoos all over his bald head and his foot encased in what looked alarmingly like a block of wood. Licking his finger, he was flicking through the Rodent Operators Gazette. Looking up, he caught sight of Cassie and winked. Cassie wished he knew that among all the women he'd probably already winked at that day, it was a virtual certainty that not a single one of them had felt the urge to wink back. Glancing over at reception she saw with relief that Zadie seemed to have finished filling in forms and one of the efficient-looking women was explaining something to her – with luck they'd soon be coming to sit down.

There was a group of empty chairs in the middle of

a row halfway down the room. She leant down. 'Come on, kiddo, let's grab those seats, and when the others join us we'll go and check out those vending machines, Okay? Looks like they've got loads of different drinks and stuff.'

She didn't spot Ivo till they'd made their way halfway down the row, stepping cautiously over bandaged feet, picking up dropped teddy bears and dummies and twice nearly tripping over a pair of crutches. She was bending down to murmur encouragement to Brooklyn when she stopped dead. Ivo was huddled in a chair at the end of the row in front, elbows resting on his thighs, scowling at his phone (calling *her*?). Trademark black leather jacket, hair gleaming with product, booted right foot tapping an uncontrollable tattoo on the smeared lino. Instinctively she backed away, fast – stopped abruptly as she heard a hoarse shout of rage behind her. Spun round, horrified to see that in her terror she'd almost caused an elderly man in dark glasses carrying a cane to collide with her. Ignoring her abject apologies, he tottered past her, muttering imprecations, as all the waiting patients capable of movement swivelled in their seats and glared accusingly at Cassie. Including Ivo. *Except that it wasn't Ivo*; a shock of relief swept through her as she saw that this casualty had sallow, pockmarked skin and an overbite that rivalled Butt-Head's. A stained surgical dressing covered his right eye; his left eye, if further evidence was required, proved to be not chocolate brown but a pale watery blue.

Choking down the hysterical laughter that threatened to erupt as she imagined Ivo's fury at being taken for such an unprepossessing specimen she shepherded Brooklyn on down the row. They'd barely got settled when the others joined them. Bronx settled down on Zadie's lap, too worn out with shock to protest, while David threw himself down beside Cassie. 'Shouldn't have to wait too long while they sort triage – depends how many emergencies come in with top priority.'

'No worries, Brooklyn and I are about to go for Cokes. Coming, Brookie? Better bring Darth, he'll love it.' She turned to Zadie. 'Fancy a tea? Or they probably have coffee and stuff too –'

'A tea'd be great.' She managed a smile.

David hauled a handful of silver from his pocket. 'Keep coins on me for the toll booth at Swinford. Mine's a double Scotch, hold the ice.' He grinned. 'Keep an eye on that Darth, if I were you.'

Cassie took the coins gratefully, forcing her hands to stop shaking, and retraced her steps down the row, keeping an eye out for the crutches, apologising when she almost tripped over a prosthetic metal leg suddenly stretched in her path. Brooklyn, hanging on to the hem of her tee shirt, gasped with horrified delight. 'Cass! Cass! Look! It's like in Forrest Gump, where they had to saw *the real legs off* Lootenant Dan cos –'

'Hey, there's the drinks machine, Brookie! Great, there's loads of stuff –' Brooklyn rushed ahead and pressed his nose to the impressive machine's window, round eyed. 'Look! They got Mars bars! And them biscuits in little packets!' He jumped up and down excitedly. 'Can I put some dosh in?'

Cassie proffered the handful of coins. 'Course you

can, sweetheart –'

'KEITH!!!'

She stood motionless, gripping the coins, unaware of the pain as they ground into her palm. *Somebody was calling Ivo. She was wrong, it had been him all the time* – Suddenly the floor was tilting beneath her feet, her heart hammering against her ribs, the vivid colours of the confectionary packets blurring, the buzz of patients' chatter fading to an echoing silence.

'*KEITH*?' The voice was sharper now, clearly expecting a response. *Which meant he must be close, now…*

Somewhere nearby plastic chair legs scraped on worn tiles – *no, please no* – and the coins slid from her hands, cascading with a crash to roll beneath the vending machine. She felt a sharp pain somewhere, getting worse as she clenched her hand to stop herself screaming – where was he? Oh God, *what was he going to do?* – and then a shadow was looming in the vending machine's glass door, hand outstretched, and she remembered Brookie – funny, spunky little Brookie, terrified his brother was going to die – was with her. With a sob, she forced herself to turn –

'Cassie?' David stood beside her, a hand on her shoulder, looking worried.

People were turning in their seats, staring.

'Mrs Perkins?' The receptionist's voice was exaggeratedly restrained. 'Time for little Keith to see the doctor again. Treatment Room 14, all right? And no biting, this time, please.'

There was a scuffle, accompanied by roars of childish rage and weary maternal pleas. Finally an exhausted-looking woman managed to prise a small shaven-headed child with an arm encased plaster from the chair beside her. The cast was liberally decorated with drawings of varying offensiveness, the child sported the ragged remains of a tee shirt bearing a mercifully indecipherable logo. Cassie blinked, then burst out laughing as accompanied by the bolder patients' irritable protests, progress was slowly made down the row until a door slammed, hard, and the roars and pleas diminished.

'Cass? You okay?'

'Sorry – sorry! It's just the idea of little Keith – you know, Perkins –' She made herself stop laughing. '– *Perkins*, right, not *Jennings* –' Oh thank God '– biting the doctor was funny. Well, sort of –'

'No kidding. Hope the doc's up to date with his tetanus jabs –'

'There's a dead spider under there! 'S bigger than a – a – *dog*!' Beaming, Brooklyn backed out from under the vending machine, clutching the errant coins in his grubby little hands, and began to feed them with intense concentration into the slot. Cassie slowly opened her painful hand, wincing as she extracted the fifty pence piece she'd been grinding into the tender skin of her palm, just in time to lean forward and catch the first Mars bar. At last she and David made their way back to their seats carrying plastic cups of tea and coffee, followed by Brooklyn balancing cans of Diet Coke, several packets of crisps and Mars bars (with two more stashed in Cassie's bag for later, after she'd explained that Bronx just might need treatment that meant he couldn't eat anything right now). Brooklyn stared up at her wide-eyed. 'Like...like...when they cut your chest open and put plastic boobies inside you?' Cassie ruffled hi hair. 'God no, nothing like that, sweetheart, I mean if Bronx needs some...special Elastoplast or something –'

'With monsters on?'

'Well –'

Luckily two impossibly youthful policemen strode into the waiting room at that point, either side of a struggling handcuffed youth wearing a black pea jacket with a swastika emblazoned on the back, and EVIL tattooed in scarlet letters on his forehead. Looking to neither right nor left they marched him along the aisle beneath the giant flat screen telly, past the kids' play area, and disappeared through an unmarked door. As before, the waiting patients able to move swivelled as one to watch; now they faced front once more, and apparently unperturbed, resumed their conversations.

Brooklyn clutched Darth Vader to him, ecstatic. 'Wow, awesome! Wait till I tell my dad!'

They sat down again. Zadie, looking exhausted, had passed Bronx to David, where he sat leaning comfortably against his shoulder as David quietly related all the really *really* terrible accidents he and his very *very* naughty brothers had when they were kids, heavens, much *much* worse than a bit of a nose bleed. It was a long wait, and when Brooklyn began to fidget Cassie, inspired, fished her notebook from her bag and showed him how to play Noughts and Crosses, followed by Battleships, followed by Hangman. Several hours later, a friendly young nurse came and shepherded Zadie and Bronx away to a treatment room, at which Brooklyn burst into tears of terror. 'Gonna die, ain't he – can't be hardly no blood left –'

'Hell no, buddy – you know how much blood we've all got inside us?' David reached for one of the empty Coke cans and held it up. 'Least eight of these cans, right? Massive amount. Reckon your brother's lost a tiny, *tiny* teaspoon's worth – don't you agree, Cassie –'

'For sure, probably not even that much –'

'– so he's got loads to spare!'

They were playing an enthusiastic game of I-Spy when Zadie and Bronx returned twenty minutes later, Zadie weak with relief, Bronx skipping happily along beside her as if the accident had never happened. They stood waiting at the end of the row. 'Hey, guys.' David ruffled Bronx's hair and raised an eyebrow at Zadie. 'Everything okay?'

''S all good – hey, the doc said we done everythin right with the ice 'n' all, bleedin' ad stopped already by the time we sat down –'

'Yeah, and he looked up my nose with a telescope thing 'bout *that* big!' Bronx held his hands up a good meter apart, looking important.

Brooklyn's jaw dropped, then he recalled himself, fast. ''Spect you'll have to come back tomorrow so he can look up your bum, too, butt-wipe.'

'Mum...' Bronx was on the verge of tears.

Zadie sighed. 'Can it, Brookie. Course we don't.'

Brooklyn gave his brother a friendly shove. 'Hey bro, only kidding.' He paused. '*Or maybe not...*'

'Just got to take it easy now, keep him quiet.' Zadie shook her head. 'Yeah, some hopes.'

David put an arm round each of the boys. 'What say we head back to the car, see what's happening on Kiss FM?'

Waving enthusiastically to the friendlier-looking patients, and with a chorus of grateful goodbyes to the receptionists, they trooped out.

It was gone seven by the time they arrived back at Poplar Street. As the boys shuffled up the path, subdued now, and Zadie scrabbled in her bag for her keys, David watched for a moment, then hurried after them. 'Just a thought, guys, but if you're as hungry as I am you could eat a horse. Can't manage a horse, but how about I send out for pizza?'

There was a chorus of agreement. David turned to Cassie. 'You've been great – join us?'

'Yeah, go on, Cass – stay.' Zadie finally got her front door open and stood aside as the boys shot past her into the hall and disappeared into the living room, arguing about whose turn it was to choose a movie.

By the time the pizzas arrived, David had nipped home to fetch a couple of San Pellegrino lemonades and an almost full wine box, and they were all settled comfortably on the battered mauve plush sofas, engrossed in *Home Alone 2*. Allowing that it was a special occasion, Zadie agreed to a second film before bed. As she located *Toy Story 3* on the vast entertainment system (Lloyd's contribution after an Extra Job, apparently, the nature of which wasn't specified) David yanked a broken rocket from the depths of the gaping cushion he was sprawling on and discreetly dropped it behind the sofa. Catching

Cassie's eye, he raised his glass to her with a wink, and a smile so warm it was impossible not to return it. She took a sip of wine, her cheeks hot. Why on earth *wouldn't* she have returned it? He hadn't meant it personally, for heaven's sake, it was just that he was looking forward to watching Toy Story 3. She sat up straighter, crossed her legs, and was about to adjust her skirt more elegantly when she glanced down. Froze. *She wasn't wearing a skirt.* She'd spent the whole day – *the whole day!* – in her disgusting work jeans and a tatty green tee shirt!

Oh well. Nothing to be done now, least said soonest mended, no use crying over spilt milk, and all that. None of which bracing sayings were any bloody help at all.

She took a much larger sip of wine, and doing her best to look dignified, concentrated hard on watching the film.

It was late when she and David left. A full moon hung low over the roofs opposite, guitar music drifted from the open window of a nearby students' house, the faint scent of chicken curry hung in the air. He strolled beside her to the back gate, a gentle hand on her arm as they navigated an outcrop of nettles. Yawning, she rummaged in her bag among the litter of chocolate wrappers and discarded papers scrawled with the kids' games she'd taught Brooklyn earlier that day. *That day?* It seemed a lifetime ago.

She found her keys at last. David reached out and touched her cheek. 'Sleep well.'

'You, too.'

'See you soon?'

She smiled. 'Definitely.'

Halfway across the grass she turned, waving as he walked away. Gazed up for a last glimpse of the moon, buried her face briefly in the white roses climbing the kitchen wall, inhaling their heady fragrance.

Then she slid her key in the lock and opened the door.

CHAPTER ELEVEN

SHE STOOD STOCK still as she entered the kitchen, hardly able to believe what she was seeing. Moonlight filtered through the open door, illuminating the pool of liquid – no, not liquid, *slurry* – issuing from the dark maw of the fridge, its door hanging open like a broken limb. The pool had spread – no, *was spreading*, there was sluggish movement, bubbles occasionally erupting on the surface – as far as the rug. A scatter of fragments – glass? No, impossible – gleamed beside a table leg. More – a lot more – glittered near the work bench.

She clapped a hand to her mouth, trying to mask the putrid odour, realised with a shock that she was still clinging tightly to the door – the *wide open* door – handle with the other. *Move. Now.* Slamming the door, she locked it, shoved the chain into place, checked all the blinds were closed, switched on the lamps and backed against the counter. Jumped as she caught sight of a white face reflected in the kettle, glaring at her. Oh God –

the dreadful apparition in The Innocents, *pale and ominous – standing motionless, watching. Waiting...*

She was here. In the kitchen. With her. She stood

rooted to the spot. Realised with dread that there was nothing for it but to face the horror, be ready to run when – and then she made sense of the image, a sob of relief as she realised her mistake followed by a moan. God, she really was turning into a basket case. Sinking into a chair at the table, she stared into space. After a moment she found herself focusing on the slew of flyers beside the pile of brown envelopes. On top was the colourful advert for Domino pizzas, the vivid slices of tomatoes and peppers and sweaty coins of pepperoni a comforting reminder of normality. She was about to get up when she noticed the corner of another flyer protruding from the rest. Less colourful than the others – well, not colourful at all, from the bit she could see; the background was a misty grey, and the Gothic-type lettering was black. It was the two words that were visible that caught her attention; curious, she reached for it – '*king tour*'. What on earth was a '*king tour*'? Gingerly she reached over and pulled out the entire flyer – and almost dropped it again. Forget '*king tour*'. No, the event being advertised was '*A ghostly walking tour*.' Underneath was an image of a sweet little old man in Victorian evening dress – no, wait. That was an undertaker's outfit, wasn't it?

Cassie shuddered, and was about to screw up the flyer and chuck it at the bin when the next line of type caught her eye. '*An evening of fun and laughter on the Oxford Ghost Trail!*'

Laughter? No way. Despite herself, she read on. '*Illustrated with Props and Illusions! Your Costumed Guide will Entertain You!*'

Props. Illusions. Fun. Cassie hesitated. Remembered

the terror she'd felt just now, when she thought – okay, *imagined* – she'd seen…

standing motionless, watching. Waiting

She exhaled slowly. People scared of flying did courses, didn't they? Feel the fear and do it anyway, wasn't that what they said?

Might not a brief stint on this jokey Ghost Trail, where the old guy admitted right off it was all a bit of fun – *Illusions*, that was the word he used – be just what she needed to put an end to her ridiculous fantasies, once and for all? And if after *that* she didn't realise she was imagining things that didn't exist, she'd need her head examining.

There was a comment from a satisfied customer at the bottom of the flyer, beside a sweet little sketch of a harmless-looking cobweb. '*Brilliant – we loved every minute!*'

Right. She was going. She checked the information beside the cobweb. '*Meet outside the Tourist Information Centre on Broad Street at 6.50 pm every Wednesday and Friday till September. No Need to Book.*' She'd go this coming Friday, if she was ahead with her work…Reaching for a pencil, she scribbled Friday's date at the bottom, and drew a star beside it. '*Loved every minute!*' Smiling, she turned up the protruding corner, slipped the flyer in with the others – she didn't necessarily want to *keep* looking at it – took a deep breath, and made herself turn and face the mess on the tiles. Recalled her desperate haste that morning, the echoing crash of the fridge door – *the unreliable fridge door with the worn catch* – behind her as she fled with the ice.

Stopped smiling, as she realised with a thrill of horror what she'd done.

CHAPTER TWELVE

CASSIE WASN'T SURE how long she stood staring, willing herself to start clearing up. If only she'd made sure the fridge door had actually shut – for heaven's sake, she *knew* the catch was shaky. She'd double checked the iron when she ran back for her purse, why hadn't she checked the fridge, too? Oh well, too late now.

Edging sideways, she leant against the workbench and shook her head, trying to clear the headache that was beginning Definitely shouldn't have had that last glass of wine, everything looked slightly blurred round the edges and she had to concentrate to focus. As she brushed a loose curl off her face she realised she was smiling. *Smiling? Why on earth was she…?* Of course. David had reached out and gently touched her cheek when he said goodnight. Her spirits lifted. It had been a brilliant day, she wasn't going to let a little puddle – actually the bubbles were gleaming with a rather attractive range of colours in the lamp light – spoil it. Best thing would be to leave it, clear up first thing in the morning. Simple. *Just needed a security check of front and back doors, quick – very quick – visit to the bathroom, teeth would have to wait till morning.*

Discard clothes leaving them where they fell, pull on dear old friend kimono. Burrow under duvet with nasty crumpled cover – time for new look? Definitely. Something with flowers would be nice. Maybe blue and purple. Yes. Or maybe...

She slept.

CHAPTER THIRTEEN

HER HEAD HURT. She felt sick, too, plus she needed the loo. And if she didn't get her hands on a large glass of water soon she'd…she'd…Moving very carefully she sat up. Lay down again. Edged to the side of the bed on her back and sat up once more, much slower this time. Closed her eyes. Why oh why had she had that fourth glass? And why oh why were bloody Zadie's Royal Wedding glasses (free gift with fuel purchase) as big as flower vases…? Taking a shuddering breath, she shuffled towards the doorway.

Nearly at the bathroom. Something was lying on the landing floor. Postcard? Not very likely these days. Be nice if it was from somewhere exotic, though, all palm trees and ruined temples…Hadn't Mia from Zumba class said she was planning a trip to Turkey or somewhere? Bracing herself with one hand against the wall she lowered herself carefully until she was able to pick it up, and slipped it into her kimono pocket. She'd read it after she'd drunk that glass of water, rummaged in the cupboard for paracetamol and cleaned her teeth. Always felt better when she'd cleaned her teeth. And she did, a bit, though not enough to drag a flannel over her face or pull a hairbrush through her tangles.

She leaned against the wash basin, touched her cheek lightly. Stopped. Later. She'd check it later.

It was hard to determine the strength of the sunlight as she squinted up at the frosted glass window but it sure as hell felt seriously early. She'd go downstairs very slowly, make a mug of tea and bring it back to bed. Not too strong and definitely no sugar. Pile the pillows up, lean back, close her eyes and think about…things. Tourmaline spacers? Variegated rows of pearls? No, more likely a shock of dark brown hair with a hint of grey, and a slightly hawk-like nose. Blue eyes – well, dark green, really – a tiny chip in a front tooth.

First though, another glass of water. The first had been lukewarm, she'd been too thirsty to wait. She turned the tap on full and stood leaning against the basin, watching the water gradually become colder, admiring the froth of foaming bubbles – they reminded her of something, she couldn't remember what – and when the glass was full to overflowing, picked it up. She was about to take the first luxurious sip when she caught sight of an overturned bottle of her favourite skin lotion amongst the clutter on top of the cupboard, the first expensive drops about to slide down the mirror. Oh for God's sake, what next? Stretching up, she reached for the bottle and lost her balance, bare feet slipping on the damp lino, glass tilting and sending icy water cascading down her front.

She gritted her teeth. At least it was summer, her sodden kimono would be even more uncomfortable if it was winter, the bathroom was always freezing.

And the glass hadn't broken. That was good too, wasn't it? Even if it was one she didn't particularly like. Still, enough. A quick dab at her chest with a couple of towels, then for that second glass of water – maybe. Because no way was she getting out of bed and traipsing back to the bathroom once she'd untangled the duvet, plumped up the pillows and climbed back in again with her tea.

As she sat down on the loo and hitched up her skirts she felt something digging into her side. Must be the postcard, might as well read it now. Prising it from her pocket, she peered at it hopefully. Far from technicolour views of far-off lands there was a scarlet logo at the top she vaguely recognised, with a printed message. Lower down there was a note scrawled in green biro:

called with delivry at 9.00am,
will call back round 12.00
cos it needs a signiture see ya Vic

Oh God. Better check the time, see how long she'd got for her lie-in. It was good Vic was coming, really, she needed that order for the drop earrings. She washed her hands, then dawdled into the bedroom to check the bedside clock. Stood rooted to the spot as with a loud click the clock registered 12.11, and simultaneously there was a knock at the back door. She sighed. Better go, she'd have to pay Precious Gems a fortune to re-deliver. Holding tightly on to the banister she edged her way down the stairs, vaguely aware as she shuffled across the kitchen floor that there seemed to be some sort of leak. Another knock, louder this time. She cleared her throat. 'Coming…'

It came out as a hoarse squeak. She tried again; it sounded even worse the second time.

'Allo? Aven't got trouble again ave you, darlin?'

Raising the blind in a series of erratic jerks, Casie managed what she hoped was a reassuring wave, and after a tussle with the chain, got the door open.

Vic stood there looking anxious, sporting tiny round sunglasses with bright blue lens and a shrunken black tee shirt featuring Madonna Doing Something Unusual in a leather leotard. 'Blimey, got me worried there for a moment, thought you must ave gone down with that Covoid.' He peered at her. 'Still, not exactly in the pink by the look of you – not sure I should be giving you them jewels and that, ask me you should be in bed, not messing around with –'

'I'm fine, really – thanks.' She reached for the package, grabbing for the door handle as her bare feet slipped in the mess and she lost her balance. Stepping forward smartly, Vic seized her elbow, doing a dramatic double take as he took in the state of the floor. Cassie edged away, holding the package to her chest 'It's nothing, no worries – had a bit of a problem with the fridge, door didn't shut properly and everything defrosted, you know, soup and stuff –'

'Smells more like sewage, don't mind me saying.' He moved nearer, forcing her to retreat. 'Nasty, could damage your wiring worse than your iron running amok, flood like that. Lucky your Uncle Vic's a dab hand with a mop.' As he turned and pushed the back door to, a shaft of bright sunlight refracted off his glasses, making it impossible to see his eyes behind the bright blue lens.

'No, honestly – it's kind of you, Vic, but I can manage –'

Too late. He was already shoving the sunglasses into his torn back pocket and pushing past her, gazing appreciatively round the kitchen as he headed for the sink. 'Nice little place you got here, lady. Cosy.' He jerked his head towards the flowered cream jugs on the dresser. 'Go down a treat on Antiques Roadshow, those would.' Turning, he winked, then froze, eyes bulging, as he took in the state of her kimono.

'Dear oh deary me…' Without taking his eyes off her, he reached for the teacloth hanging on the hook beside the sink and approached, shaking his head. 'Catch your death, this rate.' Cassie glanced down, suddenly realising she was still in her kimono, now clinging to her front and leaving nothing to the imagination. Grabbing the tea towel before he could start dabbing at her she backed away, holding it tightly to her chest. 'Better get changed – started work at crack of dawn this morning, forgot I hadn't –' She tossed the soaking tea towel in the direction of the sink, not caring when she missed and it flopped wetly on the floorboards, turned and headed for the stairs.

He took a step forwards. 'Give you a hand with the floor before I go.' Another step. 'Got a mop?'

There was a faint sound behind him. 'Scuse me, Ms ?...'

Cassie whipped round. Gave a smile of relief as she saw Eddie standing hesitantly in the doorway. 'Hi there!'

'Knocked at the front door a bit earlier but no luck, thought I'd try round the back like last time –'

Vic scowled. 'Last time?'

'He's fixing the cooker, aren't you Eddie?'

He adjusted his lanyard so Vic could see his ID, set down his toolbox and looked proudly at Cassie. 'Managed to get my hands on those replacement gas injectors I mentioned.'

'Wow, that's great. Be with you in a sec –'

'Yeah, great.' Vic smirked at Cassie. 'Sure start 'em young these days…Still, my advice is go for a bit of experience, know what I mean?' He came closer – *sweat, stale cigarette smoke, whiff of overpowering aftershave* – and produced his digital screen. Polished it on the hem of his tee shirt, causing Madonna to contort herself even more suggestively, and held it out for Cassie to sign. She scribbled her initials quickly. 'Anything else I can do, let me know. Phone's on the docket.' He shot Eddie a venomous look and headed for the open door. 'Back soon.'

'Great. Thanks, Vic – think I'd better get on with some work, now.'

As he strode off, ignoring her wave, she turned to Eddie. 'Sorry about the mess – left in a hurry yesterday and didn't shut the fridge door properly, such an *idiot*. Do please carry on with the replacements, I'll get dressed and make some tea when I come back.'

'Thanks.'

Upstairs in the bedroom Cassie stripped off the kimono, flung it in the corner, yanked on a pair of old jeans, pulled a baggy jumper with a hole in the elbow over her head and trudged to the bathroom, cursing herself for not getting dressed before bloody Vic arrived. Oh well, he was probably harmless enough, probably tried it on with all his female customers… Still, lucky Eddie arrived when he did. Downing a couple of paracetamols, she gulped more water, massaged her temples briefly, patted concealer over the bruise on her cheek, wincing, brushed her hair, twisted it roughly into a scrunchie, took a deep breath and headed back downstairs. Back in the kitchen Eddie was busy working on something in the depths of the oven. Good. Quickly she tuned the radio to a worthy classical music station, opened the Italian art book containing the portrait of an eighteenth-century noblewoman wearing the magnificent pearl brooch Cassie was planning to incorporate into the tiara design, and placed it on the work bench. Now for the hard part. Restraining a groan, she made her way to the shed, retrieved the bucket and mop, shuffled back to the kitchen and slowly began to clean up the mess on the floor.

She was taking a break when Eddie turned.

'Hmm. Tricky. Have to deal with this later.' He held up a blackened metal object.

'Oh. Is it – um – important?'

'Yep.' Crouching, he rummaged in his toolbox.

'Sorry, silly question' She sighed. 'Time to put the kettle on, I reckon.' She propped the mop in the bucket of dirty water and surveyed the remaining gloop on the floor. 'Just glad my Gran can't see this mess – she'd have a breakdown.'

He looked up. 'Coming round, is she?

'No – no, she's – passed on.' She collected mugs and biscuit tin and set them on the table. 'It's just this little house was her pride and joy, she'd hate me being careless closing the fridge door, not bothering to use the ironing board –'

'Why wouldn't you use –'

'Sockets are crazy, pre-historic basically – have to use the iron on the landing. Easiest to do it on the floor. Keep my hairdryer plugged in there, too – handy to use in the bathroom.' She switched on the kettle. 'At least this works.'

He was frowning. 'Don't think you're s'posed –'

Oh God, she must sound like a spoiled brat. 'Don't get me wrong, I was over the moon when she left me this place –'

'You mean like a *present*?'

'Well, yes –'

He looked about him. 'Amazing.'

'I know. I'm very lucky.' She hunted for the tea bags.

He reddened. 'Sorry, we're not s'posed to make personal comments to customers.'

'No problem, I'm glad you –'

'Just it reminds me of being at my Nan's. The little cottage…homely, bit like this…snow on the roof, wisp of smoke drifting from the chimney into the winter sky…it's nearly dark.' He stared at the floor. 'But there's lamps glowing in the windows, and through the downstairs one you can see a log fire burning and a Christmas tree with all little twinkling lights.'

'It sounds stunning.' She hesitated. 'Hey, maybe you'll get lucky like me, and one day she'll leave you –'

He blinked and looked up. 'In a care home, isn't she. Telling you about her latest jigsaw.' He chucked the metal object into his toolbox.

'Oh Eddie, I'm so sorry.' She reached for the teabags,

trying to think of something helpful to say, when there was a light tap on the open kitchen door. 'Hi Cassie – sorry to interrupt, thought a quick check on the patient might be a good idea?'

She clutched at the tea bags. The thing was to sound casual. Unfazed. 'Oh hi, David, sweet of you to call –'

'Meant to ask how it was going the other day when we got back from the hospital, but there was too much going on.'

He caught sight of the remaining mess on the floor, and grinned. 'No ill effects, I hope?'

She laughed, then stopped as she realised the Gas Engineer had stiffened and was standing watching them. 'Sorry, Eddie – this is my neighbour, David.'

'Neighbour.' He relaxed. 'Oh.'

'He's keeping an eye on my sickly lemon tree.' She gestured towards the windowsill. 'David, this is Eddie, he's sorting out the gas cooker –'

Eddie adjusted his lanyard so it sat dead centre on his chest. 'Complete renovation, more like.'

David glanced at the bright yellow tape swathing the cooker. 'Impressive!' He grinned. 'Place looks like a crime scene from one of those –'

'Actually, it's an important safety regulation. Customers often don't realise –'

A small green lemon fell into the sink with a thud. 'Oops.' Turning away, David scooped it up and examined it. 'Not so much sickly as defunct, I'm afraid. Beyond my power to resuscitate.'

Cassie sighed. 'It's because I overwatered it, isn't it?'

'Didn't help, but Dwarf Meyers are tricky little buggers at the best of times – got to watch the soil PH levels, various pests and diseases.'

'Think I'd better follow Zadie's example. Only plant she's got in the house is a plastic rose that came free with her one of her fancy underwear catalogues.'

'Hey, come on – never say never, we'll make a horticulturist of you yet. Tell you what, I'm on my way to the garden centre to get a cherry tree for my mother's garden – why not come along and we'll get a new lemon tree?'

'But what if I mess it up again –'

'No worries, I'll show you what to look out for.' He grinned. 'then there's various pests and diseases I'm always available for house calls.'

Behind them, Edie kicked his tool box.

'Only thing is I'm expecting a call from a client about a ring she's concerned about, can't afford to miss it –'

'Bring your phone, no problem.'

A garden centre. Perfect, a change of scene was just what she needed. And it was days since Ivo had phoned – he'd obviously lost interest once he realised harassing her wasn't going to get a result.

'Brilliant. Hope you don't mind my rushing off, Eddie – I'll fix you that tea before I sort myself out –' She poured boiling water onto a tea bag, added milk and pushed the biscuit tin towards him.

'Finish fitting these gas injectors then I'll be on my way.' He puffed out his chest. 'Got an important visit to make myself, got a contact for those O ring replacements.'

As she headed for the stairs, she heard David laugh. 'Sounds like you're working on a dodgy space shuttle, rather than a defunct gas cooker.'

No laughter in response, just a grunt. Oh well. Better get a move on, swap the ancient jeans and tatty jumper for something a bit more summery. Fix concealer, brush hair. Lipstick? Definitely.

Downstairs again, fast. 'Ready –' She stopped dead. The Gas Engineer guy – no, *Eddie* – was straightening up at the cooker, wiping his hands on a rag, looking pleased with himself. There was no sign of David. 'Hello? Where's –'

'Good job, if I do say so myself. Can be a pain, gas injectors, but these…' He stuffed the rag in the tool box and secured the lid. 'Sweet.'

'Brilliant. Um…where did David go?'

'Sink this then I'll be off.' He picked up his tea and gulped at it, looking her up and down over the rim of the mug.

'My neighbour –'

'Guy with the green fingers?'

'David, yes –'

Picking up his tool box, he headed for the open back door. 'Said he was going to take a look at your rockery. Prob'ly an expert on rocks, too.'

'Thanks, Eddie –' He waited, clearly expecting something more. *Got it.* 'Really appreciate you tracking down those new gas injectors, fantastic.'

She followed him into the garden, watching as he walked away – then stopped. No sign of David. Oh God, he'd gone, she should never have kept him waiting so long, what on earth had she been thinking? Disappointed (ridiculous, what was so great about a visit to a garden centre, for heaven's sake?) she was about to return to the kitchen – get the back door safely secured, check the front door, too – when she noticed the shed door was open. *Which must mean she hadn't bothered to close it when she fetched the mop and bucket earlier.* Like she hadn't bothered to close the blasted fridge door properly yesterday, either... She shook her head; she was going to have to get a grip. Concentrate on what she was actually *doing*, instead of imagining things all the time. She'd start making errors with her work, at this rate. *Enough.* Marching forward she began to push the door shut – heard a sound and stopped, peering into the gloom. *Ivo stood by the shelves, his back to her, reaching for something.*

'Ivo? What the hell are you –?' Her throat was dry, her voice little more than a whisper.

'Cassie?'

The figure turned; she felt a rush of relief so great she thought she'd fall over. 'David!'

'Hey, hope you don't mind, saw the door was open and couldn't resist taking a look – always loved sheds.'

'It's fine –'

'The smell of creosote, the stash of garden stuff, the immaculate tools –'

He was holding something. Stepping closer, she saw it was the putty knife with the dangling price tag. Except it wasn't gleaming any more; he was brushing little flakes of white paint off the blade. He smiled. 'Can't let this one spoil the show.' Producing a crumpled tissue from a pocket he picked up a half-full bottle of turps, thoroughly cleaned the knife, swept the flakes of paint onto the damp tissue, screwed it up and thrust it back in his pocket.

'Honestly, you really didn't need to bother –' She

frowned. 'Can't believe I didn't notice it myself.'

He smiled. 'No problem.' Glancing at his watch, he indicated the doorway. 'Better get going if you still fancy a trip to the garden centre, they close at six.'

'Lovely – sorry I kept you waiting so long.'

'Worth the wait. Love the tank top.'

'Thanks.' She closed the door firmly behind them. 'I'll just get my bag and lock up –'

He paused as they passed the rockery. 'May I?' Picking a handful of lavender, he rubbed some on his palms. 'Get rid of the smell of turps.'

She laughed, wondering how she could ever have imagined it had been Ivo lurking in the gloom. 'Clever.'

With an exaggerated bow, he presented her with a single long-stemmed pink from the rockery. 'See you at the car.'

She was heading for the kitchen, trying to remember exactly where she'd left her phone and whether she could actually *afford* a lemon tree – time to chase her overdue invoices, didn't they realise she had bills to pay? – when she stopped dead. Was that a movement at next door's upper window? She glanced up, expecting to see a tall thin figure in black staring down at her, but as she watched a pigeon rose from the window sill with a great flapping of wings and flew off towards the copse of trees down the lane. Cassie smiled. *A bird.* Just a bird…

Quickly she collected her things, slid the chain off the front door – the obvious exit since David's car was parked outside, and she'd only be out for a couple of hours – and checked the back door was secure. Then, her mind full of images of flowering lemon trees –

no, Dwarf Meyers – laden with fruit, imagining air fragrant with perfume, she hurried away to find David.

CHAPTER FOURTEEN

'ALL SET?'

Cassie secured her seat belt. 'Sure.' She felt a sudden wave of panic. Had she closed the front door securely? 'Though actually – I'm terribly sorry, would you mind if I just –' Seat belt off, car door open 'Won't be a sec –' Tripping over a cracked paving stone, she ran.

Eight minutes later she was back, breathless as she climbed back in the car. 'Forgot something, so stupid –'

'No problem, do it all the time myself.' They drew away from the kerb, slowing as they approached a small white van. 'Hey, isn't that…?'

A familiar figure in an over-sized hi-vis jacket was opening the van's back doors and chucking in his tool box.

'Eddie, yes –'

David gave a cheery double toot as they overtook. Cassie waved as they passed, shrugged as the greeting was ignored. 'Don't think he recognised us.'

'Probably worrying about those O rings.'

Cassie laughed, and settled lower in her seat, relaxing, her thoughts turning to the problem her client was having with her ring. That was the trouble with princess cut diamond rings, elegant as the shape was, the corners were always alarmingly fragile. One solution would be…

'Cassie?' Someone was touching her gently on her bare shoulder, sunlight was warm on her face. She stirred. If this was a dream, she didn't want to wake up.

'We're here.'

She opened her eyes reluctantly. David – *David*? – was smiling down at her. She looked about her. What on earth…? She was sitting – well, practically lying – in the front seat of a car. Through the windscreen she could see a beautiful old country house, the foreground crowded with old-fashioned wheelbarrows full of flowering plants and stacks of huge terracotta pots. Over there was a hand-lettered sign saying *Garden Centre*…Suddenly she remembered settling down in the front seat of the Audi, pondering the common weakness in the design of princess cut diamond rings as they set off down the Iffley Road.

She had no idea how long it was before she actually fell asleep, and despite the seat belt, slipped down the sun-warmed leather. She looked down now, horrified, at the rucked up poplin skirt, the bag that had slipped off her lap and spilt its contents all over the foot well (even from here she could see half a Crunchie bar, a flattened box of Tampax, and the crumpled flyer for the Ghost Trail). Had she snored? Please *please* God she hadn't dribbled…David was getting out and coming round to open her door. Hastily repacking her bag she scrambled out and looked around, squinting up at the golden cockerel weathervane glinting on the roof.

David was already disappearing round the corner of the house, beckoning her to follow. Past a little wooden hut where people were queueing to pay, down a narrow track that led to…well, Fairy Land, really. Cassie had never been to a garden centre in her life and had been vaguely expecting to see a giant polythene tent crammed with rows of unidentifiable green shoots with unpronounceable labels, and a selection of hanging baskets containing a few rather tired pansies. She'd been wrong. She stood motionless, gazing at a network of shady paths that stretched as far as the eye could see, bordered by rustic stands crammed with a riot of blooms; tray after tray of dahlias, varying in size from pompoms to dinner plates in a rainbow of vivid colours, huge sunflowers (van Gogh yellow) frilly little pinks (the delicate shade reminded her of the pearls in her bangle) and best of all hydrangeas, a mist of blues and lilacs and purples so ravishing it made her catch her breath.

She wandered on. After a while, the abundance of flowers gave way to racks of exotic plants, their huge leaves all shapes and sizes in every conceivable shade of green, their labels unintelligible. Occasionally other customers strolled past; a cheerful couple pushing a wire trolley loaded with trays of bright orange marigolds, a woman in a wax jacket and fuchsia headscarf clutching a container crammed with lethal-looking cacti, an old man carefully carrying a flowerpot overflowing with trailing scarlet rosebuds. She was fishing in her bag for paper – an old receipt, anything, plus something to draw with – when she felt a hand on her shoulder. She jumped, whirled round. Saw David.

'Hey, only me –'

Weak with relief she managed to smile. 'God, sorry – I was miles away –'

'Like it?'

'*Like* it? It's heaven, I had no idea…'

'Fancy a cup of tea before we get on with the serious stuff?'

'It'd be great, but I couldn't bear to leave yet –'

'Not a problem.' He doffed an imaginary cap. 'Follow me, Ma'am.'

He set off down a little pebbled path overhung by massive palm trees, and took a turning that led into a clearing containing a wooden hut and several green metal tables and chairs, mostly occupied by families, the kids playing with various electronic gizmos and devouring ice creams. A hand-lettered sign beside the hut invited patrons to help themselves to free tea and coffee, and avail themselves of the homemade cakes offered within for a small charge. As they approached she could see a wall-mounted hot drinks machine and an array of glass cloches covering an array of perfect sponge cakes, set out on a blue and white checked cloth.

David gestured to a vacant table beneath a magnificent chestnut tree. 'Let's have a coffee – unless you'd prefer tea? Self-service, obviously.' Cassie put her bag on one of the metal chairs and rummaged for her purse, knocking the edge of the table, horrified as a half-full plastic glass of orange squash left behind by a previous customer tipped over. '*Idiot*…Hang on, sure I've got some tissues somewhere…'

Reaching into a pocket, David whipped out the clump of tissues he'd used earlier to clean the putty knife. 'Allow me –'

'But –'

'My speciality, cleaning up' He got to work. 'Looks weird, I know.'

'Well –'

'My ex, Erica –'

oh please, not bloody Erica

'– can't stand any sort of mess, untidiness –'

lucky she didn't see the kitchen floor, then

'It's a medical condition – Ataxaphobia.'

so not just a controlling bitch

'Oh dear. What causes –'

'Mother was an alcoholic, plastered twenty-four seven. Three kids under eight, Erica was the eldest. Other two were boys. House made a pig-sty look like a show home, apparently.' He wrung out the sodden heap of tissue on the grass, screwed it up again. ''Fraid I've got used to jumping whenever there's a problem. Which is – *was*, now she's moving out – often.'

Cassie tried to feel sorry for her – and failed. Still, trying to cope with two small brothers couldn't have been much fun. No wonder she wasn't exactly keen on Brooklyn and Bronx – lucky she was away skiing that time they decided to set up a homemade chocolate fountain on the pavement and forcibly charge hapless passersby for a slurp. All had gone relatively well until Blanco had taken a keen interest in the venture and knocked over the whole caboodle, flooding the pavement with melted chocolate. It had taken Zadie days to scrub off the mess.

'Oh well – nothing lasts for ever.' He straightened a couple of chairs, and grimaced. 'Thank God.'

'No kidding.' She instinctively touched a hand to her cheek.

'So what about you, Cassie?'

She hesitated. Met his eyes, and saw nothing but kindness there. Took a deep breath... then another... And I told him about Tom.

Afterwards there was a long pause. 'Know what?' The warmest of smiles, deepening the lines at the corner of his eyes. 'Think you deserve that tea.'

She smiled back. 'Reckon we both do.' Retrieving her purse from her bag, she made to follow him.

'My treat.' He turned back. 'No good asking if you fancy a slice of Victoria sponge, I suppose?'

Bliss. 'Nothing I'd like more.'

Whistling, David chucked the used tissues into a nearby rubbish bin and strolled away.

By the time he returned, Cassie had placed her phone on the table and was surreptitiously sketching an alarmingly sun-tanned woman in a leopardskin-printed sundress, sitting at a nearby table sharing an ice cream with her elaborately coiffed miniature poodle. He peered over her shoulder, laughing, as he set out the contents of the tray and sat down. 'So, how's the work going?'

She took the proffered container of tea, and told him about the rose gold bangle with the tricky lobster clasp she'd finished that morning, and the earrings with circular blister pearls above pear-shaped amethysts with tourmaline spacers that had to be ready in two weeks. Oh yes, and the complicated tiara she was working on.

'Fabulous. Like the sound of that lobster clasp.'

They sat companionably drinking tea. Cassie slipped a forkful of Victoria sponge into her mouth, closing her eyes with pleasure as it melted on her tongue. When she opened them again David was looking at her intently. Oh God, he was probably afraid she was going to fall asleep again. She sat up straighter. 'Actually, I was wondering what exactly it is that you do?'

'Currently working on my projected series of putatively upmarket pocket-books for European travellers on little-known carvings – stone, wood, marble, whatever – unicorns, angels, demons, *putti* etcetera – and where to find 'em.'

'Sounds great.'

'Glad somebody thinks so. Erica thinks it's a terribly *vulgar* idea.'

'But –'

'For 'vulgar' read 'commercial'. And for 'commercial' read 'popular''. He took a swig of tea and set down the container. Hard. 'She doesn't know the half of it, luckily. Pete, my editor – guy I was having a row with on the phone when you came round yesterday, think bloody ridiculous oversize Groucho Marx specs, a grubby Shane MacGowan tee shirt two sizes too small and an MBA from Harvard – is busting a gut to get a TV series green-lit.'

Cassie gasped. 'That's fantastic!'

He adopted an affected falsetto. 'But my students might see it! The *embarrassment*!'

'You're kidding. So what does Erica do that's so –'

He grinned. 'Strikes terror into the Upper Sixth at a swish private school. Private tuition at the weekends to foreign students desperate to get into Oxford, poor bastards. Symbolism, semantics and suchlike. Makes a fortune.'

'Think I'll stick to lobster clasps.' She cut a piece of sponge with the side of her fork and was about to lift it to her lips when her phone rang, the ringtone amplified by the ornate wrought-iron tabletop. The fork fell with a clatter as she half-rose to her feet.

David reached out a hand, concerned. 'Cassie?'

She sat down again, managed to laugh. 'Sorry – gave me a fright.' She took a sip of tea and picked up her phone. 'India? Hi…' She listened. 'Fine, thanks. And I think I've decided on a solution to the problem with your lovely ring; I plan to reset the stone in a claw setting that will protect those fragile corners.' She listened again. 'Rose gold, yes? And I'll give the stone a polish that'll make those facets sparkle like a thousand stars.' She smiled. 'Looking forward to it – a princess cut diamond of that calibre will be a joy to work with.' She listened. 'A couple of weeks? I'll give you a call when it's ready to collect. Bye, India.'

She replaced her phone on the table and reached for her tea.

'Amazing. Makes little-known carvings sound positively dull.'

'No way, I think they sound great.' She pushed back her chair. 'Is there a loo?'

He waved a hand. 'Behind the tea hut, little log cabin, very discreet.'

Discreet it might have been but as Cassie pushed the ill-fitting door to it was clear from the rustlings in the sudden darkness that it was also the residence of who knew what species of wildlife. *Mice. Insects. Frogs.* No, not frogs, they needed water. Bats? No caves were their thing…*weren't they?* But definitely – Oh God – *spiders.* Still, needs must…Quickly she sat down on the wooden toilet seat. *Concentrate on India's ring. Fifty-eight carats – glorious, the more carats a diamond possessed the more light it would reflect. It had been a birthday present from her late husband, and she'd been distraught when the corners began to show signs of wear. A claw setting would definitely –*

She felt a slight tickle on her bare ankle. Without even thinking about it she found herself outside again, pulling up her pants, brushing at her legs, straightening her skirt, laughing with relief. Slowly, enjoying the warm sunshine on her bare arms, looking forward to finishing the remains of her cake – maybe getting them both another tea? – she headed back to their table.

Stopped as she saw David, standing now, frowning at the phone in his hand – hers, she recognised the colour – holding it out to her as he saw her approach, shaking his head and looking embarrassed. 'Cassie, huge apologies – should have left it but it rang three times on the trot, thought it might be your client ringing back with a query –?'

Even as she took it Cassie could hear Ivo ranting. She held it gingerly to her ear. 'Ivo? What on earth –'

Her knees weak, she sat down hard on her chair.

'Don't *what on earth* me, you stupid cow –' Several loud gulps, the crash of a bottle being set down, followed by a loud burp. 'So who the fuck's the jerk who answered?'

Oh God, it was on speaker! She fumbled for the mute button. 'Just a neighbour –'

'And where the hell are you – dogs barking and fucking birds singing –'

'In a garden centre –'

'Oh how *super.*'

'I wanted to replace the dying lemon tree and David –'

'*David?*' Ivo made vomiting noises.

Damp with sweat, her fingers slid uselessly over the buttons.

'– needs to buy a cherry tree for his mother –'

'Ah, *sweet.*'

'So he gave me a lift.'

'Had his hand down your pants yet?'

Another hopeless stab at the bloody, bloody mute button. 'Ivo –'

A loud guffaw. 'Hope you're enjoying all the flora and fucking fauna.' More loud gulps. 'Always did love flowers, right?'

'Ivo, what's the point of all this –'

She tried the mute again. This time she heard a click. *Success.* 'Gonna come back, that's what. Can't take kipping on Dave's floor any more, stinks of cat's pee.'

'Dave?'

'Fellow shelf stacker. Can't stand that fucking job any more either, but my useless bitch of a mother won't let me go home – too busy with her bingo nights and her new *fancy man.*' His tone changed from aggression to self-pity. '*Said* I'll pay rent this time, wouldn't be like last time – keep my tunes down, right, clean up after the fry-ups –'

the handles of the old pine store cupboard slammed into her back, agony exploding in her kidneys, shooting up her spine, a dazzling display of scarlet fireworks fading to black as she collapsed

Cassie shut her eyes. 'No, Ivo.'

'Say fucking *what* –?'

'Sorry.'

Silence. Then the bottle was set down again, harder this time 'Well you have fun, queen of my heart, light of my fucking life.' When he next spoke, it was a whisper. '*While you can…*'

She snapped her phone case shut, fast, and opened her eyes. The sun-tanned woman in the leopardskin-printed sundress was casting nervous looks over her shoulder at Cassie as she hurried away, tripping over her lavishly mirror-sequinned wrap, clutching her miniature poodle protectively to her chest.

'You okay?' David was watching her, concerned. 'Guy sounds a bit of a case.'

'You *heard*?'

'On speaker.'

So much for success. She shut her eyes. 'Cassie? Is there anything I can –'

'No, honestly, it'll be fine, he just gets a bit –'

you'll pay for this, you fucking bitch

'– het up.' Hands shaking, Cassie attempted to tidy

the tea things, almost knocking over the remains of her cold tea. She recoiled as David reflexively steadied the container – looked up and caught his eye. Shaking his head, he burst out laughing 'Tell you what.' He picked up her bag and slid the strap onto her shoulder. 'Reckon it's time to find that lemon tree.'

CHAPTER FIFTEEN

IT WAS NEARLY seven o'clock by the time they arrived back at Poplar Street, with a perfect lemon tree and an equally perfect cherry tree stashed on the Audi's back seat. Cassie managed to make small talk during the journey; the danger of No 42's overflowing rubbish bins attracting foxes – suspicious noises had been heard at night – and the pros and cons of traffic calming devices proving to be useful topics. This time she couldn't wait for the journey to be over, desperate to settle down in the kitchen, immerse herself in her work and forget that David had heard every word – *every word! Fresh perspiration bloomed under her arms, her cheeks blazed* – of the conversation with Ivo.

'Great.' David was hauling the lemon tree out of the car. 'Let me carry this in for you – love to invite you for a drink but I'm off to town for a couple of days. Give you a call when I get back, if that's –'

'Honestly, I can manage –' She practically snatched the tree out of his arms, almost overbalancing as she underestimated the weight of the pot, stepping back smartly as he put out a hand to steady her. 'Thanks so much for the tree and – and – everything, it's been lovely.' Smiling as hard as she could she managed a quick wave, then, tripping over the cracked bloody paving stone yet again, turned and headed for the back lane and home.

She found herself in the kitchen at last, front door safely chained once more, lemon tree dumped on the windowsill over the sink, phone switched off and slung in a drawer. Weak with relief she stood for a moment, simply looking about her – even the bright yellow *DANGER DO NOT USE* tape festooning the body of the oven looked welcoming. There was a slight odour in the air – Oh God, she hadn't finished cleaning up the revolting spillage on the floor. Suddenly she was galvanized into action, mopping and rinsing, chucking the remaining contents of the fridge in the bin. Washing her hands, she took a deep breath. Exhaled. Lamps on, music on, mug of coffee at her elbow (*tea? No thanks*), notes on the drop earrings for Mrs Langley Smith's daughter in front of her on the bench; she settled down to work.

Two hours later, the drawings and measurements were completed. More coffee; then she took an array of circular blister pearls, pear-cut summery green peridots and vibrant tourmaline spacers from the little safe and sat gazing at them as they glowed in the lamplight. After a while, composure restored at last, she laid out her most delicate tools, and donning a headband magnifier, began to work.

Early morning light was seeping beneath the bottom of the closed blinds when the last amethyst was finally set in place. Setting down the delicate solder pick she removed the headband magnifier, and mindful of the bruised area on her back, stretched to ease her aching muscles, picked up her illuminated jeweller's loupe and began a detailed inspection of the exquisite finished earrings. Satisfied at last, she laid them gently in one of her trademark velvet lined boxes; ready to be photographed in the morning before she stashed them in the safe – she was too tired to do it now, getting the lighting right was always tricky. Then she'd send the image to Mrs Langley Smith for her approval – hopefully she wouldn't have to wait for months to be paid. Automatically cleaning her tools first, she put them away, levered herself up from the work bench, switched off the lamps, trying as always not to wonder what on earth the electricity bill was going to be, and shuffled towards the stairs, managing to avoid glancing at the lemon tree as she passed.

She reached the landing and making a huge effort, forced herself to perform the usual ritual of checking that the security chain was firmly in place. Stepped back, feeling sick. Far from being slotted securely into place, the chain dangled limply against the dark wood. *What…? How…? Think…* She remembered panicking earlier as she and David were about to leave, and rushing back to check the front door. *Hadn't* she? Or was panicking the problem, and she'd been in such a state about David thinking what an idiot she was that *she'd actually slipped the chain off just now*? More than likely, given – well, everything. Like the time she thought she'd switched the iron off, only to discover… Still, no good crying over spilt milk, as Granny Jackson would say; she'd just have to be more careful in future.

At least the house had only been left unprotected for a few hours – not even a night, thank God. Speaking of which, if she didn't get into bed soon, she'd collapse. She thrust the chain into place, and was about to head for the open bedroom door when she glanced down. A scatter of brightly coloured envelopes lay on the mat. Cards? Bending down effortfully she picked them up, carried them through to the bedroom and opened them, frowning. Of course! It was her birthday! She read the cards, smiling at the humorous ones (her brother Ted, teaching European Politics at Harvard, Zadie and Lloyd AND CO, Merrill who taught the Zumba class and insisted on listing everyone's birthdays) and admiring the arty ones (Kurdish tile designs from Wendy, an old friend from one of her jewellery courses, Toulouse Lautrec's can-can dancers at the Moulin Rouge from her father). Her father's card contained a note:

Happy birthday, darling girl!
Dinner tonight if you've no other plans?
Will call at 11 am to check xxx

Relieved that there was nothing from Ivo, she glanced in the bathroom mirror after she'd cleaned her teeth and gently touched her cheek. The livid purple bruise had begun to turn varying shades of yellow and green, like a rotting apple, and looked if anything even worse than before. With a shudder, she climbed into bed and set the alarm for 10.45, ready for her father's call. She hadn't seen him since Christmas, and dinner out would be a treat. Browns in Woodstock Road, hopefully. Brilliant. With a sigh of pleasure, she pulled the duvet round her shoulders, settled the pillows more comfortably. Tried to smile as she remembered the humorous cards, instead found herself recalling her reflection in the bathroom mirror.

After a moment, she pulled the duvet over her head. Finally, slept.

CHAPTER SIXTEEN

CASSIE WOKE WHEN the alarm shrilled, over-heated and struggling to breathe. Throwing off the duvet she reached for the glass of water on the bedside table, misjudged it and drenched the little pile of cards and flyers she'd left on top of the Redouté Rose book. Stumbling into the bathroom she did her best to towel the cards and book dry, and nearly burst into tears when she found the page featuring the little white climbing rose was ruined. Huh, great start to her birthday. Better grab her phone ready for her father's call, at least she had tonight to look forward to. Hurrying back to the bedroom she checked the folds of the abandoned duvet and groped in vain beneath the pillows. Stood listening, bewildered, to a muted buzzing sound that seemed to emanate from somewhere downstairs. A trapped insect? Better go and check.

Yawning, she stumbled down to the kitchen, and tossed the cards and flyers on the end of the table. As she passed the dresser the buzzing increased. Stopping suddenly, she yanked open the drawer. Almost managed a grin as she remembered chucking her phone in when she got back from the bloody garden centre. She snatched it up. 'Dad?'

'Hey, birthday girl! All good for tonight?'

'You bet, can't wait to see you. Where –?'

'Hang on, call on the other line –'

She grinned. Probably Warren Buffett or Jeff Bezos – her father was a top Investment Banker, and travelled all over the world.

'Pick you up at half-six, sweetheart. Have a good day!' He was gone.

She felt better already – better still when she caught sight of the flawless earrings lying in their little box on the work bench, waiting to be photographed. She'd made coffee, and was about to set up the lights she'd need to photograph them when her stomach rumbled. She was starving – not surprising, since the last thing she'd eaten was – *no, don't go there*. Better eat something before she concentrated on the pics, though, getting the settings right was always tricky. Toast perhaps, or cereal. Except that she had neither bread nor milk, and the bloody fridge was empty. She'd nip into town – it wasn't far to Sainsbury's, and a stroll in the morning sunshine would do her good. And after she'd finished the pics, she'd concentrate on getting ready for tonight.

She focused on the design for the tiara as she walked; that headband was going to be tricky. She was still debating the merits of silver versus rose gold as she entered the supermarket, picked up a wire basket and headed for the shelves of bread. She was reaching for a small sliced white when she felt a nudge. 'Hiya!' Zadie stood beside her, beaming, skimpy sundress patterned with huge sunflowers, braids threaded with scarlet ribbon, silver hoop earrings clattering. 'Happy birthday, girlfriend!' Cassie's heart lifted. 'Hey Zades!' As they hugged, Cassie glanced down at her neighbour's basket, overflowing with packets of mince, onions, red and green peppers, limes, tomatoes, avocados and a tub of crème fraîche. Two enormous boxes of corn tacos were balanced precariously on top of the avocados. 'Bloody hell, Zades! Feeding the five thousand or what?'

'Be a doddle, that would.' She rolled her eyes. 'Lloyd'll be home later. Wasn't laughing a lot when he called last night – said he'd been cut up at lunch time by a load of Lycra boys on some poncey cyclin holiday, nearly made him rear-end some old bloke's caravan –'

'God, Zades, that's –'

'– so he forced the lot of em off the road, got down outta the cab and said he'd better warn em it's a fuckin – pardon my French – bad idea to mess with a 44 tonne 12 wheeled DAF XF lorry cos it's a killing machine when it wants to be, if they got his drift.'

'*No…*So what…?'

'Whole lot turned tail and vamoosed.' Zadie burst out laughing. 'Practically wettin their shiny little shorts, Lloyd said.'

The tacos began to slide slowly off the rest of the shopping. Grinning, Cassie bent down and retrieved them.

'Anyway, thought I'd make him his fave dinner tonight – e's been livin on Chinese takeaways 'n' dodgy sausage sandwiches from them layby vans all week.

Tell you what, why don't you join us? Birthday treat –
play your cards right and you'll get extra guacamole.'

'Oh Zades, thank you, I'd have loved to, but –'

'Kids'd go ape, still talkin about the way you let
Brookie loose on the vendin machine up the hospital.'

'They were great that day –'

'Yeah, well, at the moment not so much.'

'Why, what –?

Zadie set her basket down, took a quick look behind
her and leaned closer. 'Know No 42? Bins need sortin?
Weird barkin 'n' screamin's been heard late at night,
people been complainin, say it's foxes.' She plucked a
plum tomato from her shopping. 'Know what?' She
took a bite. 'They're right.'

'*No –*'

'My two been hidin peanut butter sandwiches in the
rubbish. Wanna catch one 'n' bring one home for a
pet.'

Cassie burst out laughing.

'I know.' She wiped tomato juice off her chin.
'Bronx's got a carton stashed in his room for its bed,
little bugger's stuffed my best cardi in it. Plannin to
send that David Attenborough a pic, got a bet with
his mates he'll get an invite on the show with his little
furry friend.'

'Oh my –'

'No worries…' Zadie stuffed the rest of the tomato
in her mouth. 'Lloyd'll sort the little buggers out.' She
picked up her basket. 'See you later, then?'

'Really wish I could, but Dad's picking me up at half
past six. Next weekend any good?'

'For sure. Where's he takin you, then?'

'Browns, I expect.'

'Ooh, posh. Never forget that time he come round when you moved in to make sure you'd settled in okay, and I thought Harrison Ford'd come callin'. Just tell me you're not wearin those godawful jeans, girlfriend. And I gotta tell you, that tee shirt's seen better days.'

'No worries. Bound to be something stashed at the back of the wardrobe.'

'Yeah, old dungarees full of moth holes if I know you. Have a lend of my hot pink poppy print with the split skirt if you want, if you can't find nothin'.' Zadie moved away, screeching with laughter, narrowly avoiding a customer irritably pushing a loaded trolley with a screaming toddler crammed in the child seat. Giving the woman a cheerful smile, that wasn't returned, Cassie dropped the loaf in her basket, and was about to head for the chilled section to get some milk when she caught sight of a display of croissants at the end of the bread shelves. She hesitated. God, they looked delicious. And it *was* her birthday, after all. A packet of croissants joined the bread, and crossing her eyes at the screaming toddler, whose mouth snapped shut in disbelief, she went in search of a litre of semi-skimmed.

She'd set out mug, plate and butter, switched on the kettle and was taking the croissants from their bag when she remembered the oven was unusable. Still, even cold they'd be delicious. Sunlight poured though the kitchen window – she'd raised the blind when she returned, before going outside to cut a celebratory spray of white roses from the bush climbing the kitchen wall. She'd hesitated briefly, debating whether to leave the door open to the August sunshine while she ate her breakfast. Winced at the ache in her back as she reached up to adjust the roller on a blind. Was she *stupid*? Quickly she locked the door, slid the chain into place and lowered the other blinds. Right, time to get on; adjust the Anglepoise lamps and set out her notebook. She'd concentrate on checking her drawings for the tiara while she ate, refuse to think about Ivo –

thrusting a forkful of chicken in his mouth, chewing angrily, mouth half-open, gravy running down his chin

– then work on the headband –

dropping the fork, snatching up handfuls of little seed pearls and flicking them at her one by one

– till it was finished.

She'd double-checked her measurements, made another coffee and eaten most of the second croissant when she heard a sound. *Coming from outside. Close to the back door.* She froze, heart thudding. Ivo had remembered her birthday after all? Planned to surprise her? Oh please God, no. She got silently to her feet, listening, careful not to jar the leg of the chair. She'd seen an old black and white film once, about a female British secret agent; intelligent, brave, resourceful.

On the run, on the verge of being tracked down, she'd been forced to hide under the floorboards of a Japanese army outpost where a meeting was taking place. Pitch black. Airless. After a few moments dust began to clog her nostrils and coat the back of her throat as she struggled soundlessly to breathe, eyes watering, nails digging into her palms – silence was imperative, a matter of life and death. Then, at last, the sound of officers' boots stamping over the floorboards. Fading. The sound of a door opening – they were leaving. Desperate, the agent risked a silent, shuddering intake of breath – and sneezed.

Disbelieving silence. Followed by pandemonium, followed by the clatter of boots returning, fast this time, followed by the sound of floorboards being ripped up followed by –

Where the hell had she left her phone? Another sound, a sort of crackling this time. Outside the back door? More crackling. What…? Suddenly a shadow appeared on the blind. Cassie froze, heart pounding. Maybe if she –

'Hallo? A woman's voice. Zadie, pretending to be posh? Ruth from Zumba? Relief swept through her. Knees suddenly weak, she clung to the edge of the table.

'Coming –' Taking a deep breath, she moved to the door and raised the blind.

Erica stood there, scowling. Cassie tried to manage a smile, noting the immaculate bob and pristine cream linen outfit, wishing she wasn't wearing jeans badly in need of a wash and a tee shirt with a scorch mark on the sleeve courtesy of the soldering iron. After a brief tussle with the chain she unlocked the door and opened it.

'Heavens, it's like visiting Fort Knox.'

'I know, silly really –'

Erica surged towards her, forcing Cassie to step

back. 'These came earlier. You were out, apparently –'

'Yes, I –'

'– so I had no option but to accept them.'

'Sorry –'

'– appallingly pushy, these delivery people.' Brandishing a large bouquet of yellow roses wrapped in crackling florist's paper, she pushed past Cassie and stood looking about her. She made a moue of distaste. 'How cosy.'

'Thanks –'

'Of course, we updated ours the *moment* we moved in. My husband adores that clean Scandinavian look.'

'I've got a friend who did her whole kitchen in Ikea, and it's –'

'*Broste* Copenhagen, actually.' Erica arched an eyebrow in exaggerated surprise at the tape-swathed cooker. 'Heavens. When are you expecting the new model to arrive?'

'Oh, this one's being –'

'And all those floral plates! Sweet...' Turning, she took in the dilapidated fridge. Caught sight of Cassie's workbench, with its array of complicated-looking machines and neatly labelled drawers of tools, and stopped dead. 'What on earth...?'

'My workbench.'

'*Work...*?'

'Bench, yes.'

a princess cut diamond of that calibre will be a joy to work with

Cassie smiled. 'I'm a jeweller.'

With a sceptical look Erica reached for the leather box containing the earrings Cassie had completed the previous night, and opened it. She stood staring at the contents – Cassie could have sworn she had no idea her mouth had fallen open.

'Circular blister pearls, pear-shaped amethysts and tourmaline spacers.' Cassie touched an earring affectionately. 'I always think tourmaline –'

'Such fun to have a hobby. I only wish I had the time.' Erica snapped the lid shut. 'I must be getting back, I've a very important Zoom conference call scheduled for 12.30.' A lightning cut of narrowed eyes at the neatly arranged breakfast table, then she was darting forward, heels clicking sharply on the flagstones. 'I'll leave these here, shall I?' She dumped the bouquet on top of the croissants, turning away as Cassie put out a hand to stop her. Turned back. '*Silly* me! Such a butterfingers! Oh dear – your *delicious* breakfast!' She seized the bouquet and set it down again, this time in the middle of the table. The almost full mug tilted, seemed for a long moment to pause, then toppled over. A river of cold coffee streamed towards the open notebook as Cassie, horrified, lunged to save it.

Too late.

Erica squealed, stretched out an ineffectual hand. 'Oh no! All those charming little doodles!' Hurrying to the sink, she picked up a teacloth between finger and thumb, returned to the table and began flapping it at the ruined notebook, making things worse.

Yanking a handful of used tissues from her jeans pocket Cassie dabbed at the sodden pages, trying not to cry as she saw detailed sketches and lists of measurements and charts of colour comparisons disintegrate under her hand.

'I'm *so* sorry!' Erica opened her eyes wide. 'It's not like me to be clumsy – in fact Davie always says –'

Cassie gritted her teeth. 'No problem.' She hoped Erica wouldn't notice the splashes of black coffee on her hitherto immaculate cream linen sleeve until the bloody Zoom conference call was well under way.

'Still, you can always turn out some more, I expect.' Erica glanced at her gleaming wristwatch and gave a little gasp. 'Simply *must* fly – there's a desperately important meeting with the Planning Committee tomorrow I need to prepare for before the conference call.'

She headed for the back door. 'Don't bother to see me out…'

She was gone.

CHAPTER SEVENTEEN

WHEN A DOUBLE toot on the horn announced her father's arrival in Poplar Street on the dot of six-thirty, Cassie was ready. She'd spent hours on her hair and makeup, and ironing (on her knees, with difficulty) a favourite sundress, the back cut just high enough to conceal the dark bruises still blooming on her back. With a last glance in the bathroom mirror – smoky eyes to draw attention from the heavily camouflaged bruise, a casually messy loose bun, the beautiful freshwater pearl earrings inherited from her grandmother – she slipped her feet into neutral-coloured wedge espadrilles (borrowed in a panic at the last moment from Zadie, when it became clear that neither sneakers nor ancient Uggs were going to fit the bill) and hurried to the front door.

It took a moment to deal with the front door's lock and chain, and when she finally stepped outside she burst out laughing. Her father's navy-blue Porsche Boxter GTS convertible was parked at a careless angle at the kerb, wheel rims sparkling in the sunshine, velvety black hood folded down. It was sandwiched between a filthy black van with CLEAN US scrawled in the dirt on the back door, and a battered little lime-green deux-chevaux that belonged to the students in the house opposite and was clearly on its last legs. As she approached the driver's side, she saw that her father was talking on his phone, looking serious. 'Absolutely – in fact I as I told Warren last week –'

Bloody hell, no way she was going to interrupt *that* conversation. As she edged away, she heard No 26's front door open and saw Bronx and Brooklyn standing, staring speechlessly at the Porsche, open-mouthed. Then they were pounding down the path, fast, hopping from foot to foot as they peered at the trademark badge, traced the silver letters. ''s a POSH!!!' Gasps of delight. 'Yeah! 's a Boxer GIT' Restraining a grin – even from here she could see their tee shirts were covered with paint and melted chocolate was much in evidence on hands and mouths – she reached out a restraining hand. Too late. Scrabbling for a foothold, the kids hauled themselves up on the immaculate chassis, and leaning in at a perilous angle, screamed with delight as they pointed out the *lit* hi-tech gizmos to each other. Turning in his seat, her father raised an amused eyebrow, murmured something briefly into the phone, placed it in an inside jacket pocket and began to demonstrate various instruments and gadgets to the riveted kids. Retracing her steps, Cassie ruffled Bronx's hair, tweaked Brooklyn's nose and slid into the passenger seat. 'Hey, Dad – great to see you! And huge thanks for the stunning roses!'

'Sandy!' Despite the limited space, he drew her towards him and enveloped her in a bear hug. Rugged features with their usual tan, sharp grey eyes, silver hair curling on the collar of his sea-green shirt. The faint fragrance of his usual Acqua di Parma cologne.

Bronx shot her father a scornful look. 'S'not Sandy, it's *Cass*, dumbo.'

Knowing she'd probably regret it, Cassie explained she hadn't been able to say 'Cassandra' when she was little. Their shrieks of scorn were drowned out by Beethoven's fourth piano concerto, *fortissimo*, as Brooklyn jabbed a finger at the Spotify play button on the leather dashboard. Hands clapped over ears and vomiting noises ensued. Her father switched it off. 'Okay guys – gotta head out now.'

Their faces fell.

'Might possibly – only possibly, mind – bring you some chocs back from the restaurant, if you behave yourselves.'

'*Wowza*!!' Sliding swiftly back onto the pavement they shot down the path and barrelled through their front door, yelling for Zadie.

Grinning, Cassie made to open the passenger door.

'Hang on, sweetheart –'

'Let's walk, Dad, it's not far –'

'Ten miles or so.' Her father glanced at his Rolex. 'Take about fifteen minutes to drive it.' He started the engine.

'But where –?

He grinned, and manoeuvred the Porsche expertly out of the cramped space. 'Magical mystery tour for the birthday girl.'

And it was.

After turning off the busy A40 they slowed down, and travelled at a more leisurely speed through the lush

Oxfordshire countryside. The summer sunshine, the quiet hum of the engine, the smell of warm leather… Cassie concentrated on hunting for the tube of mints at the bottom of her bag, determined to avoid thinking about the last time she'd been a passenger in a car, or the way Ivo's phone call had been overheard by everyone – *everyone* – in the garden centre.

guy sounds a bit of a case

David's expression.

Cassie? Is there anything I can –

tripping over the bloody paving stone, hurrying to –

Her father shot her a swift glance. 'Sandy? You okay?'

She jumped, managed a smile. 'Fine, Dad, this is just –' She waved a hand at the stunning view. 'Perfect.'

He smiled back, and continued the resume of his recent travels as they drove – constant business flights to advise international financiers and politicians, from Dubai to Tokyo, with occasional trips to Zurich and San Francisco by way of light relief. He was recounting a scurrilous tale about a particularly unpleasant American magnate who'd been in the news recently when he slowed at a signpost: Great Milton village hall 1 mile. Village hall? Didn't sound like Dad – maybe he'd read there was a traditional country fair, with an Aunt Sally, and a maypole, or whatever, and thought she'd like it. She patted his sleeve, smiling. He was right, she would. And there was bound to be an ancient pub – thatched, probably, with tiny leaded windows, and hanging baskets of pansies beside the porch, where they could go for dinner afterwards –

And then they were entering a car park, drawing smoothly to a halt as a young man approached. Her father handed him the keys, took his jacket (Paul Smith – Cassie grinned. She didn't think it would be Gap) from the hook on the back of his seat and slipped it on, then came round to Cassie's side and helped her out.

'*Dad?*'

'Birthday treat.' He slipped an arm through hers, and they began to stroll down a lavender-scented flagstone path towards an exquisite honey-coloured manor house. 'Fifteenth century. Superb.' He shook his head. 'Look at those chimneys, the mullioned windows…Two Michelin stars. Beloved of the late Queen's mother.'

'You don't mean –' Cassie stopped dead. 'This isn't –'

'Le Manoir aux Quat'Saisons? Think it might be – afraid McDonalds was fully booked, so I thought –'

Cassie had read an article about le Manoir once, in an exclusive magazine abandoned in the dentist's waiting room. She'd thought then how extraordinary it was, never dreamed she'd ever actually visit it. '*Oh…*' She hugged him, hard. 'Thank you.'

'I'm so sorry Isabelle can't be with us, my darling, or that dear man, Tom. They'd both have been so proud to see what you've become.'

Tears stung Cassie's eyes. Her mother had died from pancreatic cancer when Cassie was eleven; one of the last memories she had was of a figure bending over her, indistinct in the shadows cast by the flickering bedside night light, fragrant with a perfume that reminded the eleven year old Cassie of barley sugar. Long auburn curls tickled her daughter's cheek as she bent over her, whispering good night as she set off with Cassie's father to some party, or private view, promising faithfully to pop in for a goodnight kiss when they returned home. Unknown to Cassie, her mother had been experiencing jaundiced skin, digestive problems and rapid weight loss for some time. Three weeks after she finally saw a doctor, her beloved mother was dead. Numb with grief, her father sent eleven-year old Cassie to stay with her strict maternal grandmother in the French countryside. *The open casement opposite the child's enormous brass bed was hung with a sheer white voile curtain; when she woke in the early hours that first night it was shimmering in the moonlight, rippling and billowing in a breeze heavily perfumed by the night stocks beneath the window, for all the world as if it was alive. Her appalled grandmother could not assuage Cassie's screams of terror – 'Mon dieu – sois calme!' – or Cassie's belief that her mother had returned from the grave to haunt her – 'Ne sois pas ridicule!'. Still the child sobbed. La petite vilaine Cassandra was packed off home the following day.*

Her father bent and picked a single stem of lavender and held it out to her. 'Happy birthday, dearest Sandy.' She held it to her nose, breathing in the delicate fragrance –

to get rid of the smell of turps

– and carefully threaded it through a strap on her sundress.

'Come on, let's take a look at the gardens before dinner. Apparently there's a rather fine terrace where pre-dinner cocktails might be procured.'

They set off, wandering across manicured lawns to gardens full of perfectly planned flower beds, each a palette of pale summer pastels, and on to fruit orchards carpeted with wildflowers, past greenhouses and an organic walled vegetable garden, and immaculately ordered herb beds. Stopping occasionally to point out a particularly delicate spray of lace-cap hydrangeas (Cassie), or a bronze statue of a little boy playing cricket (her father), they came to the beginning of a narrow path bordered with rocks and boulders. 'Looks interesting, Dad, let's –'

Before he could answer, his phone rang. With a frown, he extracted it from his pocket, pressed a red button she hadn't noticed before, and turned away before answering. Listened, then turned back. 'Got to take this, sweetheart, it's Warren.'

'Not…*Beatty*? Oh my God, Dad –'

He grinned. 'Warren *Buffett*, brilliant investment strategist – far more interesting than any film star. You go on, I'll follow in a sec…' He turned away again, looking concerned.

Cassie glanced up. The sky was a deepening blue, shafts of late sunlight pierced the branches of the surrounding trees. She began to follow the path, and stopped to admire the lake it bordered, a deeper blue sky contained in its still reflection. On the opposite bank stood a tiny thatched Japanese tea house, a hint of pink amidst the smooth teak wood lines of the veranda, a sliver of tatami mat just visible through the open door. It was surrounded by miniature trees and a thicket of bamboo, close to a rockery where a pair of bronze herons were poised to take flight and a stone lantern was set deep in a recess.

She stood and simply gazed. It was magical, the stuff of fairy tales. She wished she knew the names of the miniature trees, or what the strange cream cone-shaped flowers they'd seen in one of the flowerbeds they'd passed earlier were called. If David was here, he'd know. And if he'd enjoyed visiting the garden centre, he'd adore this. In fact next time she saw him –

let me carry this in for you

Oh God.

practically snatching the tree out of his arms –
almost overbalancing

stepping back smartly as he put out a
hand to steady her

If only she'd explained it was just that she was embarrassed that he'd heard Ivo's rant!

you have fun, queen of my heart, light of my fucking
life

Except that she hadn't been embarrassed.

while you can

She'd been terrified.

A sudden breeze rattled the slender branches of a nearby ash tree, changing the light entirely, deepening the shadows and dappling the surface of the pond with silver. She shivered. Time to retrace her steps. To go and find her father.

Cassie looked up, smiling, as with a bow the waiter set a tall chilled glass fizzing with delicate orange bubbles in front of her. 'Champagne Negroni Cocktail,

Madam.' As he set another in front of her father, she looked about her. Browns would have been wonderful, but this...this was perfection.

'Happy birthday, sweetheart.' They clinked glasses. Cassie took a sip, closed her eyes as the bubbles dissolved on her tongue. 'Bliss...'

'And here's to many, many more.' He took a long, slow swallow. Grinned. 'Definitely beats a synthetically sweetened vanilla milkshake.' The grin faded. 'Wish you'd told me before that the bastard had become even more of a pain. Never did like him –'

'I know, Dad.' She took another sip of her cocktail. This time it didn't taste quite as delicious. Her father had only met Ivo twice; the first time at a party after the opening night of a play written by a friend of the director (the words 'HARROWING' and 'SEARING' in red caps were prominent on the posters). The party took place in a room above the pub where the play had been performed, and Ivo, the star of the show, held court in the crowded, airless space, decorated with beer-stained posters of previous productions. Ignoring Cassie, Ivo flattered her father shamelessly, pumping him for contacts and forcing free tickets for subsequent performances on him. So, what was his opinion of the 'work'? Her father had grinned. 'Can't wait for the musical.'

For a fleeting moment Ivo's expression had been murderous, before he managed a hollow laugh.

The second time was more recent. Her father had been taking part in a symposium on International Finance at one of the Oxford colleges, and had called in unexpectedly on the last day, after the farewell lunch. Ivo's agent had phoned that morning, to tell him he hadn't got the non-speaking part he'd auditioned for the previous afternoon (comatose patient in hospital drama – apparently Ivo's palsied twitches and agonised grimaces to indicate that he was starting to regain consciousness hadn't gone down well with the director). When Cassie's sympathetic hug was met by a violent shove followed by a volley of insults, followed by the front door being slammed so hard as he made his exit a watercolour fell off the wall, she had burst into tears. She was still sobbing when there was a knock at the front door. She hurried to answer it, thinking it was Ivo, repentant, returning to apologise.

It was her father.

By the time Cassie had finished recounting a severely edited version of the recent months with Ivo, the other tables on the terrace had begun to empty, as the elegantly dressed guests drifted towards the open glass doors of the dining room.

'Loathsome little tyke – thank God he's gone. Good riddance to bad rubbish – don't know how you put up with him for so long, frankly.' They raised their glasses in a toast, and drank the remains of the second round of Negronis the waiter brought in instant response to her father's nod. 'Hungry?'

'Starving!'

He pulled out her chair for her, placing a hand on the small of her back as he steered her towards the open glass doors from which tantalising aromas wafted. She winced.

'Sandy?' They stopped walking. 'Darling girl – did

he *hit* you?'

'No! No, Dad, it's fine – I just lost my balance in the kitchen – these silly wedges –' *thank you, Zadie* – 'banged my back against the handles on the old store cupboard –'

agony exploding in her kidneys, shooting up her spine, a dazzling display of scarlet fireworks fading to black as she collapsed

'Bit of a bruise, but it's almost gone now.' She took his arm quickly, smiling. 'Hey, something smells good.'

As they entered the almost full dining room, all starched linen tablecloths, tall white candles and gleaming wine glasses, an immaculately uniformed young waiter showed them to their table. Once settled in the elegantly upholstered chairs, menus were proffered, the Seven Course Tasting Menu being highly recommended, and the wine list discussed. As they waited for the first course to arrive, Cassie told him about her latest commissions. She was describing the painting inspiring the design of the tiara (omitting the fact that she'd had to salvage the little seed pearls from the gaps in the kitchen flagstones) when the first course of pot caught Cornish crab was served with a flourish. Confit of duck liver was followed by courgette and lemongrass bisque. A short break was requested as they savoured a glass of her father's favourite Nuits-Saint-George premier Cru (this isn't wine, my girl, this is nectar!). Then it was time for milk-fed lamb with asparagus and wild garlic, and when the waiter assured them that this was a pudding it was impossible to refuse, a Yorkshire rhubarb baba. As Cassie set down her spoon with a sigh of contentment, she looked around her at the tables of quietly chatting guests, the waiters gliding discreetly between the tables, the dark green plants reflected in the polished windows. As she sipped her coffee, she saw that the moon was rising in the evening sky.

'Dad?' She leaned forwards and took his hands in hers. 'Thank you – *thank* you! Tonight was the best surprise I've ever had, it's been absolutely…The lamb with asparagus and wild garlic! The –'

He squeezed her hands, laughing. 'I'm so glad you enjoyed it, darling girl. Must say I think it might have the edge on chicken McNuggets.'

'And as for the rhubarb baba –'

A tinkling laugh somewhere nearby. Cassie looked up. Erica, clad in a beaded black evening jacket accessorised by a double rope of gleaming jet beads, was approaching their table, followed by a short bald man with pop eyes and a mouth like a wet rosebud. 'Heavens, Cassandra! Such a surprise to see you here!' She gave the sundress a scornful look, followed by a double take at the espadrilles. 'And looking so summery, too!' She cast a sideways glance at Cassie's father. Scorn was replaced by surprise as she took in the handsome features, the expensive jacket, the Rolex watch. Fluttered. 'Why, I don't believe we've met.'

Her father rose. 'Richard.' He held out his hand, smiling politely. 'Delighted.'

Rosebud Lips edged forward. Erica waved a hand in his direction. 'A colleague. Mervyn. Problems to discuss after a frightfully difficult meeting.'

'A pleasure.' Her father sat down again as the waiter approached and discreetly presented the bill on a polished salver. Erica blinked as he slipped an American Express Centurion card from his wallet. As the waiter presented the receipt with a bow and glided away, he grinned at Cassie 'Oops! Mustn't forget those chocolates.'

Erica clasped her hands. 'Chocolates too! You *are* a lucky girl.'

'Oh, they're not for me.' Cassie delicately touched an earring. 'We promised Brooklyn and Bronx –'

'Brooklyn and Bronx?' Rosebud Lips winced.

Cassie grinned. 'Their dad's a big Beckham fan. Drew the line at Romeo, though.'

Rosebud Lips goggled at Erica. 'They're surely not the brats you're always complaining about? Charging about on supermarket trollies – endangering the traffic with their skateboards and so on?'

Erica tightened her lips. 'I fear the parents simply don't –'

Cassie's father looked surprised. 'I found them quite delightful, myself. Asking highly technical questions about the Boxter, the meaning of GTS –'

'GTS?' Erica's grip on her matching evening bag tightened.

'Gran Turismo Sport.'

Cassie gave a careless shrug. 'It's a Porsche.'

'– both riveted by the Beethoven, bless them.'

'*Beethoven*?' Erica gave her head a disbelieving little shake. 'Well, we must be going.' The immaculate bob fell smoothly into place. 'Such a pleasure to meet you, Richard.' A tight smile. 'Lovely to see you, too, Cassandra.' She let a beat fall. 'Take care.'

Followed at a respectful distance by Rosebud Lips,

she stalked towards the exit.

There was a brief silence as they disappeared, then Cassie and her father exchanged looks. 'Ghastly creature. How...?'

'Afraid she's a neighbour.'

'Well, God help her husband.'

Cassie picked up her water glass and took a sip. 'You were great about the kids, Dad.'

'Bright little buggers – liked 'em. Next time I visit, I'll take 'em for a spin.' He glanced out of the window at the sunset, flaring amongst the trees in a blaze of scarlet and orange. 'Hey – the visuals are right on cue.' He grinned. 'I'm thinking of your neighbour heading for the car park – Ride of the Valkyries blaring *fortissimo* in the background – her little flunky trotting along behind...'

Cassie shuddered. 'Only hope we don't bump into them.'

'Tell you what, birthday girl, how about a Stambecco Tiramisu Liqueur for you before we leave?' He signalled to the waiter. 'Just a fizzy water for me, thanks, I'm driving.'

'I'd love one.' She hesitated. 'Dad? Do you think we could...?

'Stop by a late-night supermarket on the way back to buy chocs for Poplar Street's Junior Spawn of Satan Chapter?' He lowered his voice. 'Ye shall know them by their stolen supermarket trollies and – *whisper it* – scruffy skateboards.' He grinned. 'Just try and stop me.'

CHAPTER EIGHTEEN

NEXT MORNING CASSIE woke early and lay for a while, relaxing, re-living the events of the previous evening. Hard to decide what she'd enjoyed most – her first glimpse of the lavender-scented flagstone path leading towards the honey-coloured manor house – the tiny thatched Japanese teahouse, with its hint of pink amidst the smooth teak wood lines of the veranda – the little crown of caviar nestling atop the salad of pot caught wild Cornish crab...She stretched luxuriously. Giggled. *No.* It was the look on bloody Erica's face when her father said he found Brooklyn and Bronx quite delightful...

Excellent. She couldn't remember when she'd last felt this happy, this – *normal.* She'd send a text – no, a card – to thank him. Swinging her legs out of bed she pulled on jeans and tee shirt, then headed for the bathroom, used the toilet, cleaned her teeth, and padded downstairs. Coffee first, then she'd get to work recreating the detailed sketches, lists of measurements and charts of colour comparisons Erica had ruined. By lunchtime, she'd be ready to start work on the actual tiara.

But first she opened the elegant little leather box

containing the drop earrings she'd left lying on the table, waiting to be photographed. She smiled. Perfect. Stopped smiling, and sighed. Better get on.

She was concentrating on re-calculating the measurements for the tiara band when there was a light tap on the back door. Heart racing, she jumped up, dropping her pencil on the floor. Too late to switch off the lamps, or silence the radio. Please God it was Zadie, dying to hear the details of last night's d inner; the tap had been light, so there was a good chance. *Wasn't there…?* She edged towards the door. Called Zadie's name, softly. Waited. Silence. Maybe it was Vic, delivering the moonstones and aquamarines she'd ordered. But he'd beat his usual tattoo, keep going till she answered. *Wouldn't he…?* Unless he was playing a game, doing what he called 'having a laugh', like that time ages ago when Ivo was away and Vic had pretended to be the police, and ordered her sternly to Open Up, he had a Warrant. She called his name tentatively, and waited. Still nothing. Her heart thudding in her chest, she reached out a hand and edged the blind aside – blinked, blinded by the sudden flood of sunlight.

Screamed, rearing back in shock as flattened features pressed against the glass.

Hand clapped over her mouth she retreated, letting the blind fall – *oh God, Quint, the dead governess Miss Jessel's evil lover in The Innocents* –

'Hello…? Ms Fitton…? Everything all right in there? Eddie from the Gas Board here–'

Wait. Eddie. Gas Board. Cooker. Repairs. *Only Eddie!* This was like the time she thought she saw Miss Jessel reflected in the kettle – the *kettle* for God's sake! She shivered. She was in worse shape than she thought; the sooner she did that Ghost Trail the better.

'Eddie!' Thank God. Hands shaking, she raised the blind. Glanced through the window – yes, it really was Eddie – fumbled with the chain, unlocked the door and opened it. 'So sorry! Couldn't see properly, the sunlight – made me jump, ridiculous. Great to see you, come in –'

She held the door wide.

Casting her a worried look he entered. Set his toolbox down beside the cooker and turned to look at her. 'I'm dead sorry, Ms Fitton –'

'No, honestly –' she gestured at the notebook on the table '– it's just that I was concentrating on some figures –'

He backed towards the table and peered awkwardly at the page of calculations. ''Tiara band.'' He looked up. 'Sure looks complicated.'

He'd started to move away when he did a double take at the leather jewellery box lying open on the table, and stopped. 'OMG. Not s'posed to do this, and hope you don't mind me asking, but –' he jerked his head towards the drop earrings, amethysts, pearls and tourmalines glittering in the sunlight pouring through the open back door. '– *you*…?'

Cassie nodded, touched. 'Sure.'

'*Wow.*' He shook his head, ran a hand over his punishingly short hair. '– I mean how d'you learn how to do this stuff?'

'I did a course in London.'

'Yeah?' He eyed the earrings. 'Take a long time, does

it?'

'Well, about three years. Though –'

'Cost a lot, I 'spect.'

It must have done, though she'd never asked. It had been a birthday present from her father.

'I guess. I mean yes. It did…So hey, what's the plan today for the oven?'

He blinked. 'Oven…?'

She laughed. Gestured at the bright yellow *DANGER DO NOT USE* tape wound round the cooker.

'Oh. Yeah.' He rummaged in his toolbox and held up a delicate coil of transparent flex, with a complicated little plug attached to the end. 'Got a new spark electrode for you.'

'Brilliant. Thanks, Eddie.' She smiled. 'Pretty! It'd make a great pendant.'

'A…?' He held it up to the light, turned it this way and that. 'See what you mean.' He turned away, looking thoughtful, and moved to the cooker. A brief rattling sound, and he turned back. 'Hey! *Idea!*' He produced a finger-nail-size six-sided metal bolt with a neatly turned thread, shining in the sunshine. 'Make a great ring – fact there's loads of gizmos you could make into necklaces and earrings and that.' He gazed at her. 'Loads. Start a whole new fashion, call it… dunno… TechnoTat.' He snickered. ''cept the stuff would cost a bleeding fortune.' He caught Cassie's eye. 'Sorry –'

'Lord, don't be sorry – sounds fun. And you've certainly got an eye!' Laughing, she moved towards the table. 'I'll leave you to it, I'd better get on with those colour comparison charts.' Drawing her notebook towards her, she settled down to work.

It took less time than she expected to complete the charts. She stretched, relieved, and realised Eddie was still tapping away. She put the kettle on. 'Eddie? Cup of tea?'

He turned, a hammer with a bright yellow handle in his hand. 'Well if it's no trouble, Ms Fitton…'

'Think there's some biscuits somewhere.' She set out the tea things. 'And Eddie –'

He polished the hammer's head on his sleeve, looking apprehensive.

'– call me Cassie, okay?'

He ran a hand through his hair again, the blood rising in his cheeks. ''kay.' He grinned.

Restraining the urge to hug him – he looked like a kid with his favourite toy in his hand – she hunted for the ginger biscuits.

They were sitting at the table, discussing the merits of custard creams versus fig rolls, when he set down his mug.

Cassie got to her feet. 'Refill?' She reached for his mug, and picked up her own.

'No thanks, Ms Fitton –'

'Cassie.'

'– Cassie. Thing is, I was wondering if I could ask –'

'Bet you're thinking about Jaffa cakes. Excellent. I'll get some in for next time.'

'No. No…' He cleared his throat. 'It's just –'

'Bourbons? Hmm, never been keen on –'

'– I've been – you know – thinking.' He reached out a hand towards the earrings. 'Like I said, I was wondering if I could ask –' He touched an amethyst with a delicate forefinger. Withdrew it, fast. '– if you'd teach me how to do it?'

Cassie blinked. 'Sorry…?'

'How to do it. Make earrings and stuff.'

'Make…?'

'I could pay you – not as much as one of those posh courses, course, but –' He leant forward eagerly.

'Oh Eddie, I'd love to –'

A sharp intake of breath.

'But –'

His face fell. 'But…?'

'It's just not possible. For starters, I'm no teacher –'

'You'd be great. I'd pick it up fast, I'm used to working with dead delicate stuff in the work I already do, you've seen the O rings and that, but it's just not, I dunno, rewarding…'

'It's not only that, Eddie, I simply don't have the time. I'm way behind on my commissions as it is, and once we get into September the Christmas orders'll start.'

'You said yourself I got an eye…'

'For sure – I remember the comment you made about the oven needing half a dead cow in the oven and a sparkly skull on the grill if it was going to win the Turner Prize – brilliant!'

He added a heaped spoonful of sugar to his tea. 'So –'

'Tell you what, how about a part-time course?' She picked up a gingernut. 'I'm pretty sure there's an evening class at the City of Oxford College –'

'I don't want a course, I want –'

'Eddie –' She broke the gingernut in half. 'There's a lot to learn about different materials and techniques and stuff. Sawing – soldering – annealing – that's when heat's used to reduce the hardness of a metal, makes silver more pliable, easier to work with –'

He stirred his tea. 'I know what it is. Do it all the time.'

'Sorry, of course you do. I'm just saying –'

'Noticed your workbench, all the tools and stuff, the first day. Knew straight away that's what I want to do.'

'Look, check out local courses, I'm sure they won't be expensive –'

He closed his eyes. Opened them again. Stirred his tea harder. 'I said I –'

'You'll race through the Beginners stuff – be working with freeform and angled stones before you know it.'

'Well if I'll get on so fast, why couldn't *you* –'

Cassie restrained a sigh; she really needed to get on with the tiara. ''Fraid there'll still be a lot more to learn.' She slipped the piece of gingernut in her mouth and crunched it, trying not to feel irritated. 'Precision measuring and cutting – decorative finishes – wax carving – design skills – honestly, Eddie, I just wouldn't have the –'

'– time.' He set the spoon down beside his mug.

'But there's bound to be advanced part-time courses you could –'

He pushed back his chair. 'Thanks Ms Fitton, 's really good advice, sorry I banged on. Gotta go and…and…' He dropped the hammer in his toolbox, sniffed, wiped his eyes and then his nose on his sleeve and headed for the open back door. As Cassie looked after him she saw the holes in the soles of his cheap work boots, the worn elbows of his fleece.

She got to her feet, calling. 'Eddie…'

He was already halfway across the lawn, head down. As he passed through the gate there was a knock at the front door. Without even thinking about it she closed and locked the back door, thrust the chain into place and pulled down the blind. Stood motionless, waiting, wishing Eddie was still there. If it was Ivo at the front door –

A rap at the glass.

'Ms Fitton? You there? Customer knocking at the front door, showed her round the back.'

A customer? She wasn't expecting anyone. 'Thanks so much, Eddie –'

She raised the blind, fumbled with key and chain, and finally got the door open. An elderly woman in a vintage floral tea dress, her hair held back with silver combs, stood smiling tremulously at her. 'My dear, I've been so looking forward to meeting you! I've brought the set I told your husband about when I called.'

Husband? Oh God. 'Please, do come in. I'm afraid I...'

'He was so helpful!' She held out a green leather case. 'Assured me the job would take you a mere few hours, and cost next to nothing.'

She tottered to the chair Eddie had just vacated and sat looking about her. 'Charming, quite charming.' Her gaze fell on the cooker. She politely averted her gaze.

Cassie opened the box, to see a set of perfectly carved antique ivory chess pieces nestled amid copious folds of black silk, the customary black team dyed a delicate celadon green.

'Exquisite, aren't they? I bought them in a darling

antique shop in Putney.' The old lady picked out the intricately modelled black King. 'Why, one could swear he's about to speak.'

'I wonder...' Cassie swallowed. 'When exactly did you call?'

'Let me see. Yes, it would have been the afternoon of the 15th.'

The 15th...A swift calculation. The afternoon she'd been at the garden centre with David, the afternoon she'd taken the chain off the front door, *the afternoon Ivo knew she wasn't at home.* Somehow he'd managed to get in – no, wait. Hadn't she read somewhere once that that all it took was a credit card? She closed her eyes. Stupid stupid *stupid*. Why the hell hadn't she left the back way? God knows what he'd *planned* to do. What the bastard had actually *done* was answer the landline. He must have been cock-a-hoop at his luck.

'– the day I made my purchase –'

She opened her eyes. 'The day they were *sold*?'

'– and had my brilliant idea, as I told your husband. He thought it was tremendous.'

'I'm sorry, but...the idea?'

'Oh! Your husband didn't...? She replaced the tiny ivory King and picked out the slightly larger Queen. 'He said you'd simply love – no, *adore* was the word he used – to make them.'

'Make...'

'Why, cufflinks.'

'Cufflinks.'

'For my darling Edgar. Chess is his great hobby, you see. He already has several sets, he certainly doesn't need another, so I thought well, how about –'

A tide of anger rose in Cassie's chest. She forced herself to smile. 'I'm terribly sorry, Mrs –'

'Lady –'

Christ. 'Lady –'

'– Chudleigh.' She smiled. 'I know, it's tricky. I had to spell it twice for your husband while he was writing it down in the diary.'

Cassie hurried to the workbench, picked up the desk diary and riffled through it. Today's page was blank.

you'll pay for this, you fucking bitch

She returned to the table and sat down. 'I'm terribly sorry, Lady Chudleigh.' She moved the two mugs closer together. 'The thing is, my husband has been unwell recently –' *or he bloody well will be soon* '– and he isn't quite – you know –'

The old lady adjusted the antique Wedgwood brooch at her silk neckline. '*Au courant?*'

God knows. 'Exactly. I can't apologise enough, but there's nothing in the diary –'

'Well, I'm here now.' She leaned forward conspiratorially. 'And I have to tell you – *I have another idea!*' She took several chess pieces from their box, arranged them on the table, and held up the Bishops and Knights. 'Cufflinks for Orlando and Oberon, my nephews!' After a moment's thought, she replaced the Bishop and Knight with two pawns. 'Only the smaller pieces, of course.'

Cassie positioned the milk jug beside the mugs. 'I'm afraid there's something else I have to tell you. Lady Chudleigh. I can't tell you how sorry I am, but there's been another mistake. I fear my …my husband must have forgotten the recent law, or he'd have explained –'

'Law?'

'The government banned the sale of ivory recently –'

'Banned? Why, pray?'

Cassie thought of the countless photographs she'd seen of dying elephants, their perfect ivory tusks hacked off, leaving bloody stumps. She dug her nails into her palms and tried to smile pleasantly. 'To protect elephants from being tortured by thousands of unscrupulous poachers. The sale of ivory in any form now is forbidden –' a law long overdue, in Cassie's opinion '– the penalty to any vendor or dealer being a lengthy prison term or unlimited fine.'

'*Prison*?'

'If the chess set had been inherited there would have been no problem, but as it's a recent purchase –'

Her visitor was already replacing the lid on the box. She rose. Cast a disapproving look at the flyers. The old girl probably disliked the Domino's ad on top of the pile – she didn't look as if she ordered a lot of takeaways. With a moue of distaste at the drop earrings sparkling in their open box, she stalked towards the open door.

Trying not to cry, Cassie hurried after her. 'May I call you a taxi?'

'A taxi?' She stepped into the garden. 'My driver is waiting.'

She made her way across the grass. Cassie wasn't surprised when she didn't look back.

CHAPTER NINETEEN

SHE LOCKED AND chained the back door automatically, returned to the table and stood leaning against it, staring into space, not thinking about anything at all. After a while she glanced down.

Pity the table had been in such a mess. Pity she'd been makeup-free, with chronic bed-hair. Pity she'd been wearing rubbish jeans and the tee shirt bearing a bright pink Percy Pig logo, a present last Christmas from Brooklyn and Bronx. Slowly she collected the mugs and put them in the sink. Added the milk jug. Then the biscuit tin. No. That wasn't right. She replaced the milk jug in the fridge, put the tin back on the shelf, leant against the table again. There was half a gingernut lying amid a scatter of crumbs near the box containing the drop earrings. Messy. Lady Chudleigh must have thought…Better get rid of it. She shoved the piece of biscuit in her mouth, swept the crumbs into her cupped hand and made for the rubbish bin. Stopped abruptly. Gagged. Spat out the half-chewed mess, lobbed it into the bin with the crumbs, washed her hands twice, and returned yet again to the table. Picking up the jewellery box, she closed the lid, carried it carefully to the workbench and placed it in the little safe. Touched the notebook she'd left open beside the row of tools in the hope that it would slowly dry out. Still sodden…Cassie turned away.

She'd arranged the birthday bouquet from her father in one of Granny Jackson's best vases as soon as Erica left the previous morning, and placed it on top of the bookcase. Picking it up, she set it on the table, arranged the cards and made to tidy the usual litter of post and flyers. Odd, the stack of mostly brown envelopes was neater than she remembered, the flyers an orderly pile. Must have done it automatically when she set out the tea things for Eddie earlier. She stood back. There. That was better. Wouldn't matter if a hundred unexpected clients turned up now –

my dear, I've been so looking forward to meeting you

– she gripped the back of a chair. Not bloody much, it wouldn't, only permanently damage her reputation… She sank down on the chair, put her elbows on the table, dropped her head in her hands and closed her eyes. Opened them again, to see Peppa Pig's bosky little eyes beaming up at her. Oh God. Must get changed – Never Think Lightning Won't Strike Twice, Granny Jackson had frequently advised. Still, if she wasn't home, she wouldn't have to deal with it…Levering herself to her feet, she crawled up the stairs and into the bathroom. Fifteen long minutes later, after cleansing, moisturising and concealing her bruises, adding a touch of mascara and a dab of lipstick, and punishing her hair with a strong bristle brush and a painfully tight scrunchie, she trudged into the bedroom, to emerge almost immediately wearing her long poplin skirt and a plain blue tee shirt.

She checked the chain on the front door and hurried down to the kitchen, desperate to leave the stifling kitchen and its ever-worsening memories, and stroll among the cheerful visitors in the Water Lily House at the Botanic Gardens, or better yet, the Ashmolean Museum, with its staggering wealth of ancient artefacts; a few hours spent among the mysterious treasures of the Ancient Egyptians couldn't help but restore a sense of perspective.

A cup of tea and a slice of chocolate cake in their delightful café wouldn't do any harm, either.

She checked her bag for her wallet, slipped the strap on her shoulder and was about to leave when she hesitated. Ran upstairs and checked the chain on the front door. Fine. Ran downstairs. Hesitated once more. Dashed upstairs for a second time to re-check the chain. Still fine. Downstairs again. Unlocked and unchained the back door, checked the blind.

At last she stepped outside, into the hot summer afternoon.

CHAPTER TWENTY

SHE SIMPLY STOOD for a moment, face turned up to the sun, relishing the noisy birdsong emanating from the trees down the lane – must mean Blanco was on the prowl – admiring the chalk-white clouds scudding across the Wedgwood blue sky. Wedgwood? No thanks, call it the…uh…*delphinium blue* sky, that was better. Still, the mood was broken; time to move on. She'd decide whether her destination would be water lilies with pale pink petals and enormous pie-tin shaped leaves, or mysterious hieroglyphics inscribing inscrutable mummies, while she made her way across Magdalen Bridge.

What a choice! God, she was lucky. Time to stop having a breakdown because Ivo had persuaded some rich old lady –

my driver is waiting

– that Cassie would make cufflinks for her nephews – Oswald and Oscar? Sure couldn't have been called Walt and Wayne – from some poor bloody elephant's hacked off tusks, or beating herself up because there were a few biscuit crumbs on the table. Pity it hadn't been the remains of a spliff, or an empty vodka bottle lying rakishly on its side…Grinning, she turned to close the back door when she stopped, wondering if it was worth nipping back to exchange her long-sleeved tee shirt for something sleeveless. No, she'd be fine, it had begun to get chilly in the – Just a minute. *The smell.* Where on earth was that god-awful smell coming from? *The kitchen?* She sniffed. Gagged. *No, it was out here in the garden.* On her left…

She turned her head, and saw the rose bush. Recoiled. The once flawless sprays of diminutive white petals were now tinged a rusty brown, the luxuriant blooms sparse, drooping, revealing the fragile branches that had been painstakingly trained along the trellis by her grandmother. Fed with the finest nutrients every March and July, pruned early every spring.

Once a sweet fragrance had perfumed the whole garden. But now…She touched a petal, ran a finger gently down an exposed branch. Realised how parched it felt. Oh God, it was her fault. When had she last watered it? She pushed a hand through her hair, dislodging the scrunchy, felt perspiration break out under her arms. She couldn't remember. Lowering her gaze, she saw the once rich soil was now shrunken and withered, bubbles forming on the faintly steaming surface. And the smell…

And then she was on her feet, shoulder bag banging against her hip, streaking across the grass, into the shed, seizing the watering can, rushing to the kitchen, filling the watering can to overflowing, rushing back to the rose bush again and –

Casssie stopped dead. What if there was some sort of Plant First Aid you had to administer before dispensing a dose of cold water to a seriously sickly shrub? And maybe the water should be slightly warm, to lessen the shock? She was no expert, look at the mistake she'd made with the bloody chef's extra – okay, two, if truth be told – for the lemon tree…

But she knew a man who was.

Swiftly she locked the back door, shoved her hair back into its scrunchie, and ran.

David's car was parked outside, but there was no sign of Erica's Mini. Perfect. Taking a deep breath, she knocked on the door. Silence. Maybe he was in the bathroom? On the phone? She thought of the rose bush, parched, struggling for life in the August heat, and knocked again, harder this time. At last the door opened. David stood there. Was she imagining it, or did he actually take a step back?

'Yes?' The lines round his eyes were more deeply etched, his hair was uncombed and he badly needed a shave. Maybe he'd been having a nap and hadn't surfaced yet.

'David! Really sorry to bother you –' She waited for him to say she wasn't. He didn't. '– got a bit of a problem, and I don't know –' He looked away from her, focused on something – oh God, *someone*? – over her shoulder. She whirled round. Nothing. She turned back, tried to smile. '– it's the rose bush outside the back door –'

'Vine.'

'You know, the one with the little white flowers –'

"Darlow's Rosa Enigma."

'I've been a bit – uh – *preoccupied* –'

queen of my heart, light of my fucking life

'– recently –'

His lip curled. 'Yes?'

'– and I've been forgetting to water it –'

'Minimal water, what it requires.'

'But it's been so hot –'

'Thrives in full sun.'

'But the petals are turning brown! The branches look all dried up –'

He sighed. 'It's one of the toughest climbing roses there is.'

'But –'

'It'll be fine.'

Was she imagining it, or was he starting to close the door?

'David, please –' Her eyes filled with tears.

'Look, Cassandra, I really don't have the time. You want gardening advice, check out Monty Don. Bet he's rich as Croesus.'

The door shut with a sharp click.

Slowly she walked away. He wasn't well, that must be it. Or maybe he'd had a serious row with Erica and she'd buggered off, hence the absent Mini. Could have been a bit more friendly, though. Until now, he'd always been...in fact she'd thought he just might... Suddenly she found herself stumbling over a pile of rubbish that had spilled from an overflowing rubbish bin. She looked up, frowning. Saw she was outside No 42. What...? Must have crossed the road by mistake when she left David's house. *Stupid*...Retracing her steps, she wandered along Poplar Street, wincing at the uneven paving stones, the ugly pollarded trees with their dusty trunks, the fag ends and greasy fast-food wrappers littering the gutters, the disgusting state of the student houses at the end of the street. She hated summer, she really did. As she trailed along the back lane she thought of Eddie's grandmother's jigsaw – *the little cottage with snow on the roof, wisp of smoke drifting from the chimney into the winter sky…* God, that birdsong was annoying – *lamps glowing in the windows, log fire burning* – and forget delphinium blue, that sky was merely washed out.

She wished now she'd said she'd teach him. He'd been a bit upset when she'd said it wasn't possible, but had he been unpleasant? He had not. She kicked open the back gate. Huh, not like some she could mention…

Bronx and Brooklyn were splashing about in their leaking paddling pool as Cassie passed next door's fence, screaming with laughter and yelling colourful expletives as they did unspeakable things to limbless Wedding Barbie and headless Buzz Lightyear. She stopped grinning as she reached the climbing rose. The drooping petals were edged with a darker brown, now, more bubbles had emerged from the sickly-looking soil, and the smell was worse than ever. She stopped dead. Maybe the little vine had caught some sort of plant-type virus? If animals could, why not plants? And if it was as tough as bloody David said it was, weren't the chances good that with plenty of TLC, it would recover? The full watering can was still where she'd left it earlier; blowing a kiss to the fragile blossoms, she hurried to the shed. Grabbed the bright pink vat of Bloom 'n Gro Advanced Fertiliser Granny Jackson used to use on the rockery plants, the giant pack of Best Quality Enriched Plant Soil she'd been planning to use on a projected window box, bucket, trowel, and an empty plastic spray bottle. Hesitated, as she caught sight of the ancient pair of gardening gloves lying on the end of a shelf. Strange, they looked even more worn than she remembered…she shrugged. Must be imagining it. Clutching her stash of equipment to her chest, she ran back to the vine, knelt down and got to work.

Two hours later, she'd dug out all the sodden soil surrounding the roots, instinctively including an extra cuff of undamaged earth for safety's sake, and dumped it in the bucket, relieved to find that as soon as the bubbles burst, the smell evaporated. Carefully she stirred Advanced Fertiliser into the pack of Enriched Plant Soil and refilled the gaping hole, wishing it didn't remind her so much of the root canal she'd endured as a result of a broken upper molar one Christmas when she was eighteen. She hadn't eaten dates containing pits since.

So far, so good. Wiping a sweaty sleeve across her forehead, she sat back on her heels and regarded the rich, peaty surface of the soil with satisfaction, picturing the roots slowly beginning to absorb the nutrients. Right. Now for the actual roses. Getting to her feet, she filled the plastic spray bottle from the watering can. Looked up at the fast-deepening azure sky, and sent a heartfelt plea for support to Granny Jackson. Stepped back a little. Then, holding her breath, with the lightest of touches she misted the scorched petals, the abundance of creamy little buds on the verge of opening.

She'd done her best. Painfully, her bruised back aching from her exertions, she gathered everything except the vat of Bloom 'n Gro Advanced Fertiliser and the bucket of discarded sludge and schlepped it all back to the shed. The kids were still creating mayhem in their paddling pool, waving at her over the fence as she passed and inviting her to come and paddle. Screaming with laughter, they assured her they'd trained the piranhas not to bite. On her second trip, lugging the fertiliser and the bucket – whatever virus had infected the soil it was clearly lethal (Lloyd would know what to do with it) – Zadie was emerging from her kitchen, waving a wooden spoon coated in a bright red sauce in one hand, a glass of wine in the other. 'Hiya, Cass! A'right? Wotcha doin gardenin this time of night?'

'Hey, Zades.' Cassie approached the fence. 'Been sorting out the little rose bush, you know, by the back door.'

'Yeah? Prob'ly needs extra waterin, this weather.' She brandished the glass. 'Know I do – want one?'

'Thanks, but –' *She hadn't been imagining it. Face it. He did take a step back.* Shoulders sagging, she held on to the top of the fence. 'You know what? I'd kill for one.'

'You got it. Back in one, babe.'

And she was, clutching her own refill and a large tumbler brimming with red wine. 'Medicinal, right?' With a wink, Zadie passed it over the fence.

'Thanks, you're a life saver.' They clinked glasses. Cassie took a large gulp.

'Gonna say you should check Davie out bout the

rose tree, but I bumped into him earlier and he looked like somethin the cat dragged in.' She eyed Cassie shrewdly. 'Bit like you, if ya don't mind me sayin.'

'I called round ...' She took another gulp of wine. 'But he didn't want to know.'

'Yeah? He told Lloyd when he was helpin him fix the clutch on the Fiesta you'd been up some posh gardenin place together.' She raised her glass in a toast. 'Nice goin, girlfriend!' She frowned. 'Okay then, was he?'

'Lovely.' She drank more wine, remembering. 'But Ivo phoned while we were there – '

'Keith, Cass, *Keith!* Keep up, woman...' Zadie polished off the remains of her wine.

'David was fine about it –'

> *off to town for a couple of days.*
> *Give you a call when I get back*

'– maybe I was a bit distant when we got back, but –'

'Should've explained.'

'I just didn't expect – you know, today, why he was suddenly so curt –' Tears filled her eyes.

'Hey.' Suddenly Zadie spun round. 'Brookie! *Cut that out!*' She turned back, voice gentle again. 'Got it bad, ain't cha, kid?'

'Course not. But up till now he seemed – I thought – oh, I don't know –'

'Tell you what. You wanna know what's goin on, you gotta see Mystic Marge.'

'Who?'

'Psycho to the Stars, right?' She belched. 'Pardon. No, Psychic. Saw her advert in the newsagent's window. *Your Life in the Cards! Ask Any Question!*' Her cards got little pictures on, dead weird some of 'em.'

'Tarot, that'd be.'

'You say so. She's brilliant, went to her when I was worried about Lloyd. Thought the wanker was up to somethin –'

Cassie thought of Lloyd; with his ever-thinning comb-over, beer belly bulging over the elasticated waistband of his baggy Bermuda shorts, and mercifully indecipherable tattoo on his beefy forearm. 'No way.'

'Yes way, though it wasn't what I was thinkin.' Zadie snorted. 'Marge done the Cards, clocked the daft bugger was meetin his mates down the bookies, plannin to use his winnin's on new wheels.'

'She sounds amazing! So has he –'

'Loses every time, doesn't he. Still, least s'not women.'

Women. Cassie shivered. Dusk was falling, she could practically feel the dew settling. Maybe David had a girlfriend, he'd have had no reason to mention it – after all, all he'd actually done with Cassie was order a pendant for his mother and give her a lift to get a new lemon tree.

But the way he'd gently touched her cheek the other night…His interest in her work…'Zades? Wonder if –'

'Blackbird Leys, £40 for one question. Cash. Pop her info round tomorrow.'

The shouts and laughter from the paddling pool had gradually become full-blown fighting. Sighing, Zadie yelled over the fence. 'That's it, guys. Dinner. Inside, *now*!!' She turned back to Cassie. 'Keep your pecker up girlfriend, 's all good. Hey, forgot to ask, how was Browns?'

'Went to le Manoir instead, birthday treat.'

'Seen it in the Cowley Road. Nice. Have a steak?'

'Um…similar, sure…Nearly forgot, Dad bought a couple of chocolate bars for the kids.'

'Gawd, they'll go mental. Pick 'em up tomorrow when I drop off Marge's info.'

Cassie passed over her empty glass. 'Better finish clearing up. Night, Zades.'

Clasping the severely depleted vat of Advanced Fertiliser to her chest with one hand, and lugging the bucket of sludge in the other, she plodded back to the shed. Set the bucket down with a sigh of relief, and shoved the Fertiliser into the space beside the Roundup Total Weedkiller.

She yawned. She'd had enough for one day. She'd check the little vine tomorrow, with a bit of luck it would be looking a bit healthier. Replacing the weedkiller and dumping the bucket in the corner behind the door, she shut the shed door behind her and set off across the grass.

The light was almost gone now, and there was a definite chill in the air. Apart from Zadie's kitchen, the rest of the row was in darkness.

She ran the rest of the way to the back door.

CHAPTER TWENTY-ONE

'CASH ONLY, DEAR. No cheques.'

'Yes, of course. Could I just ask –'

'Magnolia front door, brass leprechaun door knocker. Two-thirty I've got you down for, all right?'

'Thank you, I'm looking forward to –' The line went dead.

Cassie switched off her phone and glanced at her watch. Ten past one. If she caught the next bus heading to Blackbird Leys she'd be at Laurel Way by one forty-five, giving her plenty of time to find the right address. She was nervous enough, without a last minute panic making things worse. She'd locate the house first, then stroll about a bit until it was two twenty-five. God, this was worse than going to the dentist. Which was ridiculous, people did this all the time, and it wasn't as if she didn't know what to expect, Zadie had given her a blow-by-blow account of her reading, Apparently Lloyd had got a taste for gambling after having a bit of luck with the scratch cards, and though he definitely needed reining in before he got into serious financial trouble, evinced by the Five of Pentacles (skeletal paupers in rags limping through the falling snow, described with delighted horror by Zadie) he had no interest in Other Women.

At last the bus shuddered into view and the queue surged forward, jostling and complaining, carrying Cassie with it. For a moment she resisted – *what on earth was she doing*? She should be at home working on the tiara not paying some weirdo forty quid to tell her David was happily involved elsewhere and had no interest whatsoever in Cassie; he'd just tried to be helpful when the lemon tree was poorly. Well the new lemon tree was doing just fine, thanks, and – joy of joys – Rosa 'Darlow's Enigma' was looking a lot healthier this morning. Most of the brown-edged blooms had fallen off, and the little buds were starting to open. Even the leaves looked perkier, so – without warning she was given a shove by the enormous woman behind her, clutching a collection of bulging carrier bags in one hand and a half-eaten hamburger reeking of fried onions in the other, and told sharply to get a move on. Sensing it would definitely be wiser to obey, judging from the way the woman was snarling at the small boy clinging to her skirt and whining for a bite of the burger, before she knew it Cassie was sitting at the back of the bus beside an old man muttering darkly to himself as he perused the Daily Mirror.

The journey seemed to take a lot longer than twenty minutes, and it was a relief to fight her way through the crush of passengers standing in the aisle, trying not to notice the pervading odour of cheap sunscreen and sweat, or step on bejewelled flip-flops and unlaced trainers. She stood at the bus stop as the bus drew away with yet more passengers aboard, breathing in traffic fumes and wishing it wasn't so hot. Still, look on the bright side, as Granny Jackson would say. Though actually, she wouldn't; Granny Jackson had no truck with what she called soothsayers and gypsies. Cassie checked her watch. Better get a move on, though presumably Mystic Marge would know sort of psychically that she was on her way?

She started walking.

Laurel Way was a cul de sac, containing semi-detached houses with fake Tudor beams and diamond-paned windows, each with a pocket-handkerchief-sized fake front lawn and pastel-coloured saloon car in the drive. Thanks to the leprechaun door knocker it was easy to identify the right house, though the heavy opaque net curtains weren't exactly welcoming. Two twenty-five. For heaven's sake, how bad could it be? Taking a deep breath, she ventured down the front path. Raising a shaking hand, she lifted the leprechaun's pointy little boots, and knocked.

She must have got the wrong house, despite the leprechaun. Surely Mystic Marge, Psychic to the Stars, would be all extravagant hair extensions, dramatic purple eye shadow and flowing robes embossed with gold crescent moons? But no, the woman standing in the doorway and smiling pleasantly was short and dumpy, with permed hair and pink-rimmed spectacles, wearing a dowdy summer dress Cassie remembered seeing displayed in M&S's window.

'Cassie? Come in, dear. Through here.'

She led the way into the room with the net curtains. If Cassie had been disappointed by Mystic Marge's appearance, the decor was equally unprepossessing. Trying not to look as if she *was* looking, she noted the beige Dralon-covered suite, the enormous television set, the neat row of china figures ranged along the mantelpiece. It was just a lounge – not so much as a scented candle, let alone a crystal ball and faint sounds of chanting.

'*Your Life in the Cards! Ask any Question!*' Fat chance – she'd have something to say to Zadie when she saw her later.

'Take a seat, dear.'

For the first time, Cassie noticed a little card table covered with a black velvet cloth that stood in front of the window. As she obeyed, Mystic Marge sat down opposite her and pulled a cord, drawing heavy curtains across the nets, plunging the room into darkness. Cassie was wondering how the hell she was going to make a run for it if she couldn't remember where the bloody door was when there was a click and the figures on the mantelpiece began to glow, faintly, swaying and dancing, clearly creatures from some mysterious allegory. Enough. Cassie fumbled in her bag for the envelope containing the two twenty-pound notes she'd brought. 'I'm terribly sorry, I'm afraid I've just remembered –'

'Let's begin, shall we, dear?'

Suddenly there was a curiously worked silver tealight holder in the middle of the table, beside a deck of cards. Another click, and the little tealight was flickering, filling the corners of the room with shadows.

Picking up the cards her hostess began to shuffle

skilfully, until the cards became a blur. Cassie watched, mesmerised. After a while – two minutes? Several hours? – Mystic Marge split the deck into three, cut it, then cut it again, then reshuffled the entire pack, then with a flick of the wrist laid out the cards in a wide semi-circle, face down, and waited. Cassie looked up. What now?

'So…' Her hostess's eyes gleamed green in the half-light. 'What's your question, dear?'

Basically, what time's the next bus? Cassie gave a casual shrug. 'Oh, you know – just – er how are things sort of generally, I suppose.' The tealight flickered wildly.

There was a brief silence. 'Take five cards, dear.'

Better do as she was told. She reached out a shaking hand.

'One at time, please.'

'Yes of course, sorry –'

Carefully Cassie drew out five cards and placed them face-down on the table in front of her. Mystic Marge gathered up the remainder, shuffled, briskly remade the pack, held out a scarlet-nailed hand for Cassie's selection, set them down in a neat horse-shoe pattern, still face-down, and leaned forward.

'One. The Present Position: The Hermit.' Mystic Marge turned the card over and regarded it expressionlessly, then held it up to Cassie, revealing an old man in trailing robes, leaning on a stick, holding up a lantern illuminating an empty sky. 'Isolated. Lonely. Disturbed.' Mystic Marge leant forward, frowning. 'There is an urgent need for the Seeker to work things out.'

Was she supposed to answer? Cassie settled for nodding intelligently.

'Two. Your Expectations: The Moon.' An unsettling image of a grim, bone-white Moon hanging in an ominous sky above baying hounds was revealed. Hallo? Surely the Moon should look pleasingly serene amid a delicate veil of clouds, with perhaps a few stars in the background? Cassie shifted in her seat.

'Doubt and uncertainty. Volatility. Poor judgement.' Mystic Marge tapped a fingernail on the image of a crayfish struggling out of a pool. 'Unpleasant memories returning to haunt the Seeker.'

Maybe she could walk home…?

'Next, Three. What you're Not Expecting: The Page of Swords.' The card depicted a young man in a pale blue tunic brandishing a sword. 'A young man of ruthless character, cold and calculating and of deceptively strong will.' She narrowed her eyes. 'A deceitful fellow not to be trusted.'

Cassie blinked. Recoiled. *Ivo.*

'Four. The Short-Term Future: The Seven of Wands.' Six wands rise up to attack a fellow who, though in possession of a mere single wand himself, fights on courageously. Strength and determination will be required if success is to be achieved.

Strength. Determination. Cassie sat up straighter. *Better watch your back, Keith.*

'Five. The Long-Term Future: The Knight of Pentacles.' A Knight in Armour was revealed, mounted on a gentle black steed. The Knights visor was raised, exposing ruffled hair, handsome features, a thoughtful expression. 'A peaceful, gentle fellow.'

Mystic Marge's expression softened. 'Tolerant and kind.' She scowled at Cassie. 'And most important of all…' Cassie held her breath. 'Trustworthy.'

Good news at last. She looked closer. Just a minute – he looked a bit – no, a lot – like –

'All right?' Mystic Marge was gathering up the cards.

'Brilliant – thank you!' She hesitated. 'Though could I just ask when – I mean how long till –'

Mystic Marge looked pained. 'The Beyond doesn't do Timing, dear.' She shuffled the cards briskly. 'That'll be forty pounds, cash, like I –' Without warning, a single card bearing the legend THE TOWER flipped out of the pack and landed face-up on the black velvet cloth.

An ancient Tower was pictured, perched precariously upon a high mountain peak. The sky was pitch black, clouds blew past the base of the Tower. A storm was in full spate; lightning flashes struck the top of the Tower; flames leapt from the windows.

Cassie reared back in her seat, horrified. 'What…?'

Mystic Marge sat gazing at the card. Then, using thumb and forefinger as pincers, she seized it, thrust it back into the pack, pushed back her chair and got to her feet.

'Nothing to worry about, dear.' She gave a little laugh. 'New cards, so they're a bit slippery. Need to concentrate more on my shuffling.'

She pulled a cord, and with a couple of clicks the room reverted to the way it had looked when Cassie first entered. Her hostess hurried to the door and held it open. Slowly Cassie followed, holding out the envelope containing payment.

'*No!*' She held the door open wider. 'No need for that, dear.'

'But –'

'Every twenty-first consultation's free, all right?' She gestured to Cassie to pass through the doorway.

'Thank you so much, it's been –'

'Don't mean to hurry you, dear, but my next client's due any –'

'I'm so sorry! And thank you again –'

And then they were in the hall, and the front door was shutting behind her. She was halfway down the path when something made her turn, just in time to see a figure watching at the window before the net curtains fell swiftly back into place.

CHAPTER TWENTY-TWO

THE JOURNEY HOME was delightful. Although the bus was crowded, this time sunscreen and sweat were merely the inevitable consequence of the August heat, flipflops and trainers the obvious choice of leisure wear. Cassie looked about her, admiring her surroundings; reds had never been so red, blues had never been so blue, sunshine had never been so sunny. Even the juddering stops and starts at the numerous bus stops, the blaring horns as other traffic dared to overtake, the elderly bus driver's resulting imprecations and violent gestures were welcome, since they signalled the approach to her destination.

She was smiling as she alighted from the bus on Cowley Road

the long-term future

and made her way to Sainsbury's. A chilled bottle of Sauvignon for tonight was in order, and by the time she'd done some serious work on the pendant she'd be hungry. Maybe she'd do some work on the tiara, too.

Adding a cheese and onion quiche and a bag of rocket to her basket, but giving the croissants a miss this time, she strolled along Cowley Road, stopping to drop coins into the cardboard cup of an old man busking on an out-of-tune fiddle beside an empty bench, then bending to stroke a cross-looking mongrel tied to a street lamp outside the chemist while his dishevelled owner frantically searched his pockets for his prescription. As she turned into Poplar Street she saw Erica getting into her car in the distance. As she screeched past Cassie she bestowed a radiant smile, waggling her fingers in a skittish manner. Surprised, Cassie turned, automatically waggling her fingers in response, and stood rooted to the spot as David came round the corner, carrying a bulging Sainsbury's carrier bag, a dry-cleaning bag slung over his shoulder. As he caught up with her, he jerked his head in Erica's fast-disappearing Mini's direction and raised an eyebrow. 'Best friends, eh?'

She blinked. 'What? She just waved to me – I bumped into her the other night at –'

'I know. Le Manoir. She said. Good evening, I hope?' He carried on walking.

'Brilliant! It was my birthday – I don't usually – you know – but my Father wanted to take me to –'

He stopped. 'Your father?'

'Richard, yes –'

'The guy was your *father*? Erica said – she thought –'

Cassie frowned. 'Thought what?' After a moment, she burst out laughing. 'You're kidding me! I mean Dad's in pretty good shape for his age – works out, still got all his own teeth, thanks to his Harley Street dentist, but –'

'Oh God, I'm sorry, Cass.'

Cass.

'I thought –' he smacked his forehead lightly '– I'm a

fool, and unforgivably rude, too. It's just I'd thought –
hoped you might –' he cleared his throat. Checked his
shopping.

Cassie looked surprised as tins clanked. Somehow
Fray Bentos steak and kidney pies didn't seem a likely
choice for tonight's supper.

'Picked up a few tins of Whiskas for Blanco's supper –
pretty sure the poor little bugger's a stray, he's made a
pathetic little den for himself at the end of the lane. I'll
leave some grub out behind the conservatory for him.

tolerant and kind

He sighed. 'Don't tell Erica, she can't stand cats.'

Cassie gazed at him, wondering yet again how he'd
got that tiny chip on his front tooth.

'Anyway, how are those roses doing?'

'The '*vine*', you mean?' She grinned.

He grinned back. 'Touché! God, what a tosser…'

'Much better, thanks to the industrial quantities of
Enriched Plant Soil and Advanced Fertiliser lurking
in the shed. Well, I think it is, anyway…'

Would she feel the chip if he kissed her?

'Look, let me dump this lot, and I'll nip back and
take a look.' He looked worried. 'If you'd like me to,
that is –'

trustworthy

'I would.'

He began to walk away. Turned back. 'Cass?'

She waited.

'Playing rugby. Winger. Got buried in the scrum.' he
winked. 'Didn't stop me getting a try, though.'

'Sorry, I didn't mean to stare – just wondering –'

'I know.' The corners of his mouth twitched. 'Back in a sec.' He walked on.

A quick check on Rosa 'Darlow's Enigma' as she passed – mercifully it was continuing to thrive – a dash upstairs to pin her hair into a loose bun, apply a touch of kohl to her eyelashes and fix her lipstick – down again to stash the shopping in the fridge. A quick check of the landline yielded a request from a new customer for a rose gold pendant with two hearts entwined, needed for his sick fiancée's birthday next week, if she could possibly manage it? Well, she'd certainly try; she made a note in the diary to call him back. She'd left the back door open, expecting David to arrive, and turned smiling as she heard a tap on the glass.

'Hi, Cass.' Eddie stood in the doorway. 'Just wanted to check that spark electrode's settled in.' He looked serious. 'Tricky things, spark electrodes.'

'I can imagine – it certainly looked delicate.'

'You said it'd make a great pendant, remember?' He shot her an admiring look. 'Genius.'

He moved towards the workbench. 'So how's the jewellery going, if you don't mind me asking?'

'Pardon?' *Damn, the wine wouldn't be chilled enough to offer David a glass after he'd taken a look at the vine.* 'Oh, the tiara…' *Should have bought a bottle of red, too.* 'Going to be nice, I think.'

'*Nice*? It'll be *fab*! By the way, hope you don't mind me asking, but is it hard to make the circlet?'

What?

'Always had an interest in jewellery – been reading

up on it. Apparently you need 18-20 gauge for the binding wire, but I wondered if –'

There was a tap at the back door. David entered, wearing a white shirt under a black linen jacket, and bearing a single dark red rose. He held it out to Cassie. 'From my garden.'

She felt the colour rise in her cheeks. 'Thank you.' She held it to her nose and closed her eyes. 'My God, the perfume...'

Eddie made for the cooker. 'Big fan of lupins, myself.'

David raised a hand. 'Hey, Eddie – how's it going?'

'Just saying to Cass –'

David glanced at his watch. 'Quick look at the patient, if I may?' He stepped outside. 'Back in a sec.'

'Brilliant.' Cassie stood looking after him as he left.

Eddie turned away. 'I'll get on, then.' He began to tinker with the cooker.

'Thanks, Eddie.' She tidied the collapsing pile of post on the table, washed a couple of mugs she'd left in the sink, straightened the cushion Ivo had once hurled her phone at. Then, trying to look unhurried, she drifted towards the open door, and saw David striding towards the shed. He waved as he returned, carrying the little fork, then crouched down and began to gently lift and turn the soil surrounding the vine's roots.

a peaceful, gentle fellow

Cassie leaned against the doorway, watching. After a while he stuck the fork in the soil, and stood up, smiling. 'Looking good – let's hear it for Enriched Plant Soil and Advanced Fertiliser. Reckon it'll be fine, best to let it get on with it for a bit.' He looked stern. 'No chef's extras, okay?'

Cassie giggled.

Eddie began to pick up the hob pan supports, inspect them, and bang them back into place again.

'Sorry to interrupt the good work, Eddie.' David shot an amused glance at the cooker. 'So how's Exhibit A coming along?'

Eddie scowled. 'Fine, thanks.'

'It's a very tricky job, isn't it, Eddie? Honestly, David, you wouldn't believe how hard it is to get the parts for these old cookers, most people would give up – I remember how difficult it was to find the O ring replacements –'

'Apologies for interrupting, guys, but I've got to rush – off to London to see my editor and traffic's always hell on a Friday.'

Cassie smiled. 'Wondered what was in the dry cleaner's bag.'

'Got meetings with the publishers all day tomorrow – got to impress the buggers somehow.'

'God, sounds scary – hope it goes well.'

She shivered. *At least David wouldn't turn up blind drunk and spoiling for a fight if it didn't.*

'Cassie? You okay?'

She managed to laugh. 'Think a ghost just walked over my grave.'

'Come on, that's just an old wives' tale.' He headed for the door. 'By the way, I finished cleaning that little putty knife just now, must have missed a couple of flakes last time. Put it back with the others.'

'Thanks –'

'It looked so out of place when the others have been

so well-cared for.'

Eddie shook his head. 'Got to take care of your tools.'

David stepped into the garden. Turned back. 'Home Sunday afternoon.' He raised an eyebrow at Cassie. 'Fancy a drink in the evening? Be pleasant to sit beside the river at The Trout.'

She swallowed. 'Lovely.'

'I'll give you a ring when I get back.' He raised a hand in Eddie's direction. 'See you, Eddie.'

He hurried away. Cassie drifted over to her workbench. *The sundress she'd worn on her birthday? No, trying too hard. Jeans, and a plain white shirt? Or maybe –*

'So what was wrong with the rose bush, then?'

'Vine – David says it's not a bush.'

'Vine. Right.'

'Had some sort of disease, or infection, or something. It's fine now, though.'

He began to repack his toolbox. 'Got another customer to visit.'

Hair down. Wash it in the morning. 'No peace for the wicked…'

He picked up the toolbox. Padded towards her. Stopped and gazed at the paraphernalia on the workbench. Set down his toolbox. 'Hope you don't mind me asking, but I don't suppose you've thought any more about teaching me? Been reading up on circlets, like I said, and –'

'I'm terribly sorry, Eddie, but I simply don't have the time. Just had a new customer ring wanting a double heart pendant urgently, plus I've got various other jobs to finish.' She sketched a helpless gesture. 'Not to mention any day now orders will start rolling in for Christmas –'

A short silence. Then, looking downcast, he picked up the toolbox again. 'Better get that pendant sorted before Sunday evening, then.'

He stumbled into the garden and trailed across the grass. Cassie stood watching, hoping he'd turn and see her waiting to wave. But he closed the gate quietly behind him without looking back; she wasn't sure, but she thought he was crying as he turned into the lane. She'd never felt so mean in her life. She'd check out the details of suitable local courses herself, so she'd have something concrete to suggest next time he called in.

She was about to secure the back door when she saw that in his hurry to get away, David had left the garden fork stuck in the soil beside the rose vine. After taking a moment to admire the burgeoning buds' progress anew, she took the fork back to the shed, luxuriating in the sun's delightful warmth, the cheerful chorus of birdsong, and the joyful prospect of the following night's trip to The Trout. The aroma of creosote amid the gloom of the shed was equally pleasant; easing off her sneakers, she flexed her toes luxuriously. She took her time cleaning the fork's tines. As she reached up to put it back in place, she miscalculated and knocked the container of Roundup Total Weedkiller off the shelf below, flinching as it fell and landed with an inexplicably hollow sound on the concrete floor. She stopped dead. The container fell because it was so light, and it was light because it was almost empty. Which was odd, because it should have been full. Granny Jackson bought it to get rid of plantains, but refused to use it once she realised it would kill the daisies, too. Cassie bent to pick it up, wincing as the bruises on her back throbbed. Carried it to the door and examined it in the light.

Saw Roundup Total Weedkiller was indeed now almost empty. Saw the label saying POISON in heavy black capitals. Lethal.

She slumped against the wooden wall as it hit her. *It was no virus that had attacked her adored Rosa Darlow's Enigma, Ivo – bloody, bloody Ivo – had poisoned it.* She shivered – she hadn't been imagining the ancient pair of gardening gloves looked even dirtier than she remembered. *Ivo had worn the gloves to protect his hands.* He must have rushed over the minute he knew she was at the Garden Centre –

you always did love flowers

– got inside, and with the luck of the devil found himself in the right place at the right time to intercept Lady Chudleigh's phone call. *Bastard.* After a while she began to straighten up. Oh well, look on the bright side – at least she no longer had to get Lloyd's help with the bucket of sludge; she'd do the wildlife a favour and dump it herself on the massive clump of giant hogweed in the lane.

She froze. *What if he was planning to poison her, too?* No, if she knew Ivo he was having too much fun freaking her out with his phone calls, messing with her adored roses, and screwing her reputation with potential clients. Thank God he'd only managed to get in once.

Hadn't he…?

She levered herself upright and returned to the row

of tools. Grabbed the putty knife and stood staring at it, remembering the flakes of paint. Without even thinking about it, she found herself in the area at the side of the house, knocking into the old bike, stubbing her toe on the wonky wheelbarrow, shrivelled scraps of yellowing white confetti adhering to the soles of her feet. She stood motionless, staring at the old sash window. Only now remembering how, aiming for security, Grandpa Jackson had once painted over the weak catch with white gloss paint. It had been impossible to open ever since.

She closed her eyes. Took a deep breath. After a moment she opened her eyes – saw where the paint had been carefully chipped away, the exposed ancient catch. *Do it.* Slowly she raised the putty knife to the window frame. The blade fitted the peeling scars perfectly.

Standing on tiptoe, she slid the bottom half of the window up. Shivered as she thought of the over-heating iron, the defrosted fridge...

> *ought to be condemned this place*
> *bloody death trap*

Oh God. What else was he planning?

Get indoors, NOW. But first, leave the window as she found it, brush off the confetti – (she saw now that the edges were tipped with brown, reminding her of the petals on the vine) till it lay scattered on the ground again. Her sneakers, where were her sneakers? She scanned the ground. No sign. Remembered she'd left them in the shed. Okay, no way was she was going back for them, she needed to get indoors and phone KeyKwik, fast. Taking care to avoid first the bike, then the wheelbarrow, she stopped at the corner of the house. Scanned the garden. Impossibly, the birds were still singing, the sun still shining, while somewhere a car – the students' little green French car, by the sound of it – back-fired apoplectically until the sound faded into the distance. There was the shed. But something was wrong; the door was wide open. Wide open because she'd rushed out without bothering to close it when she figured it out about the putty knife – Christ, where was it? She scanned the ground. No sign. Eventually she located it on the window ledge. Face it; she was going to have to get it back, asap, as in *now*. Anyway, it was madness to leave her sneakers there, broadcasting the fact that –

She was racing across the grass again, a quick glance at Zadie's side showing that the windows and back door were closed - hadn't she said something about taking the kids to visit Lloyd's mum in Scarborough for a few days? And David would be halfway to London by now…Carefully Cassie slid the putty knife into place alongside the other tools, checked that the price tag was still dangling, grabbed her sneakers, and shoving the door shut behind her, made for the safety of the kitchen.

CHAPTER TWENTY-THREE

She was shaking so hard it took a while to lock the back door and rattle the chain into place, and check that the blinds were securely closed. A quick glance behind the blind above the sink gave no hint that the sash window had been tampered with; if she hadn't known better, the fragile hasp looked normal. Though come to think of it – didn't she recently brush a stray flake of paint off the windowsill when she was removing a dead fly? Why hadn't she wondered then where it had come from?

No good beating herself up for that now. *Beating herself up.* Funny. She attempted a cynical laugh. Regretted it – sounded as if she was choking. *Choking*...If only she could stop shaking. The first thing was to find a jacket or something, get warm – the kitchen was freezing after the warmth of the garden – the second was to call KeyKwik to fix the window, please God they'd send Merv. She hauled herself up the stairs, holding on to the banister, and stopped dead when she reached the landing. Check the front door, stupid. Everything was as it should be – safely locked, the chain in place. This time she didn't attempt to laugh. Safely? Who was she kidding?

The front door wasn't the problem, or the back door –
not when anybody could climb through the bloody
sash window any time they wanted.

Anybody? Looking at you, Ivo, you bastard.

you're going to be sorry

Goosebumps accompanied the shaking. She hurried
into the bedroom, rummaged through drawers,
searching in vain for a warm sweater to pull on over
her tee shirt, gave up and snatched a winter throw
stored for the summer at the bottom of a cupboard.
Wrapping it round her, she hurried downstairs.
Phone. Must find her phone. When the hell had she
last had it? When she went to Blackbird Leys to see
Mystic Marge? God, it seemed light years away.

a young man of ruthless character

Well the psychic had got that right, anyway...A
frantic search revealed her phone mired in the
detritus at the bottom of her bag; weak with relief,
she dialled the number. Five minutes later, relief had
given way to despair. With great regret, there were no
operatives available at this time, being either off sick
or on holiday. Of the other locksmiths she tried who
actually answered, all gave the same response. If she'd
like to call again tomorrow...

Tomorrow? Tomorrow didn't bear thinking about,
anything could have happened by then. She sank
down at the kitchen table and tried to think. Options:
call Helen or Mia from Zumba and ask if she could
kip on their sofa tonight. Contact her father and ask
if she could get the key from the night manager and
stay at his rarely used pied-a-terre in a London hotel.

In other words, run.

Cassie sat up straight. NO. This was her home, and she wasn't going to let a creep like Ivo terrify her into leaving. Think! There must be *something* she could do to help herself. As she pulled the throw more closely round her shoulders, her gaze fell on the workbench, and wandered over the various machines and drawers full of tools. Stopped dead at the wooden box beside the soldering kit labelled VARIOUS GLUES.

She took a deep breath. Worth at least giving it a try. She remembered there was a tube of J-B Weld 287 steel reinforced epoxy in there – she'd had to use it on a job once when a particularly strong adhesive was required. Hurrying over to the workbench, she rummaged in the box, found the bright scarlet and black tubes – HERCULEAN METAL TO METAL STRENGTH! PERMANENT BOND IN LESS THAN FIVE MINUTES! Herculean strength! Permanent bond! Oh, please God…Clumsily, trying to control her trembling fingers, she laid them out, together with the necessary equipment, and got to work.

Half an hour later, the damaged window lock was repaired and glued firmly in place, giving off an odour so strong it made her eyes water. The discomfort was welcome, testament, she hoped, to the strength of the sealant's components. She wished she could bang a couple of nails in the wood to secure it, but none of the screws in the drawer were long enough. Nothing to do now but wait – she'd give it the advised five minutes before she checked whether the bond was indeed permanent. She could close the blind, too, then, like the others. Sinking down at the table she looked around her. The kitchen, once so welcoming, had changed. It must be later than she thought; sunlight had been replaced by deepening twilight, bleaching the colour from painted chairs and floral plates and embroidered cushions, shadowing the corners with a murky gloom that reminded her uncomfortably of the illustrations in a book of Grimm's Fairy Tales she'd been given as a child. The images – grotesque figures lurking in sinister copses where clawlike roots emerged from shadowy undergrowth thick with rotting vegetation, and darkness settled among twisted tree trunks, had frightened her so much she'd refused to take the book to bed.

Silly to think about it now. She'd feel better when she'd closed the blind and put the lamps on – she'd give the reinforced epoxy a few extra minutes to be on the safe side. Tea, that was what she needed, and food. She'd been shopping earlier, hadn't she? Bought croissants?

oh dear your delicious breakfast

No. Erica –

all those charming little doodles

had put her off croissants for good. Some sort of quiche, wasn't it? Great, food would help a lot – as Granny Jackson always said, as she served up massive helpings of dumpling stew, or steamed ginger pudding, or lemon drizzle sponge – an army marches on its stomach. Cassie's eyes filled with tears. Best not to think about Granny Jackson right now, and she'd sure as hell never felt less like an army. She sighed. No time for self-pity; after she'd had a mug of tea and a chunk of quiche, she'd check out the sash window.

She had to concentrate hard on holding the kettle under the tap; her hands were shaking so much it was hard to keep it in place. At last she succeeded, and switched it on. She was turning away when she stopped dead. Forced herself to turn back, her breath catching in her throat. She wasn't alone in the kitchen, and her companion was worse than any invasion by Ivo.

let's not forget the apparition in black

Miss Jessel was reflected in the gleaming side of the kettle, her spectral features ghostly white, distended eyes staring straight at Cassie, her black robe stark in the deepening gloom.

the dead governess – watching, waiting...

As Cassie stared, horrified, the spectre's bloodless lips parted, about to emit a soundless scream. With a shriek of terror – God oh God *this time it's real* – Cassie leapt away from the counter, knocked into one of the chairs and fell, banging her head on the edge of the table. Curling herself into a ball, she covered her eyes with her hands, and lay still. Waiting.

Billowing steam filling the kitchen finally forced her to drag herself up. Holding onto the table, she pulled herself to her feet, shivering, and drew the throw around her. Forced herself to approach the kettle, rubbing her aching head – froze as she saw her action reflected in the shiny metal, and shaking her head in disbelief, recognised her own distorted reflection. She looked as ghostly as any wraith, her face drained of colour, hair tied back, the dark throw mimicking the governess's gown. After a moment, she took a wrenching breath, and steadying her right hand with her left, reached out and managed to switch off the kettle, the bloody, *bloody* kettle. Would she never learn?

Weak with relief, she sagged against the counter. Definitely time for that mug of tea, preferably in the cheery Clarice Cliff knock-off she'd bought in Camden market years ago, its distinctive bright orange and yellow trees flanking a tiny house perched high on a hill. As she lifted the mug from its hook, it slipped from her fingers and fell with an echoing crash onto the tiled floor. Numbly, she looked down at the shards of broken china; saw fragments of orange and yellow leaves, the house lying in ruins. She stood thinking. Remembering. The mug had slipped from her fingers because her fingers were trembling. Her fingers were trembling because…*say it. Because she was still scared.* Suddenly she wasn't numb – she was furious. She was sick of being afraid, it was time to take control. Seizing the metal pepper grinder that stood near the kettle, she hurled it at the opposite wall, where it landed with a satisfying thud. Excellent. Tossing aside the throw, she ripped the hairpins from her bun, shook out her hair and straightened her shoulders. What was it they said? *There is nothing to fear but fear itself.* Right. It was time to do the Ghost Trail.

Shoving chairs aside as she strode past, Cassie switched on the lamps, headed for the sink and checked the lock on the window. It held. She pulled down the blind, replaced the chairs and looked around the kitchen. It looked reassuringly normal, now that the clouds of steam had dispersed; she'd clear up the remains of the mug, change the water in the jug of striped tulips, and make a strong PG Tips. Hang on. Did Superwoman sit around sipping tea and nibbling gingernuts? She did not. Taking the pleasingly chilled bottle of Sauvignon from the fridge – God, it seemed a lifetime since she'd bought it – she poured herself a large glass of wine.

Now to find that flyer.

She quickly found the missive, easily identifiable by its turned back corner, and slipped it from the neat pile of post, smiling as she re-read the satisfied customer's comment – *Brilliant – we loved every minute!* – beside the little sketch of a harmless-looking cobweb, and the star she'd drawn beside today's date at the bottom. She checked the information beside the cobweb. '*Meet outside the Tourist Information Centre on Broad Street at 6.50 pm every Friday till September. No Need to Book.*'

She glanced at her watch. Nearly five o'clock – she'd have sworn it was later. She'd have to leave at half six if she was to get to Broad Street on time. She'd think about the double heart pendant in the meantime, make some sketches. At least Eddie would be pleased …She took a long swallow of wine, devoured a large slice of quiche, and set to work.

She was planning to give each ring a contrasting texture – one a matt brush finish, the other a strong hammer finish, by way of contrast – when the first doubts crept in about the wisdom of doing the Ghost

Trail. There must be *some* fairly realistic ghostly scenarios, or people would be demanding their money back, like they did at those dodgy Santa's grottos where the Christmas tree was still in its netting, a beardless Santa sat on a chair in a cupboard *sans* tinsel or fairy lights, and the reindeer was a labrador with fake antlers on its head.

No. It was too risky. She'd spend the evening working –

in possession of a mere single wand himself

– and with a bit of luck she could finish the measurements and start actually making the rings tonight –

strength and determination will be required if success is to be achieved

She dropped her pencil. Sighed. God, she was tired – it had been a long day. Picking it up again she began to make notes on the heart sizes when out of the blue she recalled a comment Ivo had made –

ghosts chrissakes pathetic

Pathetic? *Pathetic?* Incensed, Cassie spun round in her chair and flung the pencil at the old pine store cupboard, aiming at the door handles as she recalled the agony that exploded in her kidneys and shot up her spine, the dazzling display of scarlet fireworks fading to black as she collapsed –

The King of Wands fights on courageously

Cassie leapt to her feet. 'Bloody right I will! Sod apparitions and ghosts – scared? I'll show you! Watch me, Ivo – no, KEITH JENKINS, you fucking loser –'

She took a great gulp of wine. '*I'm going*!!'

She closed her notebook and retrieved the pencil, already regretting having thrown it; hopefully she'd be able to trim it down and sharpen it for future use. Hurrying upstairs, she checked the concealer masking her bruises, added a slick of lipstick for courage, and ran downstairs to grab her jacket from its peg in case the evening turned chilly. She was tucking the flyer into her bag when her phone rang. Leave it? No, it might be a client, or even David. No caller ID. Still, better respond, just in case, but make it quick. 'Hello?'

No answer, just the sound of heavy vehicles – buses? Lorries? – manoeuvering, overlaid by a cacophony of hooters blasting warnings and high-pitched reversing beeper alarms. Must be a wrong number. Still, give it one more try. 'Hello? Anybody there…?

No response. Then…'Hello? Cass?'

dragged her upright and slapped her face, hard

She shivered. Cut the call – switch off the damn phone –

'Calling from Gloucester Green coach station – hey, listen, 'spect you can hear –' The background noise increased, he must be holding up his phone.

Stuff it in a drawer and go. GO.

'– cos I'm on my way to London.'

She hesitated. London?

'I've got big news, Cass – the best!! Got a major part in a groundbreaking new political drama – think Michael Frayne crossed with Joe Orton – we're gonna change the theatrical goalposts forever!'

Her finger hovered over the red button.

'Heard last week – life's been crazy ever since,

organising digs, etcetera. On my way to The Smoke now, rehearsals start tomorrow – cast's off-book in a couple of weeks, had my head down learning lines ever since I got the news.

His voice sounded different – warm. Friendly. Maybe he really –

'God, it's good to be working again – and get this! The Powers that Be – can't mention names, obvs – say it's practically certain we'll be opening on Broadway for Christmas –'

'Ivo –'

'Cass? Just had to call before I go to say I'm sorry.' His voice broke. 'To apologise for all the shite stuff I've done.'

'I –'

'No excuse, I know, but I nearly lost my mind I was missing you so much – it was, I dunno – my way of staying in touch. Got a bit out of hand with all the breaking in and stuff, but you were doing so well with your work, while at that point I –' He began to sob. 'I'm so sorry!'

She closed her eyes. If only he'd come clean – make a clean breast of everything, accept the blame – she could forgive him. Move on.

'Ivo?'

A sob.

'Was it you breaking the sash lock? Leaving the iron on? Defrosting the fridge? Poisoning Granny Jackson's little white rose vine?'

A snort as he blew his nose loudly.

A clean breast of everything. She took a deep breath. '*All* of it?

Another sob. 'Yes.'

So she hadn't been losing it after all. A great weight seemed to lift from her shoulders.

'Please, *please* forgive me, Cass!'

No more doubting herself, no more dreading what she might find, no more fearing to answer the phone. 'I do.'

'It's a lot to ask, I know, but…can you find it in your heart to wish me well?'

'I wish –'

'Hang on.' He called to someone. 'What time you leaving, mate?'

'Now, mate – gotta go –' Must be the driver shouting.

Ivo was back again, quiet, gentle. 'Goodbye, Cass.'

'Ivo –'

'Good night, sweet lady – good night, good night. You'll never hear from me again.' His voice faded. He said something to the driver; there was a hiss as the coach door closed, followed by the low growl of the engine as it reversed then burst into life as it accelerated out of the coach station.

She was free.

She leant against the workbench, weak with relief. Her heart lifted; she didn't need to do the Ghost Trail now, she'd get on with the pendant instead. Hanging her jacket back on its peg she retrieved the broken pencil, found her sharpening knife and sat down at the table, sipping the remainder of the wine in her glass while she dealt with the damaged lead. She was pondering her sketches – maybe a polished satin texture would work better than a matt brush finish? – when it occurred to her that a cup of coffee would be a good idea before she did a trial run with the different finishes. She waved cheerfully to herself as she switched on the kettle, thinking what a fool she'd been earlier – but as she spooned coffee granules into her mug the ghastly memory resurfaced –

miserable

– and switching off the kettle she returned to the table. Yes, definitely the polished satin texture –

pale

– though maybe she'd try all three finishes and see which –

and dreadful

Okay, hammered texture first. Jumping up, she made for the work bench with her notebook and set out her tools. As she picked up the chasing hammer to check the ball-shaped side it slipped from her trembling fingers and fell with a sharp crack on the metal bench block, pitting and scratching the delicate surface; she'd have to resurface it before it could be used. *Trembling.* She backed away. *Face it*, girlfriend, as Zadie would say. If she was honest, she was still afraid of ghosts.

strength and determination will be required

Oh, for God's sake. All *right*. She strode over to the coat pegs, collected her jacket, grabbed her bag and checked the flyer was still there, half hoping it wouldn't be. It was. Probably be too late now, anyway. She checked her watch. Six thirty-five. It wasn't. She unlocked the back door, rattled out the chain –

if success is to be achieved

'All *right*! I'm *going*!'

Throwing open the door, she stepped outside and re-locked it. Pulled on her jacket, buttoned it up to the neck, turned up the collar and put on the dark glasses she found in a pocket.

Then, clutching her bag tightly to her chest, she set off for Broad Street.

CHAPTER TWENTY-FOUR

BROAD STREET WAS different at night; almost deserted and eerily quiet. No bustling tourists crowded the pavements, no students cycled three or four abreast down the middle of the road, loudly complaining to each other about their tutors' perfectly frightful inadequacies. A lone rough sleeper was stashed in his sleeping bag in a darkened shop doorway, a pigeon pecked morosely at a discarded crisp packet. Cassie glanced nervously about her. Maybe this wasn't such a great idea after all – Okay, she might know where Broad Street was, but where the hell was the Tourist Information Centre? She hurried past the immaculate railings of some imposing-looking college, its spires and towers and softly-lit windows picture postcard perfect, and on past Blackwells, not stopping to glance at the colourful book jackets displayed in its elegant windows.

Still no sign of the Tourist Information Centre. With a sigh she glanced over the road, and caught sight of the Sheldonian Theatre, illuminated now in the growing dusk, comforted by the familiar row of carved philosophers' heads gazing thoughtfully into space. Maybe she'd head back to Poplar Street;

experimenting with the different silver textures was becoming an increasingly attractive prospect. She was passing the worn stone steps of the stately Museum of the History of Science, wondering why she'd never visited it and pondering what wonders were to be seen in there – mysterious astronomical orreries, all gleaming brass and esoteric symbols? – yellowing parchment charts covered with indecipherable sepia notes, depicting the development of a cross-looking foetus? – when she saw a small crowd gathering around a white banner further down the street. Some sort of student political protest, no doubt; they'd probably want her to sign some petition before they let her pass. No problem, she'd give Erica's name and address, suggest they contact her for a donation, assure them whatever it was they were protesting about was a cause dear to Erica's heart, and urge them to persevere if she seemed reluctant at first. Hopefully they were demanding support for Marxism, or the immediate abolishment of the monarchy. But as she drew nearer she saw that rather than a group of students, the little gathering consisted of several bemused-looking foreign tourists, a giggling young couple, and a group of teenagers smoking roll-ups and quaffing cans of lager. Glancing up, she saw the legend *Tourist Information Centre* above a darkened glass door, and read the caption on the banner, *Bill Spectre's Ghost Trail*, carefully hand-painted in a luridly sinister font.

Head down, Cassie joined them. As she slipped into place behind a well-dressed elderly Japanese couple who looked as if they'd be more at home taking tea at the Randolph, a harassed-looking woman trying to control four excited young boys hurried up. Cassie's heart lifted. So the Tour *was* suitable for kids! Brilliant, she'd be fine. By the look of it things were about to get under way; a short silver-haired man in gold-rimmed spectacles, dressed in what looked like a Victorian undertaker's costume, was mounting an orange box at the front of the audience, clasping a battered attaché case in one hand. 'Welcome to my little Ghost Trail, each and every one! To an evening of Fun and Laughter, illustrated with a Positive Plethora of Props and Illusions!' The voice was plummy, confident – Cassie didn't need telling it was the voice of a trained actor. He narrowed his eyes, leaned forward. The voice was lowered, the tone became sinister. 'To meeting the Ghosts and Ghouls that lurk in the shadows of this great historic city – *the city of Oxford*!' With a dramatic sweep of his rather dusty-looking top hat he bowed low. After a moment there was a smattering of applause. 'And now, my assistant will pass amongst you and collect your pennies as we proceed to our first location.' A wintry smile. 'Let us proceed.' Stepping down from the box he strode off, bearing aloft the banner. After a moment, the group straggled after him.

They didn't go far. Their host came to a halt near the end of Broad Street opposite Balliol college, stopping so unexpectedly that the members of the group cannoned into each other, giggling nervously. They stopped as the little undertaker drew their attention to a simple cobblestone cross set in the middle of the road. 'It was the year 1555, and it is here – on this very spot – that those three brave martyrs, Latimer, Ridley and Cranmer, were burnt alive at the stake – Latimer and Ridley on October the fifteenth, Cranmer at a later date.' He shook his head. 'I believe they ran out of firelighters.' Cassie restrained a grin, and risked a glance at the French tourist beside her, who was frowning as he consulted his electronic dictionary. Mr Spectre shuddered. 'You may think *that* is bad, ladies and gentlemen. You will think it far worse when I tell you that as an act of mercy – hah! *Mercy*! – a small bag of gunpowder was hung around their necks to speed their passing.' The group gave a little gasp of horror. 'And I think it will not surprise you to hear that even now, on autumn nights when the night is dark and Broad Street is deserted, their cries can be heard, echoing faintly on the wind...I have heard them myself, many times.' He sighed. 'But I see from your expressions that what I have told you has horrified you. I fear there is more; other methods of torture no less barbaric were routinely employed in those days. For example...' He paused. '*The thumbscrews*. Allow me to demonstrate. May I have a lady volunteer?'

Amid much joshing, one of the youths pushed his girlfriend forward. With her spiky purple hair, mirrored sun glasses and ripped Chainsaw Massacre 2 tee-shirt she looked more than equal to the task. 'Excellent.' Mr Spectre beckoned her to his side, and whispered something in her ear. She nodded, giggling, and held out a hand. He took some arcane instrument from his battered bag, and attached it to her thumb. 'Let us begin the torture. I turn the screw, like so...' he demonstrated 'and the young lady's thumb will begin to swell with the pressure...' Cassie's jaw dropped. Something huge and black was starting to protrude from his victim's hand. God, this was horrible – the girl herself had stopped giggling, now, and was staring at her hand in disbelief as the swelling grew larger...and larger...the crowd was muttering anxiously now – and then the ghastly excrescence suddenly popped with a great bang. The redoubtable Mr Spectre beamed. 'A simple trick, ladies and gentlemen, to lighten the atmosphere.' He held up the ragged remains of what was clearly a balloon, and bowed. 'A big hand – if you'll pardon the expression – for my charming assistant!' Amid relieved laughter, followed by applause, the girl returned to her mates, who greeted her with loud cheers and pressed a can of lager into her willing hand.

'Phew!' Cassie grinned at her neighbour, the mother of the young boys. 'Hope that didn't upset the kids too much.'

'You kidding me? You wanna see what they watch on their Xboxes!'

It was true, she could see now they'd gone into a huddle, snorting with laughter, and were doing things to each others' thumbs she thought it was probably best she couldn't see clearly. She looked around. The Japanese couple were nodding approvingly at each other, the foreign students were happily taking selfies. Hell, it was definitely time to man up. Their host had repacked his case and was already setting off back in the direction in which they'd come, banner held jauntily aloft.

After they'd walked for a while, turning down streets Cassie didn't recognise, they came to a halt. 'And so we arrive at Trinity College.' Mr Spectre looked grave. 'Where events in the chapel of a distressingly ghostly nature have been recorded by persons of the most unimpeachable character; the utmost rectitude. Persons of standing in the university itself...'

The members of the group looked as one towards the chapel, its bulk looming against the darkening sky.

'Of the two events I shall vouchsafe, the first occurred after the organ had been restored. On the occasion of the very first service afterwards, the organist was discovered sprawled dead over the keyboards, a look of horror on his face. The second was a more recent event. One morning in 1959 the verger unlocked the chapel door at 10.00 am and went about his duties in the normal manner. On looking about him he saw the figure of a woman clad from head to foot in black –'

Cassie froze.

'– a woman of ashen visage whom he had no doubt had not been present when he arrived. She simply stood there, smiling and smiling at him –'

Cassie began to edge her way to the back of the group.

'– and with a shock that turned his very soul to ice, *he saw that it was his dead mother.*'

Cassie stopped. *His mother*, not –

'To make no 'bones' about it –' Mr Spectre allowed himself a twitch of the lips '– it was a ghost, an apparition if you will. But despite his fear – his horror – he decided to approach, looking down for the briefest moment as he hurried up the steps up to the chancel. When he looked up –' He waited, eyes closed. Opened them, and shook his head. '– the chapel was...empty.'

There was a collective intake of breath.

'It is said that often – *very often* – a strange wailing can be heard coming from within the chapel walls late – *very late* – at night.'

After a brief pause to let everyone take this in, their guide turned on his heel and set off again. With nervous backward glances they hurried after him, the mood speedily lightened by the kids having an enthusiastic wailing competition. Cassie grinned, relieved – *just his mother* – thinking how much Brooklyn and Bronx would have loved to join in. They wouldn't have been too fazed by the martyrs, either, and they'd definitely have been enthralled by the thumb screws episode...

She hoped they were nearly there, wherever they were going. The evening was warm; she'd already taken off the jacket, hung it over her arm, and returned the sunglasses to her pocket – they made it almost impossible to see in the gathering twilight. Walking on cobbles became seriously uncomfortable after a while, too, and she wished she'd eaten more of the quiche. As her stomach rumbled loudly, one of the youths ambling ahead yanked a bulging paper bag from the pocket of his stained leather jacket, and extracting double chocolate chip cookies two at a time, started shoving them into his mouth whole. Double chocolate chip, her favourite. Though even a couple of oatmeal raisin cookies would be welcome right now. Cassie looked away quickly, trying to concentrate on feeling sorry for the verger who'd had his very soul turned to ice.

Ah, they were turning down Turl Street now. As

she traipsed on with the group, she wondered what David was doing in London, and how things would go with his editor, the one he was having a row with on the phone that time she called round with his sweater. Meeting tomorrow with his publishers, he'd said. She'd never met a publisher. Would they all wear oversize Groucho Marx specs and wacky rock star tee shirts and have MBA's from Harvard, too? No, they'd probably – '*Ouch!*' The youth with the striped buzz-cut mullet, concentrating on kicking his empty lager can along the gutter to a mate, had bumped into her, hard. He grinned – '*Hey, dude!*'– and lolloped off again. She rubbed her side. It hurt. Maybe this would be a good time to slip away? No, she was here for a reason – and suddenly she realised that to her surprise it was working; Mr Spectre's exaggeratedly theatrical manner gave even his most lurid yarns an amusing twist and more to the point, all his supposed revelations were blatantly obvious urban myths.

They'd just passed Exeter College when Mr S's banner suddenly disappeared from view as he turned sharp left halfway down Turl Street and vanished. The group followed, and found themselves shuffling down a tiny dark cobbled alley. A street sign glimmered overhead in the gloom; Brasenose Lane. God, this really was spooky. Not to say chilly, and quite possibly damp. Cassie shivered, pulled on her jacket again and stopped abruptly, narrowly avoiding bumping into the foreign students, still enthusiastically taking selfies. Mr Spectre had halted beneath a flickering street lamp opposite a heavily barred window, his battered attaché case at his feet, his top hat slightly askew on his silver hair. 'And so we find ourselves, my friends, outside Brasenose College.' The Japanese couple nodded politely. 'More specifically beneath the window where one of the most heinous episodes in the history of this august university occurred. For one December night in 1828, Edward Trafford, a most disreputable undergraduate, who would have thought nothing –' he eyed the group of youths over his spectacles '– of kicking an empty beer can down the Lane, causing a rumpus quite loud enough, I suspect, to ahem –' he lowered his voice dramatically '– *waken the dead.*' Sheepishly the culprit retrieved the offending can and thrust it in his pocket.

'However, on the night in question, young Edward was engaged in a rather more shocking pastime than booting a tin can down the road. Not to put too fine a point on it, *he was celebrating a Black Mass.*'

Cassie risked a glance at the young boys. Oblivious, they were squabbling over a family-size bag of popcorn. 'Chrissakes, shut it!' Their mother, who was listening, rapt, ferreted in her capacious holdall, whipped out an outsize bag of crisps and thrust it at her offspring. Peace of a sort descended.

'That freezing winter night, a heavy snow falling, the bone-white moon peering down from the night-black sky, a Fellow of the College was returning to his rooms down this very lane. As he approached, he became aware of a frightful screaming.' The young couple, who were no longer giggling, drew closer together as Mr S leaned towards his audience, his spectacles glinting in the lamplight, and gestured grimly towards the window. 'I must tell you that in those days, this casement was not only heavily barred – strong wire netting was secured over the glass. And as the good Fellow approached, he became privy to the most fearful sight.' He paused. The entire group was holding its breath. 'A preternaturally tall, scarlet-cloaked figure was dragging a screaming man through the wire netting, *like meat through a mincer. A mincer*, ladies and gentlemen.'

The kids, having polished off the crisps, gave a cheer of approval. The Japanese man was explaining the meaning of 'mincer' to his wife, with appropriate gestures.

Mr S clasped his top hat to his chest. 'I am sorry to have to tell you it is thought that the scarlet-cloaked figure was the Devil himself, come to claim his own.'

Cassie imagined a plump satin-clad pantomime demon sprouting little horns, played by her favourite comedian, Eddie Izzard, and hid a grin.

Mr S was regarding her sternly. 'There are possibly those amongst you who doubt the tale.'

Cassie tried to look serious.

'However –' bending down, he took an imposing leather-bound tome from his case '– I have here the actual College records *for that very date.*' He read aloud a brief but alarmingly detailed account of the occurrence; the Devil was indeed cited as the evil assailant. Mr S frowned at the youths. 'But do I detect an air of disbelief? Hmm. Perhaps we might essay a little experiment?' The crowd murmured assent. 'Very well. If what has been written here, vouchsafed by the highest authority –' He held the tome aloft. '– is True, give us a sign.'

Silence.

Mr S lowered the tome. Raised it again. '*Give us a sign.*'

Still nothing.

'Hmmm.' Mr S nodded thoughtfully. 'Your participation is clearly what is required here, ladies and gentlemen; my own entreaties are not sufficient. So, on my count of three?'

Enthusiastic nods.

'Very well. One...two...three...'

A collective intake of breath, and a great shout went up, Cassie enthusiastically joining in: 'GIVE US A SIGN!!'

Suddenly, with a great burst of flame, the tome was ablaze.

Gasps of horror, delight and terror filled the air as Mr S started back, apparently appalled. The gasps were replaced by incredulous laughter as – beaming – Mr S put a finger to his lips and snapped the tome shut with a flourish, dousing the fake flames. He replaced it in his case. Rapturous – not to say relieved – applause followed, which he acknowledged with a modest bow before his smile faded. 'And now, if you will follow me, you shall hear a tale of murder most foul, involving a poor, innocent young woman; a tale I fear will chill you to the very marrow.'

Quelling the youths' ragged cheer with a look, he turned on his heel, and holding his banner aloft, set off again. Still grinning at the recent drama – she had to admit she'd been as horrified, delighted and terrified as the rest of the party – Cassie almost tripped over a cracked paving stone, and knelt to re-tie her sneaker laces as the others disappeared round the corner into Radcliffe Square. She swiftly followed them, and saw the dome of the iconic Radcliffe Camera, imposing in the deepening dusk, its stone – She stopped dead. A figure was standing in the deepening shadows at the base of the dome, her back turned to Cassie. A figure in a long black dress, her dark hair tightly plaited and coiled, pinned in a painfully tight bun at the base of her neck, a style Cassie had often seen in Victorian paintings. As Cassie stood staring, her heart pounding, her skin crawling, the figure began to slowly raise an arm from her side, a white hand pointing…For a moment Cassie stood transfixed, then, making a great effort, she took a deep breath and forced herself to look away. Ridiculous – had she learned nothing this evening? She couldn't blame Ivo now –

you'll never hear from me again

– the figure was simply a figment of her imagination. She took a quick look back at the shadows, even murkier now. Nothing. God, she was a fool. Briskly she ran a hand through her hair and brushed a shred of lint off her sleeve; time to put the stress of the past few months behind her. Casually, she strolled on to join the others by the iron railings, where they were taking selfies in front of the Camera's symmetrical, curves and pointing out the cross at the apex to each other. With a glance at his watch and a twirl of the banner, Mr S invited them to follow him, looking disapprovingly at Cassie as she tried to discreetly insinuate herself into the back of the group as they came to a halt outside the University Church of St

Mary the Virgin, its great tower with its ornamental spires and pinnacles illuminated against the purple sky.

Mr S waited patiently while camcorders were produced, selfies taken, economy bags of Monster Munch distributed to the kids. Then he turned to face the magnificent exterior, waited while the group gathered round expectantly, and began to speak in hushed tones. 'The poor innocent woman of whom I speak was one Amy Robsart, wife of Sir Robert Dudley, a nobleman well-known at the Tudor Court. Unfortunately he was a fellow much given to self-love –' Ha, sounded familiar –

> where he'd managed to declaim most of Henry Vth's
> bracing speech to a crowd of bemused Japanese
> tourists before the guide moved him on

though to be fair –

> just had to call before I go to say I'm sorry –
> to apologise for all the shite stuff I've done

even a leopard could change its spots.

Meanwhile Mr S was continuing. 'It seems that the marriage was at first a happy one, until skilful manoeuvring speedily brought Robert to the attention of the target of his ambition. The attention, ladies and gentlemen, of none other than Her Majesty Queen Elizabeth the First.

It seems the scoundrel was spending more and more time with her Majesty, who told all who would listen that he was a Most Magnificent, Princely Personage. Before long she'd made him Master of the Horse, among Other Things (he winked at the young couple) and he was spending less and less time with Mrs Robert. Well, there was gossip, wasn't there? There always is when Persons of High Birth are involved. In fact some of you might even be put in mind of the hanky-panky of more recent royals…'

The kids' mother pursed her lips and nodded sagely.

'To cut a long story short.' Mr S assumed sombre tones. 'On September 8th 1560, poor Amy was found at the bottom of a flight of stairs in her house at Cumnor Place, not far from here, her neck broken. Bruises were observed.' The youths were listening avidly. 'Couldn't have been hubby, he was busy Mastering the Horses up at Hampton Court for Good Queen Bess, right? Though some of you might think that brown envelopes containing large sums of silver pennies might have found their way to a servant or two…' Mr S looked over his spectacles at his audience. 'But where does this tragic tale end, I hear you ask?' He threw out a black-sleeved arm in the direction of the church, its looming bulk sinister now, despite the illuminations. 'There in the vaults, deep in the chancel, lie the remains of hapless Amy Robsart, rotted now to a mere handful of dust. But at midnight every year on the anniversary of her death, muffled screams are heard, echoing from the vault…'

An uneasy silence followed his words; a silence suddenly shattered by a deafening bang. Cassie jumped, and took an involuntary step backwards. What the hell was that? Couldn't have been a gun shot – a car backfiring? Something scary happening inside the church? *The stone lid of a vault cracking… opening*? Clutching her bag to her chest, she glanced round – everyone was exclaiming, looking about in alarm, when gales of raucous laughter rose above the exclamations, and Chocolate Chip Youth shambled forward, helpless with mirth, wordlessly holding aloft the tattered remains of the paper bag. Seeing the incomprehension of everyone except his delighted mates, he mimed blowing into the bag, twisting it closed and bashing the hell out of it between his open hands.

Weak smiles and a smattering of applause were brought to a summary end by Mr S, who bestowed a sharp look on the offending youth, indicated a nearby rubbish bin, turned on his heel and set off once again. Assuring each other in various languages that they had never been remotely concerned, the group hurried after the Ghost Trail's white banner as it rounded the corner smartly, and disappeared from view.

Cassie trailed after the others. The Ghost Trail was brilliant, and the exploding paper bag had actually been quite funny (*the stone lid of a vault cracking... opening? Oh for God's sake*), but she was hungrier than ever. Hang on – they were approaching the Queens Lane Coffee House. Great. She'd pop in and grab a wrap or whatever to go, then run like hell and catch the others up. She'd slowed down and was fumbling in her bag for her purse when she realised the café's windows were dark and the sign on the door said CLOSED. She glanced at her watch. Five past eight. Damn. Missed it by five minutes. Maybe she should give up and head home? Be a shame to miss the rest of the Trail, though; Mr S was great, with his dusty undertaker's costume and his repertoire of sinister voices. Smiling, she thought of the flyer. *Props*, tick. *Illusion*, tick. *Fun*. It certainly had been…

The rest of the group were ambling down the narrow lane beside the café; Cassie hastened to catch up with them. A street sign high up on the faded brick wall said Queen's Lane; it wasn't long before it narrowed and became more dimly lit, the high stone walls with their few windows barely visible in the shadowy gloom. She smiled to herself. What had she expected? Mr S was hardly likely to station himself at some cheery location on the brightly-lit High Street to deliver his next speech. Banner held high, he was stalking along beside the kids' mother, murmuring in her ear while she smiled and nodded. At last they came to a halt at a bend in the lane, beside a pair of heavy oak doors. He regarded his expectant audience gravely. 'And so we come to the end of our Ghost Trail, which I hope you have all enjoyed.' There was a chorus of approval, and enthusiastic applause. Mr S bowed. 'I had thought to end with tales of hauntings of the nearby plague pit, or perhaps the frightful occurrences energised by the spirits of those poor demented souls incarcerated in the padded cells of Oxford Prison, or the organist practising late one night in the Cathedral, who having turned out the lights upon leaving for home walked straight into a fearsome white-faced apparition. Unsurprisingly, he fled. Needless to say, the poor fellow would never again venture into the chapel after dark.' The audience, seasoned now in these matters, nodded solemnly. 'On reflection, however, considering the presence of our more junior members, whose bedtime their mother assures me is well overdue, I have decided to end on a somewhat lighter note, with a positively *jolly* ghost! Thus we find ourselves congregated outside the doors of the ancient Church of St Peter in the East. Towards the end of the lane, New College is to be found, and it is there that the subject of my last little homily, the great William Archibald Spooner, spent many illustrious years as Warden. He was a popular chap, a kindly, hospitable man, beloved by fellow academics and students alike. But his fame was not engendered by his genial character and academic prowess. Oh dear me no. For the good Doctor Spooner had a most unusual affliction: his speech contained an involuntary play on words in which corresponding vowels and consonants are switched, giving rise to curious phrases with unintentionally comic effect.' It was clear from their expressions that the members of the group had no idea what he meant, and Cassie wasn't sure either. 'For example: *it is kisstomary to cuss the bride.*' Silence. 'Allow me to interpret: *it is customary to kiss the bride.*' Relieved laughter. The young couple kissed, giggling, accompanied by piercing catcalls from the youths. 'And another example: when congratulating a young student on his well-oiled bicycle, he most unfortunately described it as '*a well-boiled icicle*'! Aha! Ahahahaha!'

Cassie grinned. Zadie would love this stuff, though the foreign students were looking more bemused than ever. 'When the good doctor finally shuffled off his mortal coil, his remains were taken to be buried in the cemetery at Grasmere – to the surprise of many, since Dr Spooner always said that the happiest years of his life were passed here in Oxford. So it is perhaps not surprising that a ghostly figure clad in academic robes has occasionally been seen shuffling cheerfully down the lane towards New College, chuckling at the memory of some inadvertently comic utterance.' He adjusted the banner at a more rakish angle. 'But I see that our young friends here are more than a little fatigued; their mother has advised me that it is long past their bedtime and they must hurry away.' The boys' mother shepherded them over to Mr Spectre, who reached into his attaché case, withdrew four little packages, quite possibly containing junior thumbscrews gift sets, presented them to the kids and waved them on their way. Cassie was surprised they didn't resist – she was sure Bronx and Brooklyn would have played merry hell at being packed off early – but tumbling over each other like puppies and yawning exaggeratedly, they trundled off down the lane, accompanied by their beaming mother, and were soon lost to sight as they rounded the bend.

The others were also getting ready to depart, buttoning their coats and winding scarves round their necks against the now chilly evening; Cassie shivered, thrusting her hands deep into her jacket pockets as Mr S stepped forward with a conspiratorial air. 'I must confess I was not entirely truthful when I spoke of ending on a lighter note. Now that our young friends have left us, I feel duty bound to tell you that there is another shade who haunts this lane, of a rather less convivial character – one who in life was a famous military figure in the seventeenth century, the Cavalier cavalry commander, Prince Rupert.

Impatient and obstinate, with an explosive temper and a contemptuous manner.' Cassie winced.

all you have to do is knock a couple of bits of tin together, stick on a few gobs of coloured glass and charge 2K a pop to some rich bitch

Wait. She wasn't being fair.

it's a lot to ask, 1 know, but...can you find it in your heart to wish me well

Contrite.

please, please forgive me, Cass

Humble…He really had changed.

'The prince fought widely in this area during the Siege of Oxford in 1646, making many enemies among fellow commanders of a more level disposition. Things did not go well for him, and after the surrender he was banished from the kingdom.' He swept the startled group with a chilly gaze. 'He was on occasion billeted close to where we now stand, and is said to return – never sighted, only *heard* – galloping helter-skelter through the twilight gloom on his phantom headless steed over the cobbles seeking…well, who knows what?' A chill breeze blew a ragged leaf down the lane towards them. It skittered past the youths; the tall one with the punishing buzz-cut helped it on its way with a kick. Mr S adjusted his top hat at a rakish angle, picked up his attaché case and bestowed a kindly smile on the youth. 'Or, indeed…*whom*…? But there is no need for concern – it is many years since such a spine-chilling din has been recorded, and thankfully I myself have never had been privy to the frightful horror.' He reached for the banner. 'And now

I must thank you for your company and bid you good night.' He bowed, and accompanied by enthusiastic applause, with piercing cat calls from the youths and polite cheers from the foreign students, began to walk away. Suddenly he stopped and turned back, as with a horrified expression he pressed a shaking finger to his lips. '*Ssssh...*' Dropping banner and attaché case, he pressed himself against the wall, eyes wide. '*He's coming...!*'

Cassie froze. The noise of galloping horses' hooves could indeed be heard approaching. Everyone else had frozen too – oh God, the noise was getting louder –then the youths broke free and raced off back towards the High Street, yelling with terror, leaving the girlfriend limping after them in her sparkly wedgies, staring back wild-eyed over her shoulder. Cassie clapped her hands over her eyes and stood shaking, wishing she was back in her kitchen, cursing herself for ever picking up the bloody flyer, whimpering. *Waiting...*The mad echoing clip-clopping was faster now – louder still. Too late to do anything except – hello? What the...? She could hear people laughing. They were clapping too, now, and laughing even harder.

Slowly she inched her hands away from her eyes, focused on the cobbles ahead. And saw the four kids, looking extremely pleased with themselves as they careered down the alley, clapping coconut half-shells together noisily as they cavorted past the now delighted group and disappeared round the bend in the wall and out of sight, the sound of galloping hooves diminishing as they went till finally they fell silent. Mr Spectre hurtled after them, brandishing chocolate bars for his little helpers by way of payment.

The group stood grinning sheepishly at each other, the men saying well of course they always knew, the women shaking their heads and smiling, the kids' mum returning, laughing and saying what a great time the kids had had, only trouble was they'd probably beg to come back tomorrow and do it all over again.

Cassie leant against the wall, weak with relief. Okay, so it'd been scary – but again, the point, *the absolutely whole point*, was that the scary stuff wasn't real. Wait till she told Zadie and David about it! Laughing and joking, the group was beginning to disperse in the direction of Broad Street, where the Trail had begun, and Mr Spectre was folding up his banner, acknowledging Cassie's wave of thanks with a gracious bow before sauntering away too, the kids mucking about behind him, scoffing their chocolate and messing about with the coconut shells – *coconut shells*! Brilliant.

Cassie turned away, smiling, and was about to retrace her steps to the coffee house and head for the bus stops in the High Street, when a movement in the depths of the dense gloom beside the old oak doors made her stop.

Slowly she turned her head – and stood rigid with terror. *This was no figment of her imagination.* The figure was there again, still in her long black dress, hair still painfully coiffed, arm still raised from her side. But there all similarity ended – for this time the creature stood facing Cassie, her head bowed. As Cassie watched, she raised her extended arm higher,

her sleeve falling back to reveal a bloodless arm, and began to beckon.

Cassie ran.

TWENTY-FIVE

AFTERWARDS, CASSIE COULDN'T remember much about the journey home. She'd planned to take the bus – her feet ached after all that walking – but she dreaded the spectre following and silently materialising at the bus stop beside her – so she ran on, down the length of the High Street – *oh where were the tourists and the bloody students when you needed them*! – constantly glancing behind her, turning at last into Cowley Road, her heart thudding so violently she feared it would burst out of her chest, panting, perspiring, tossing her cardigan to a figure sleeping in a shop doorway as she passed. Prompted by the sight of an indistinct figure on the other side of the road she put on a final burst of speed as she reached Poplar Street and found herself staggering at last through the back gate and over the grass, shaking with exhaustion and terror, fumbling with her keys at the back door. After dropping them twice she finally succeeded in opening the door and fell into the dark kitchen, getting the door closed and locked and chained before sliding to the mercifully cool flagstones.

After a while she hauled herself to her feet, and clinging to the edge of the workbench managed to switch on an Anglepoise and look about the kitchen, overcome with relief at the familiar sight surrounding her; the notebook and tools she'd been preparing to work with on the metals for the pendant, the dresser with its rows of antique Royal Worcester plates, the bright yellow tape festooning the old cooker…She was home.

She switched on more lamps, selected Billie Holiday singing Strange Fruit from her playlist and found the bulging folder containing photographs of previous commissions – exquisite earrings, bracelets and chokers crafted in a glorious spectrum of lustrous precious and semi-precious stones. She'd leaf through it while she devoured the remainder of the quiche that still lay on the table beside the half-full bottle of wine. It would reassure her, remind herself of what she was capable of doing, and then she'd get back to work on the textures for the rose gold hearts. She ate and drank slowly, savouring the flavours, gradually relaxing. As her breathing eased and her heart began to beat at something like a normal rate again, a growing feeling of embarrassment at her hysterical reaction at the Radcliffe Camera and then at the ancient oak doors to what after all could only have been a fantasy created by her own overactive imagination began to replace her relief. Hadn't she imagined seeing the odious gardener Quint peering at her? It had turned out to be poor Eddie – no wonder the poor guy had looked worried! Not to mention the times she thought she saw Miss Jessel reflected in the kettle – the *kettle*, for chrissakes! *Hello*? Plus if she thought about it rationally – not, it was becoming increasingly clear, her strong point – surely it spoke for itself that Mr Spectre had described all the horrors featuring on the Ghost Trail in detail, and never once mentioned the spectre of any governess? Despite herself Cassie shivered at the memory, and took a gulp of the warm but welcome wine. Still, at least nobody saw her idiotic dash through the city centre – though to be fair maybe it wasn't *so* surprising, given the stress she'd been under for some considerable time. Best not to think about all that now – she shook her head. It would probably take a while to get used to it's actually being over –

good night, sweet lady – good night, good night

Time to leave it in the past, where it belonged.

No need to double lock the back door any more, or keep all the blinds closed, or worry whether the steel reinforced epoxy would hold the sash window. With a surge of relief, she downed the last of the wine, and examined the photo of the delicate little gold link bracelet with the tiny lemon charms, remembering the problems she'd had getting the mould for the lemons right, but it had turned out brilliantly in the end. See, she wasn't completely useless. She aligned her empty glass with the tidy pile of post and flyers, brushed a fragment of pastry from her lap, embarrassed again as she remembered her foolishness at the Radcliffe Camera, and her lunacy near the ancient oak doors. Enough. It was over. No more imagining things, it was obvious the ghost wasn't real. She managed a smile. The kids in that stupid bloody film were probably just pretending to see ghosts to spook the stupid prissy governess…

She stretched luxuriously, wincing as the bruises on her back gave a twinge, chose Fats Waller singing Ain't Misbehavin from her playlist to cheer herself up as Strange Fruit drew to its tragic close and settled down at the workbench to resurface the chasing hammer. She was humming along to Fats and gently filing the ball-shaped side when she stopped. A faint sound had come from outside – the click of a car door closing? A front door slamming as a neighbour further down the row returned home after a night out? Zadie and Lloyd returning with the kids from Scarborough? Cassie grinned. No way, Zadie said they'd returned from holiday late at night once and the kids had been so wired on the sugar treats Lloyd's mum had showered them with for the journey they'd refused to go to bed at all. She was about to start filing again when she set the file down. Hang on – *it was over*, remember? And this was the perfect opportunity to prove to herself that she wasn't afraid any more.

Pushing back her stool she stood up, and went to the back door. Unlocked it, unchained it and opened it wide. Then she stepped into the garden and stood breathing in the heady perfume of her beloved vine, and admiring the scatter of stars beginning to prick the velvet evening sky. She heard the sound again. Probably foxes having a go at No 42's rubbish bins. It was chillier than she'd expected; autumn was definitely on its way. Then it would be winter…She thought of Eddie's Nan's jigsaw, smoke spiralling from the chimney into the glacial sky, log fire burning, wishing he hadn't been so upset when she said she couldn't teach him. She must check out local jewellery-making evening classes, there were bound to be new ones starting in September, and –

Without warning a terrifying yowling erupted in the darkness. Cassie started involuntarily, lost her balance and shrank back against the door jamb, her half-healed contusions smarting, her palm stinging as she flung out a hand and grabbed the thorny vine to steady herself. She'd righted herself and was running an exploratory hand down her back and rubbing her sore palm on her tee shirt when Blanco – *bloody* little Blanco – shot out of the darkness from the direction of the lane and hared along the fence in the direction of David's conservatory, still yowling, probably searching for his Whiskas fix.

Jesus. Definitely time to call it a night. She'd finish resurfacing the chasing hammer tomorrow; what she needed now was more Arnica, a large mug of hot chocolate, and a good night's sleep. She took a last look at the moon riding high above the trees, and was about to return to the kitchen when she thought she saw a slight movement beyond the back fence. She turned away. Must be leaves stirring in the breeze… *There was no breeze.* Or Blanco skulking in the weeds…*She'd just seen Blanco making for his dinner.* She turned back – and simply watched. Petrified.

A figure was emerging from the shifting shadows in the lane. A figure in a black robe, dark hair tightly plaited and coiled, face white as parchment, eyes dark as coals, illuminated from below by an eerie blue light.

a woman in black miserable pale and dreadful

As Cassie stood, heart racing, shaking uncontrollably, the creature's lips began to part in a smile sinister as a scythe as she slowly glided towards the back gate. Cassie heard herself groan. She knew now that Miss Jessel was looking for *her*, and if she managed to pass through the gate –

The garden was deathly quiet; the whorls and splinters in the panels of the fence, the blades of grass, the stones in the rockery all unnaturally vivid, illuminated to a cold lustre by the shafts of moonlight shining fitfully between the branches. Wait. Deathly quiet …*too quiet*. Unnaturally vivid…*too vivid*. In other words unreal, phoney, fake. *She must be dreaming again.* Weak with relief, Cassie recalled running for her life under a darkening sky, pursued by a swarm of angry wasps – remembered how her nightmare had been triggered by nothing more alarming than her phone's cheerful ring tone. She forced herself to close her eyes. She must be asleep now, too, and this – *this unspeakable terror* – was nothing more than a nightmare. All she had to do was pinch herself, and –

Suddenly the garden was no longer deathly quiet, the silence shattered by the roar of a motorbike accelerating, raucous shouts as students kicked a can down the street. She forced her eyes open. Saw that the whorls and splinters of wood and blades of grass and rockery stones were once again normal size and

and

and the wraith had reached the garden gate and was stretching out a white hand to lift the catch –

Cassie gave a shuddering moan. God help her, this was no dream! *This was real.* And then she was trying to run, stumbling, falling, dragging herself upright again, her breath coming in painfully jagged gasps as she headed blindly for the back door – oh God, *the wide open back door –*

At last she was inside, the door locked and chained, front door checked, sash window tested – mercifully, the lock held – blinds closed, every lamp burning, Status Quo blaring from her playlist. Neither notebook and tools, antique Royal Worcester plates or bright yellow tape would help her this time; forget Arnica and hot chocolate. And as for sleep…She shuddered. She couldn't imagine ever daring to sleep again. She glanced at her watch.

Twenty to twelve.

Somehow that sounded a lot better than half past eleven.

Closer to dawn. Closer to David getting back. Closer to an acceptable time to call Mystic Marge and ask if she had any experience of getting rid of evil spirits and if so could she pop round soonest. Till then she was going to light all the candles she could find and sit in a chair facing the back door, Grandpa Jackson's carving knife with the worn bone handle and lethal paper-thin blade in one hand and the bottle of sulfuric acid she used for cleaning metals, stopper removed, in the other, ready to hurl its contents at that malevolent smile should it silently materialize in front of her. Quickly she donned rubber gloves, lit candles and arranged one of the kitchen chairs so it faced the back door. Then, phone lying ready in her lap, clutching knife and bottle in each hand as if they were an orb and sceptre, she sat down to wait.

CHAPTER TWENTY-SIX

SHE WOKE WITH a start at dawn, her limbs cold, her neck painfully stiff, her bruises aching more than ever. Daylight filtered beneath the blinds, fitful moonlight replaced at last by pale sunshine. Cassie tried a gentle stretch, winced and settled for simply placing her feet together, grasping the edge of her seat and carefully levering herself to her feet. She turned her head. Saw the fruit gleaming on the miraculously healthy lemon tree, the sparkling semi-precious stones in the earrings still lying in their open box on the table, the dull gleam of the old copper milk pan hanging above the cooker. She was home, it was morning and she was still alive.

She made her way up the stairs, used the bathroom, pulled on jeans and sweater, returned to the kitchen and made tea. Still too early to call Mystic Marge, but she felt better knowing that David would be back later – maybe Zadie and Lloyd and the kids too, with a bit of luck. It was chilly at this time of the morning, and it was easy to imagine leaves beginning to fall, the scent of bonfire smoke in the air. The throw still lay where she'd tossed it yesterday – *yesterday? It seemed a hundred years ago* – maybe she'd give it to David to make Blanco's den a bit cosier, poor little bugger. She was stooping to pick it up when she stopped dead. *Hold on.* She'd read something once about cats being supersensitive to ghost and spirits; they were afraid of them, and ran screeching with hackles raised if they were in the vicinity of a haunting, according to paranormal investigators. Cassie straightened up, frowning. Surely if the lane was haunted there was no way Blanco would have made himself a den there?

Right. She'd go and see for herself.

Folding the throw into a neat little pad, she pulled on her sneakers, opened the back door and stepped out into the morning. Taking a deep breath, she made herself look at the gate. No ghostly figure illuminated by an eerie blue light hovered, white hand poised to open the gate; just a raucous chorus of birdsong, a screech of brakes as an early delivery van arrived, somewhere someone whistling Oh Danny Boy. Heartened, Cassie made her way over the damp grass, whistling too to keep morale high as she passed through the gate and set off down the lane. She hadn't gone far when she stopped; the early sunlight was glinting on something lying in the middle of the path. Bending down, she picked it up – *and recognised the little brushed silver hoop earring containing a single tiny diamond she'd created for Ivo on his birthday, soon after they met.*

Dropping the rug, she stood simply staring at it. Remembering his delight as he'd opened the box. How he swore he'd never, ever take it off.

She looked away. Focused on the clump of giant hogweed towering over the undergrowth tumbling over the side of the path. Bright green stems with purple blotches and stiff bristly hairs, irregular sharp, jagged leaves, tiny white flowers clustered on umbrella-like heads. Stunning. Except she'd heard somewhere they burned you badly if you tried to pick them.

Her mouth twisted. Best left, then.

The leaves of the trees were beginning to rustle as blackbirds began to emerge, perching on the branches, chattering noisily and shaking out their feathers ostentatiously before flying off in search of breakfast. *So it was Ivo after all…* They were actually quite annoying, the birds, if you thought about it.

you're going to be sorry – very, very sorry

Her soaking sneakers were driving her mad – bloody dew. *You bastard, Ivo.* As for Danny Boy, what kind of weirdo whistled a creepy tune like that? *Hell bent on terrifying her to the end.*

She burst into tears. Bastard. *To the end.* After a while, she stopped crying. Tried to remember exactly what he'd said in the phone call telling her that he was leaving.

on my way to The Smoke now, rehearsals start tomorrow

That was two days ago – before she went on the Ghost Trail. Before she saw Miss Jessel – twice – despite the spectral governess not being included in Mr S's ghostly inventory, and none of the others in the group seeing her. Then there was last night – she shuddered. The creep had been here all the time. The phone call had been a fake. No, not a fake – Ivo *had* been in Gloucester Green coach station when he rang; the sound of engines manoeuvring, the cacophony of hooters and beeper alarms had been real enough – but the message itself had been a falsehood – a fabrication – a lie; to convince Cassie of his departure. Her mouth twisted again. The exchange with the imaginary coach driver was genius: all Ivo had to do was shout his enquiry – 'What time you leaving, mate?' – hold out his phone at arm's length and yell back a slurred reply – 'Now, mate – gotta go –' then a pantomime of Ivo's footsteps approaching a coach – any coach – followed by the sound of said coach actually leaving the station.

Cassie thought of her terror when she thought she saw Miss Jessel drifting down the lane in the moonlight, her hand outstretched to open the gate. Imagined his pleasure as he watched her desperate flight across the grass, the slam of the back door, the fumbling rattle of the chain. Memories of endlessly listening to his lines, buying him expensive clothes so he could project an 'image', encouraging him when he failed audition after audition engulfed her. Bursting into tears, she hopelessly asked a small, iridescent insect laboriously making its way up a dock leaf stem what she had ever, ever done to Ivo to make him hate her so. If only she could call her father and tell him what had been going on. Impossible – he'd be so angry he'd probably send a hit man to teach the bastard a lesson, or worse, wait for Ivo's – no, *Keith's* – next trick and come and sort him out himself; her father was a Ninjutsu black belt and had once half-killed a couple of drunks he'd discovered trying to steal his car.

It was a while before she pulled herself together and stopped sobbing, even longer before the hiccups finally stopped. She was wiping her eyes on the back of her hand and blowing her nose on the edge of her tee shirt, managing a shaky smile when she wondered what Granny Jackson would say if she could see Cassie doing that, when she was struck by a thought that frightened her more than anything else she'd comprehended that morning. If it was Ivo masquerading as the spectre in the lane last night (not to mention on the Ghost Trail), and he didn't know she'd found his earring and knew the truth, he was almost certainly still in Oxford – and planning his next move. As for landing a major part at the Roundhouse – Christ, would she never learn? Chances were he was still shelf-filling at some supermarket in Blackbird Leys or wherever – nowhere too close to Poplar Street, in case she saw him – and dossing on some hapless colleague's floor…

The sun was warm on her skin now, the traffic increasingly noisy in Poplar Street, a radio playing Taylor Swift in a garden further down the row. Cassie clenched her fists. She was tired of being terrorised, sick of blaming herself for everything that went wrong, from overheating irons to poisoned rose vines. What was it they said? *Don't be afraid of the storm –* **be** *the storm*. She glanced down. The tiny insect that had been labouring up the dock leaf stem had finally reached the top and sat basking in the sunshine, its tiny front legs rubbing together, rainbow colours shimmering. As Cassie gazed, entranced, she noticed a long stick half-hidden in the tangle of weeds near the clump of hogweed. It reminded her of something Mystic Marge had said – something about the King of Wands –

who though in possession of a single wand himself

Slowly, she picked up the stick.

fights on courageously

Lifting her chin, she pulled back her shoulders, ignoring the pain in her bruises, and the back of her neck, and strode back down the path. 'It's your turn now, Keith, my angel, my darling. I'm going to find your boss and tell them exactly who – *or should I say what, you vile lowlife* – they're employing. I wouldn't expect a reference, if I were you.' Snapping the stick in half she threw it down. 'And if you contact me again, or come anywhere near me from now on, you'll find yourself on the end of a restraining order before your feet touch the ground.' She kicked open the gate. 'I'm on my way.'

CHAPTER TWENTY-SEVEN

THERE WAS NO way she was confronting Ivo between the shelves of discounted tins of tuna and BOGOF Special Offers and demanding a private word with the manager with tear stains enhancing the now purplish bruise on her cheek and snot liberally encrusting the bottom half of her tee shirt.

It took over an hour to shower, wash her hair, apply concealer and makeup, pin up her hair in a casual and apparently effortless style, pull on jeans and a clean tee shirt, rip them off again and replace them with the simple green sundress she'd worn to le Manoir. No neutral-coloured wedge espadrilles to complete the look this time, though; there was a good chance the bastard would try to make a run for it when he saw the look on her face as she stalked into the supermarket and he realised the game was up. She'd be right behind him; sneakers would do just fine. Cassie glared at herself in the mirror over the sink for practice, and recoiled slightly. God, she looked positively scary. Excellent. She tried parting her lips in a slow, scythe smile. Even better…

Downstairs to grab a quick coffee, collect her bag and step out into the garden. No time to linger beside the vine, or listen to the birds singing, or admire the cobalt blue sky – she had places to go, people to see. Quickly locking the back door behind her – old habits died hard – she set off.

She walked fast, fuelled by anger, not stopping to call in at the artisan gift shop or linger over the richly sequinned, elegantly fishtailed ball gowns displayed in The Ballroom Emporium's window on The Plain. Buses lurched, bicycles swerved, pedestrians dawdled. Cassie ignored them, intent only on her objective. She planned to visit the few supermarkets in the city centre, then go on to those further out, starting with Summertown and taking buses to the more distant areas; she'd invest in a One Day ticket for the GoAnywhere Zone and she wouldn't stop till she'd tracked him down.

Over Magdalen Bridge, not slowing as she negotiated the crowd of tourists thronging the pavement outside the College, not registering the fragrant girls in their bright summer dresses and designer sunglasses, or the aggressive youths in shorts and baseball caps, and their fleeting odours of aftershave and sweat and dope. Pretending to be foreign herself when a burly Australian in an outsize Hawaiian shirt blocked her path and demanded she tell him how to get to the college that starred in the Harry Potter film. On to the High Street, gritting her teeth as she passed opposite the café with the window display of giant meringues she'd been eyeing from the bus when Ivo flounced out of the café and came to a halt, scowling, jabbing at the pedestrian crossing lights. Nearly at the entrance to the Covered market, now. She wished she could call in and stroll round the stalls, maybe nip into Geogina's for an iced coffee and a salad baguette, or buy some new incense sticks from the Japanese emporium. *Not now, girlfriend. You got business to attend to.* Just the thought of Zadie made Cassie smile. She stopped smiling as she hurried on, her fury redoubled as she thought of the lengths the bastard must have gone to to create the ghastly governess's spectre; the wig, the white skin, the long black robe. He must have created the eerie blue lighting by holding a torch with a blue lens beneath the robe and directing it upwards towards his features…

She was about to brave the heavy traffic and cross the road, then turn left down St Aldates in order to visit the Sainsbury's store there, concentrating on what she planned to say if that was where she found her quarry, when her attention was caught by a large banner visible above the heads of the pedestrians milling about outside The Whitewall Galleries on the opposite pavement. The banner announced the opening of The Red Queen Café in trendy scarlet cursive; cute little caricatures of the rest of the characters from Alice in Wonderland promising free coffee to the first fifty customers filled the rest of the space.

Judging by the banner's erratic course and sluggish pace it was clear that the bearer was less than enthusiastic about the mission, and as a gap in the crowd briefly opened up she saw that the carrier was indeed The Red Queen, clad in a grubby white satin crinoline patterned with giant red hearts, sporting a large rouged heart on each cheek and oversized false eyelashes, her black wig topped by a gold crown studded with scarlet glass hearts. Cassie looked away from sheer embarrassment. Ridiculous. The bloody traffic was worse than ever; Cassie gritted her teeth, shifting from foot to foot, waiting to cross. She needed to get on, find the spiteful little prick –

I had to spell it twice for your husband while he was writing it down in the diary

and sort him out once and for all.

the thing is, my husband has been unwell recently

She stared unseeingly at the gallery window opposite, her features a mask of fury, unaware that the Red Queen had jerked to a halt, performed a violent double-take that threatened to unmoor her crown and, alarmed, had whipped round to peer in the gallery window. Or that the Queen was whirling round now to face Cassie, her cheeks drained of colour beneath the scarlet hearts, eyes wide with horror behind the false eyelashes, the painted mouth a perfect O of alarm at the sight of the once helpless female on the opposite pavement reflected in the polished glass, transformed into a vengeful Valkyrie. A Valkyrie waiting on the pavement for the moment, true. But a Valkyrie clearly about to cross the road. Towards her. And then…

he bloody well will be soon

Cassie grinned at the thought of her vengeance, which was somehow even more frightening than her furious expression had been, and casting an imperious look at the traffic, trailed one foot in the gutter, hoping the oncoming taxi would slow enough for her to risk a dash to the island in the middle of the road – *places to go, people to see*. It did. She lifted her hand in a grateful wave to the taxi driver and reflected in the gallery window, stepped into the road, concentrating on not tripping over the trailing laces of her right sneaker – not seeing the Red Queen execute a clumsy turn, and hampered by both costume and placard, make a dash for the busy Carfax crossroads, where she made the fatal mistake of expecting the very old half-blind amputee, approaching fast in his shiny new electric wheelchair, to give way to her.

CHAPTER TWENTY-EIGHT

As CASSIE REACHED the island and crouched to re-tie her laces before braving the oncoming stream of buses and delivery vans and coaches as it thundered past, out of the blue there was a deafening reverberation of metal colliding with metal, brakes squealing, glass shattering, horns blaring. Horrified screams added to the pandemonium. She rose slowly to her feet, holding on to the traffic island bollard with one hand, craning her head to see what had happened – probably some white van tailgating another as it raced to make a delivery, though please God no-one was injured. The traffic had skidded to a halt in both directions and the crowd outside the gallery was arguing and gesticulating – no point now in making for Sainsbury's in St Aldates, from the commotion it sounded like it would be some while before pedestrian access reopened. With a regretful shrug to the taxi driver, who was stationary now, looking cross, she retraced her steps. She'd take a bus up to Summertown, check out the various supermarkets there. She hesitated. That would mean passing the scene of the incident as she turned into Cornmarket, and even if it was just a dented rear bumper and a couple of irate drivers hurling insults at each other, it would remind her of Tom. There was no way she was abandoning her mission; she'd track the scumbag down tomorrow – *she remembered trying to run, stumbling, falling, dragging herself upright again, her breath coming in painfully jagged gasps as she headed blindly for the back door, while all the time the bastard watched* – oh yes, she'd be back all right. She practised the scythe smile again, frightening a small child grizzling in a pushchair. *Enjoy your last day of shelf-filling, my darling, because I don't think your boss is going to want you around any more after tomorrow.* She wasn't worried the bastard would try any more of his tricks tonight, he liked to space them out, she realised, now, while he savoured the thought of her distress and mulled over his next offensive. But for the moment, she'd forget Ivo – no, *Keith* – make the most of the sunshine, and stroll home. Her heart lifted; David would call later and when he got back they'd go and drink Pimm's together beside the river at The Trout. She'd stop at one of the little Asian shops on the way home and stock up on provisions – get something nice for lunch, she couldn't remember when she'd last eaten a proper meal – and maybe she'd call in at Annie Sloane's stunning shop, too, pick out some trendy new chalk paints for the kitchen chairs. As she quickened her step, an ambulance shot past her, siren blaring, followed immediately by a police car. People stopped to stare; Cassie averted her gaze and continued on her way. Time to get on with her life.

It was early evening when Cassie heard a knock at the

front door. She'd changed into jeans and tee shirt as soon as she got home, and after she'd put away her shopping, made herself a three-egg herb omelette, followed by too many raspberries, she settled down to work on the entwined hearts for the pendant. She'd finished fixing the chasing hammer, and experimented with all three finishes, finally deciding the first heart would have a matt brush finish, the second a strong hammer finish, by way of contrast, when she decided to make herself a coffee before she carried on working. The knock at the front door was annoying. David? No, he always came to the back door, and anyway, he hadn't rung yet to let her know he was back. Eddie? The same applied. Though she hoped he'd call in again soon, with whatever arcane but essential gizmo he'd managed to track down for the cooker. She felt a twinge of remorse; she should have been kinder when she told him she didn't have the time to teach him. She'd check out those local courses as soon as she had a moment, to show she –

The knock came again, louder this time. Switching off the kettle she hurried up the stairs, swept aside the chain, irritably unlocked the door and threw it open. Two uniformed police officers stood on the pavement, looking at her. What on earth…? Had she done something wrong? She took a step back. 'Hello? Can I help you?'

The younger one tall and thin, with acne and a pronounced Adam's apple, took off his helmet and stood twisting it in his hands. His older, female companion, short and square, with blonde spiky hair and shrewd blue eyes, produced a tight smile. 'Ms

Fitton?'

'Yes?' Without looking, Cassie reached out a hand, found the door jamb.

'It's not…?' She tried again. 'Not…? She felt a tightening in her chest. Swallowed. 'My father?'

The officers glanced sideways at each other. Away again. The young one stared at her, aghast. 'No, Ma'am –'

His companion stepped forward. 'If we might come in for a minute?'

Cassie stepped aside wordlessly and led them down the stairs. They stood looking about, registering the workbench, the empty wine bottle beside the rubbish bin, the bright yellow tape wrapped round the cooker. The older one indicated the chairs round the kitchen table. 'If we could…?'

They sat down. After a moment Cassie sat too, pushing the tins of chalk paint aside. The young one opened his notebook. 'Mr Keith Jennings has been resident recently at this address?'

'Well yes, but not –'

He squinted at his notes. 'The supermarket where, according to information found in Mr Jennings' wallet, he was employed until recently, gave this as this address.'

'Sorry? Until…?'

'Given his marching –'

His superior cleared her throat. 'Found new employment.' She adjusted a button on her tunic. 'Mr Jennings was your partner?'

'Yes – no –' She made spaces between the paint tins. 'I mean –'

'I'm very sorry to have to tell you that Mr Jennings has been involved in a fatal accident.'

Yeah, right. Laughter rose in Cassie's throat. 'Pardon?' The tosser was up to his tricks again. Must be a good one, this time, if even the police had fallen for it.

She tried to look serious. 'Thank you, but honestly – I mean how –'

'Sergeant?'

The younger one licked a forefinger and turned a page of his notebook. 'On August 27th 2024 at approximately 11.52pm an accident occurred at Carfax Oxford involving a pedestrian and a No 15 bus the pedestrian later identified as Mr Keith Jennings of No 28 Poplar Street East Oxford was pronounced DOA at A&E John Radcliffe due to multiple injuries preliminary investigation revealed according to onlookers a contributing factor was victim was hampered by fancy dress plus large placard causing him to overbalance and fall into traffic as a result of an altercation with the occupant of an electric wheelchair driven at full speed on pavement. Further investigation –

Cassie looked away as he continued, haltingly running a nicotine-stained forefinger along under the lines as he read.

causing him to overbalance

Odd, the chasing hammer was exactly where she'd left it, the coffee jar in its usual place on the counter.

multiple injuries

Cassie touched one of the tins of paint; the label

blurred, there was a ringing sound in her ears. She drew a shuddering breath. *Ask.* 'Fancy dress?'

The elder officer tightened her lips. She had a slight cast in one eye, a heavy gold signet ring gleamed on her right pinkie. 'The Red Queen. Big dress, slap, bloody great crown plus bloody great pole-mounted placard, ought to be banned on crowded pavements.'

lazy summer picnics in punts

The young one rolled his eyes. 'Advertising gig for some new café, free –'

His colleague got to her feet. 'Is there someone you can call, Ms Fitton?'

Zadie. David. Dad. Helen and Mia from Zumba? Hadn't Mia gone to Turkey? Turkey was supposed to be nice, wasn't it, all ancient ruins and colourful markets and bazaars – not to mention visits to the Colosseum and the Trevi Fountain…Wait. That was Italy, wasn't it. Or somewhere. She shook her head.

'You're sure? Only it's better not to be alone –'

passionate love-making in sunlit fields

She wasn't sure now that she'd chosen the right colours for the kitchen chairs.

'Thanks, I'll be fine.' She gestured at the workbench. 'Got to finish some work, and my neighbour will be calling in soon.'

'If you say so.' Frowning, the female officer took a leaflet from a pocket. 'Call if you have any questions, or need anything.'

a mug of hot lemon

Tears stung Cassie's eyes. 'Thank you, you've been very –'

She led them up the stairs, thanked them again as she closed the door carefully, quietly, politely, behind them. Retraced her steps, and sitting down again at the suddenly and somehow distressingly vacant table, aligned the blue sugar bowl with the red and yellow striped tulips, drooping now in their jug. Licked a finger and dabbed fruitlessly at a fleck of raspberry juice on her jeans.

Then she laid her head on her folded arms and burst into tears.

Somewhere her phone was ringing. Forget it, probably bloody Ivo calling to beg and cajole her into letting him return, or worse, screaming insults and – Cassie sat up, jerked backwards in her chair, head aching, back throbbing, and stared unseeingly at the kitchen. *He was dead.* She shook her head – come on, it was impossible, not *Ivo* – she must have dreamed it. Stress again. Tea, that was what she needed. No, coffee. Then she'd get back to work. She pushed herself up from the table, trying to remember where she'd left the chasing hammer – must be behind the tins of paint, by that leaflet thing. What *was* that? Looked a bit like the Ghost Trail flyer. *Ghost Trail.* Hadn't she…? And afterwards, didn't …? She clung to the back of her chair, a kaleidoscope of images endlessly repeating itself, reminding her of the poster of Eadweard Muybridge's Human Figure in Motion Tom had on their bedroom wall, except the human figure was really rather sweet, while Miss Jessel…

She'd throw the leaflet in the bin; stupid to have let it spook her. She picked it up. Read it. Read it several more times. Lost her balance as she sat down again. Clung on to the edge of the table, righted herself. There'd been police here, hadn't there, the tall thin one with acne and dyslexia sprawling in the grey chair – awful colour, she'd definitely change that – the short square one with spiky blonde hair and a mean smile had crouched next to him. What had they wanted?

I'm very sorry to have to tell you

Maybe someone had complained about the foxes at No 42, and they were going house to house warning people to be responsible about their bins? Or bloody Erica had complained about Brooklyn and Bronx skateboarding or writing rude words on the pavement and she wanted –

has been involved in a fatal accident

Fatal. That meant dead, didn't it. Why didn't they just say that?

Mr Keith Jennings

Oh God, Ivo would hate that. She recalled his impossibly handsome features, the rueful self-deprecating smile. The wild ambition he assured her was matched by his stupendous talent.

His lies.

practically certain we'll be opening on Broadway for Christmas

His jokes.

the little ring box that merely contained a foil-covered chocolate cherry

His insults.

all you have to do is knock a couple of bits of tin

together

The elder officer had a defect in one eye. Wore some kind of gold ring.

'You're sure? Only it's better not to be alone –'

Gold. She thought of a gold hoop earring containing a single tiny diamond, glinting in the early morning sunlight. A scrap of crinkled gold foil, stained with melted chocolate.

Covering her face with her hands, Cassie sobbed until she thought her heart would break.

CHAPTER TWENTY-NINE

THE PHONE WAS ringing again. Slowly Cassie stood up and went in search of it, found it at last buried deep in the bottom of her bag. There was a crumpled tissue underneath it; she cleared her throat, coughed, blew her nose and cleared her throat again. 'Hello?'

'Hi, Cassie – how's it going?'

David. Relief flooded her. She touched her cheek gently, felt herself trying to smile. 'Hey there!' A sob bubbled up.

'Cassie? You okay?'

Mustn't cry. 'Sure –'

'It's just you sound like you've been –'

'Crying? Lord no, just got a touch of um hay fever.'

'Ah. Be glad you're not in London, lady, the traffic fumes are appalling. Can't wait to get back and relax by the river at The Trout. You still up for it?'

She leant against the workbench. 'Sounds wonderful.'

'Great. Cassie? You sure you're all right?'

'Been a bit of a – a – difficult day. Tell you about it when I see you.'

'I'll look forward to it. Just leaving London now, be with you in about an hour and a half.'

'Lovely.'

'See you soon, sweetheart.'

sweetheart

'Take care.' He was gone.

She walked about, touching familiar things. Washed

up her plate and glass, changed the water in the tulips, adjusted the cheerful yellow tape round the cooker. Sniffled, grimacing. It wasn't true, what they said – a good cry simply gave you a headache, blocked your sinuses and made you look like Miss Piggy. There was no way she was going back to work, now, she'd ruin the finishes. Best to deal with them in the morning, she'd relax in a hot bath now with the Acqua di Parma bubble bath Ivo had left behind, and find something soothing on her playlist. Pity she didn't have any wine – hang on, where had she stashed the remains of that bottle of spiced rum Zadie gave her for Christmas last year? There'd been hardly any left after Ivo got his hands on it and passed out on the bedroom floor; Cassie had hidden the rest fast. A quick rummage in the back of the old pine store cupboard revealed the dramatically labelled bottle stashed behind a couple of Granny Jackson's oversized flower vases, a bit sticky round the screw top but otherwise fine. Excellent. She tipped the remains into a tumbler and set it on the bottom stair, ready to be carried up to the bathroom along with the tea lights she discovered in the odds and ends drawer. And after the bath, jeans, clean white tee shirt, hair down.

But first…

Taking a deep breath, she approached the back door. Slid aside the chain, turned the key in the lock and opened the door wide to the balmy August evening. The moon rode high above the trees in the lane, stars pricked the cloudless sky, the air was heavy with the vine's heady fragrance. Cassie sat down on the grass, revelling in the new sense of security, the freedom from fear – in short, the knowledge that Ivo could do no more damage. She was sad that it had ended the way it did, she wouldn't have wished such a horrible death on her worst enemy – she shivered, Ivo *was* her worst enemy – especially dressed in that dreadful costume. God, he'd have hated that. She picked a daisy and regarded it thoughtfully. *Or would he?* More likely he was entertaining Paradise right now with an impromptu drag act, lifting his skirts, crown askew, the angels in stiches at his racy dialogue…

There was a muffed clink from somewhere, quickly muted. Nearby, by the sound of it. Blanco, probably, investigating his empty food bowl. She must remind David to refill it – not that someone like David would need reminding – and give him the rug for Blanco's bed that she'd dropped in the lane.

Smiling, she blew a kiss to the brightest star, and wished Ivo well.

After a while she got to her feet and returned to the kitchen. Better hurry up if she was to be ready when David arrived – she'd wash her hair first, and blow-dry it after her bath.

As she reached the open back door she turned and gazed at the gate where the spectre had stood, hand outstretched to lift the catch, and shook her head. Enough. Shutting the back door quietly behind her, she locked it and began to reach for the chain. Stopped, as with a surge of happiness she realised there was no need for lock and chain any more. It was over.

Twenty minutes later, the bathroom resembled a

delightfully luxurious – if slightly dated – spa. A row of flickering tea lights lined the rim of the bath beside the pale-green tiled wall, the brimming glass of spiced rum was perched, waiting, beside the taps. The bath was now almost full of heavily perfumed turquoise blue hot water, topped with great peaks of sparkling bubbles; Cassie had recklessly tipped the contents of the whole bottle into the torrent of water gushing noisily from the hot tap. Spotify relayed Classical Essentials from downstairs, while Cassie's phone was strategically placed on the shelf of toiletries opposite the bath, set to Speaker in readiness for David's call to tell her he'd arrived.

It wasn't long before Cassie was rubbing the wet hair dripping onto the shoulders of her kimono with a shocking-pink bath towel, then rushing back onto the landing to check that her American state-of-the-art, ten-speed hair dryer with assorted gizmos, a Christmas present from her father many years ago, was plugged in at its usual station on the landing, thanks to the antiquated – and, in many visitors' view, illegal – electrical wiring. The hair dryer's *super-cool-dry* function stood waiting to be activated the minute she was out of the bath, dried, depilated, deodorised and moisturised, liberally sprayed with the last of Granny Jackson's Yardley lavender cologne for luck and dressed in her favourite underwear, the blast of *super-cool-dry* to be followed by the volumizing wand wafting into action.

Shrugging off the kimono, she climbed into the bath and with a sigh of pleasure, slid into the billowing clouds of delightfully perfumed, frothing bubbles. Stretching out a dripping arm, she retrieved the glass of spiced rum and held it up, admiring the luminous effect the candlelight had on the tawny golden liquid before she took a long, slow swallow. Delicious… even better, Spotify was playing her favourite Tchaikovsky melody, something to do with some unrequited love affair or other, she seemed to remember. She relaxed, enjoying the music, idly wondering how far David had got on his journey down the M25. As she took another swallow of rum and played at creating a little whirlpool among the bubbles, she heard a click. Odd. Must be the ancient boiler doing its thing – she really ought to get it serviced, maybe she'd ask Eddie when he'd finished fixing the cooker. She sighed. Delightful as it was, she'd better get out soon – it would take a while to dry her hair, work miracles with the brilliant lightweight shine spray Zadie had recommended, and brush it into shape. Maybe it would be better to –

a creak, somewhere nearby

She lay motionless, listening. No way was that the boiler. Holding her breath, she reached out, and careful not to make the slightest sound, placed the glass on the edge of the bath. *Another creak, oh God, closer this time.* Agonisingly slowly, she made herself sit up, holding her breath as foam slipped down her breasts and drifted back into the cooling water, and turning her head –

saw the eye watching her through the gap in the door jamb

Impossible. No, really, it was crazy – *absurd*, for

Christ's sake. The rum must be stronger that she thought, she wasn't used to spirits – must be a trick of the light. With a snort of laughter at her foolishness – Ivo was *gone* – Cassie retrieved her glass, slid once again beneath the bubbles into the warm, silky blue water and downed the dregs of the rum as –

the eye blinked

Cassie bit back a scream. *God oh dear bloody God there was someone in the house* – as she dropped the glass, preparing to scramble out of the bath, grab her kimono and make a run for it, her mobile rang on the other side of the bathroom. *David's voice.*

'Hello? Got held up at Hanger Lane, I'm afraid, but I'll be with you in ten – hope you're ready for a –'

Galvanised by the sound of his voice, desperate to speak to him, she hauled herself out of the tub and slipping on the bath mat as she reached for the phone to beg for help – *hurry, please, please hurry* – fell painfully to her knees. Twisting round in a desperate effort to see the intruder, she was just in time to see the quietly humming hairdryer arcing towards the bath

a deafening blinding flash
utter darkness as every light in the house fused
followed by a ringing silence

She lay curled in a foetal position, clutching the damp bath mat to her chest, listening as the back door slammed and running footsteps receded into the night. She was still lying there, trembling, when there was a light tap at the back door and suddenly David was calling her name, taking the stairs three at a time in the darkness, impatiently feeling his way into the bathroom until he was kneeling beside her.

a peaceful gentle fellow

She burrowed into him, breathing in the citrus smell of his aftershave,

tolerant and kind

the faintly exotic whiff of London fumes clinging to his pullover.

and most important of all

Cassie shivered, wondering if the police who came when David rang them would be the couple who called earlier to tell her about Ivo. No – Mr Keith Jenkins.

trustworthy

She loosened her frantic grip on his sleeve. 'David?'

Reaching for the kimono pooling on the floor beside him he draped it round her and smiling, drew her closer.

She relaxed. *Safe at last.* 'I've got a lot to tell you…' Adjusting the kimono more comfortably, she leaned against him. Hesitated.

strength and determination will be required

No kidding. She wished things had turned out differently, but she'd do it all again in a heartbeat if she had to. Taking a deep breath, she began to talk.

END

TWO YEARS LATER

A DIFFERENT CITY, now, and an attractive young woman, a potter, is struggling to move her kiln into her new house while she waits for a visit from the local council in response to her complaint about a blocked public drain in the street outside. A pleasant young man, tall and thin with dyed black hair, a lanyard identifying him as a Certified Drain Surveyor from the local council dangling over his hi-vis jacket, calls in response to her complaint. Afterwards, he offers to help with moving the heavy kiln...

ABOUT THE AUTHOR

Rosie Orr began to write poetry when her children were small, and after winning The South Bank Show's Poetry Competition her work was published in various poetry magazines, followed by a PEN Anthology and The Virago Book of Love Poetry. Several short stories were subsequently published in magazines, while her novel *Something Blue* (women's fiction) was published by Accent Press in 2016. After losing her beloved daughter Polly to leukaemia she had no desire to ever write again, but after joining Writers at the Blue Boar in Chipping Norton some years later, she tentatively began the first draft of a new novel – something darker, this time. The result is *A Trick of the Light*.

She is currently working on a new psychological thriller about an ill-assorted group of amateur artists on a painting holiday in Tuscany; relationships begin to form, and jealousy and resentment abound. Meanwhile, unknown to the others, the main protagonist, Lizzie (attractive, and worse, talented) is recovering from a laryngectomy. She can speak, but screaming would be impossible…

ACKNOWLEDGEMENTS

Pam Manix, for her invaluable advice

Richard, Nicky, Rory, Peter and Jayne of Writers at the Blue Boar, for support and encouragement (the lattes and lunches were pretty good, too)

Joe and Sarah Orr, Matt Fitton, and my lovely sister Rowena, for being there when I needed them

My beloved Isaac, Leo and Lola-Rose, for never failing to make me laugh

Old and new friends (you know who you are) for helping me through the hard times

With gratitude to the Head and Neck Team at the Churchill Hospital, for their unsurpassed expertise and unfailing kindness

To Michael, for making it all worth it

Oxford eBooks, an absolute pleasure to work with

www.ingramcontent.com/pod-product-compliance
Ingram Content Group UK Ltd.
Pitfield, Milton Keynes, MK11 3LW, UK
UKHW041441060625
459304UK00001B/1